THE BIRDS OF VERHOVINA

ÁDÁM BODOR

THE BIRDS OF VERHOVINA

VARIATIONS ON THE END OF DAYS

Translated from the Hungarian
by Peter Sherwood

JANTAR PUBLISHING
London 2021

First published in London, Great Britain, 2021 by
Jantar Publishing Ltd

First published by Magvető, Budapest, in 2011 as *Verhovina madarai*

Ádám Bodor
The Birds of Verhovina

Translation copyright © 2021 Peter Sherwood
Introduction copyright © 2021 János Szegő
Design © 2021 Davor Pukljak

The right of Peter Sherwood to be identified as the translator of this work has been asserted in accordance with the Copyright, Design and Patents Act, 1988.
No part of this book may be reproduced or utilised in any form or by any means, electronic or mechanical, including photocopying, recording, or by any information storage and retrieval system, without written permission.

A CIP catalogue record for this book is available from the British Library

ISBN
Hardback Limited edition: 978-1-914990-03-8
Paperback: 978-1-914990-04-5
Ebook: 978-1-914990-05-2

This translation has been made possible by a grant
from the Petőfi Literary Fund, Budapest

The Contents

Introduction by JÁNOS SZEGŐ: *Fowls of the air and people of the earth: on the narrative world of Ádám Bodor*   7

THE BIRDS OF VERHOVINA by ÁDÁM BODOR   21

1.	(Anatol Korkodus)	57
2.	(Delfina)	75
3.	(Nika Karanika)	11
4.	(Edmund Pochoriles)	81
5.	(Aliwanka)	117
6.	(Augustin)	125
7.	(Januszky, or rather: Roswitha)	133
8.	(Miss Clara Bursen)	155
10.	(Balwinder)	191
11.	(Nikita)	207
12.	(Stelian & Fabritius)	231
13.	(Gusty)	259

INTRODUCTION

FOWLS OF THE AIR AND PEOPLE OF THE EARTH: ON THE NARRATIVE WORLD OF ÁDÁM BODOR

Verhovina on the map

If readers tried to find Verhovina (Verkhovina, Verkhovyna) in an atlas, or perhaps on the internet, they would certainly come across more than one such place name. There is a village bearing this name in south-east Ukraine, along the river Dnieper, and another in central Ukraine, too; but these localities have precious little to do with Ádám Bodor's work of imagination. We will come much closer to the likely terrain of the novel if we seek Verhovina in today's Transcarpathia, the region where the borders of present-day Hungary, Romania and Ukraine meet. The word itself in the Slavonic languages means 'high ground, mountainous region', and one reason for emphasising the contemporary nature of this border area is that here history has wrought numerous changes in country borders and even country names. More stable and enduring than the boundaries in this region drawn by the hand of man have proven to be the divisions traced by nature: the mountains and the rivers, the gorges and the marshlands. These differences are aptly illustrated in Ádám Bodor's novel *The Archbishop's Visitation*, by the sudden overnight inundation that results in the border town of Bogdanski Dolina being swept over to the far side of a river and – thereby – into another country. And with the superimposition upon each other of these two kinds of border, the historical and the geographical, we immediately find ourselves on familiar territory: it is this topographical and anthropological space that provides the setting of Ádám Bodor's works and hence of *The Birds of Verhovina*, too.

While the Verhovina of the novel is situated somewhere in the vicinity of a real Verhovina, it is not identical with it. This technique, of playing off real and fictive areas against each other, is one of the hallmarks of Ádám Bodor, one of his recurring themes. Out of the realistic elements of existing worlds he creates a world of his own, in much the same way as the birds in the novel make their nests out of blades of grass, little twigs, donkeys' manes, and human hair. At times he is careful to hide the connections between these worlds, while at others he sharply highlights them. But before examining this distinctive realm, it is worth looking around to see precisely where we are.

At the heart of the periphery

Seen from Western Europe, this territory is located in the East; if, however, we survey the terrain from the direction of the Urals, then we find ourselves in the westernmost part of its eastern zone. Either way, there is no question that we are in borderlands that are constantly thronged with exiles, travellers on the move, and people beginning their life anew, lands rich in encounters, mysteries, and – especially – stories. At one time these areas were multilingual and multi-confessional, as well as being multicultural, while today we can't even imagine what language their folk might speak – if, that is, they spoke at all, because the silence in these parts is really quite overwhelming: some of the former churches have become at best furniture warehouses and at worst crumbling ruins, barely credible mementoes of the fact that here once lived, side by side and in relative peace, Poles, Slovaks, German-speaking Transylvanian Saxons and Swabians, Szeklers, Armenians, Jews, Rusyns, Romanians, and Hungarians.

Today's Transylvania still preserves many traces of this multicultural world and so does Bodor in his work, transforming the area into a naturalistic fiction, a utopia of the grotesque, a chillingly Kafkaesque or Beckettian parable of magical existentialism. Today what is called Transylvania makes up the western part of Romania, occupying an area approximately the size of Wales and Scotland combined, taken from the Austro-Hungarian Empire to form an expanded Kingdom of Romania when the Central Powers lost the First World War. The English term means, transparently, 'beyond the forest', and the area formed for many centuries part of the Kingdom of Hungary, later becoming an independent Grand Duchy, then a province of the Habsburg Empire, and finally part of the Austro-Hungarian Monarchy. The most famous Transylvanian is undoubtedly Count Dracula who, though an invention of Bram Stoker's in his 1897 novel, is nonetheless perceived as an authentic Transylvanian character, not least because the actor who originally portrayed him in the 1931 film adaptation was a Transylvanian, Béla Lugosi, who took his professional name from his birthplace there, Lugos (Romanian name: Lugoj).

The personal background

All this was already history when, on 22 February 1936, Ádám Bodor was born in the Transylvanian capital, Kolozsvár (Romanian name: Cluj), into a well-to-do Hungarian family (his father was a bank manager – as was, it so happens, that of Béla Lugosi at the turn of the twentieth century). Kolozsvár remains the political and cultural centre of the region, a still-prosperous university city and Romania's second biggest, with Hungarians comprising some 10 to 15 percent of the population. In 1940, early in the Second World War, part of Transylvania, including Kolozsvár, was returned to Hungary. Bodor's father was put in charge of a bank in Budapest and it was here that the young Bodor survived the fierce fighting that accompanied the Soviet siege of the city, before returning after the war to Kolozsvár, now once again part of Romania.

After the communist takeover, Bodor's father, despite having an irreproachable past but being undeniably a member of the former elite, was convicted on trumped-up charges and the family was forced to leave its former home. Years of hardship followed, and in 1952 the 16-year-old Ádám Bodor, too, landed up in prison, charged with "subversion against the state", to be set free only in 1955. The years of imprisonment left deep scars on Bodor; he gave a detailed account of how he was treated in jail in his autobiographical work *The Smell of Prison*, and the motifs of imprisonment surface in many of his works. On his release he went to work in a factory. He graduated from the Calvinist Theological Seminary in 1960, subsequently taking jobs in an archive and then a translating agency – a typical launching pad for an intellectual career in Eastern Europe.

The inexhaustible richness of the shorter form

His made his literary debut in 1965, in a journal published in the city of his birth. Thus began several decades of existence on the fringes, for the stigmatised ex-con was allowed to function only on the margins of his chosen career, where he could be sure not to make waves. This coincided with the burgeoning in Romania of an oppressive régime, reliant on a brutal secret police (the Securitate) and a vast network of terrorised informers, which even in the Eastern bloc counted as exceptionally savage. Virtually everyone was informing and being informed on. Bodor's first collection of short stories, The Witness, appeared in 1969. His early writings were inspired by Ernest Hemingway, and it was in short prose that Bodor found himself the most comfortable niche: sketches, feuilletons, short stories by the hundred poured from his pen in the decades that followed. An early selection of these, The Euphrates at Babylon, appeared in English in 1991 (Edinburgh: Polygon), translated by Richard Aczel.

He has offered the following account of the short story as a genre: "The short story is like chamber music: a noble genre, it is thoroughly mindful of the load that it can bear, of how much it is possible, or advisable, to leave unsaid, or – sometimes – to exaggerate in any story worthy of the name, and it is this that determines the pace at which it unfolds. Even more than in other genres, in short-story writing it is vital to know how, when, and where to stop. By writing too much, just as with using too much paint when painting, the colours become scorched and fade, ultimately resulting in the loss of the most honest and the most authentic features of the work of art."

The sphere into which the work of Bodor ushers the reader is not just a concrete one: it is also philosophical. In his words: "I am inspired above all by the existential image of the land of my birth and of the entire East European arena, with its rudimentary morality and its lethargic milieu; indeed, I could hardly have written about anything else, or in any other way." In these frequently ballad-like stories the mundane and the mysterious, the tragic and the grotesque are inseparably melded. The characters are generally figures in transit, people on their way from one place to another. Like his protagonists, Bodor too was obliged to move on as the ever-tightening stranglehold of the Ceaușescu régime made his life less and less bearable, and in 1982 he settled with his family in the Hungarian capital. He continued to write while taking a job as editor in a publishing house.

From Sinistra to Verhovina

The high point of his career came in 1992 with the publication of *The Sinistra Zone*, translated into English by Paul Olchváry in 2013 (New York: New Directions). In the Hungarian edition this bears the subtitle *Chapters of a Novel*: that is to say, it can be read as a novel, but also as a linked sequence of short stories, the latter being an important genre in Hungarian narrative prose. The setting is somewhere in the mountain peaks of the Carpathians, the name being a clear allusion to the dangerous and sinister nature of the area. The action takes place in this distinctive territory, the events being linked via the person of the protagonist, Andrej Bodor. While in this work he lends his surname to his hero, in *The Birds of Verhovina* it is his first name that is shared with the protagonist.

On the relationship between the real and metaphorical setting Bodor has offered the following reflections: "The setting of a narrative is most felicitous when it is also the terrain where the writer's experiences can converge; that is to say, where the writer's vision can most authentically unfold. In my case, given the nature of my life and character, this terrain is historical Eastern Europe, the labyrinthine world of border barriers and barbed wire, along with the general atmosphere and outlook on life to which these have given rise. At the same time, it is a place where, in the course of imaginative writing, its secret places are opened up and its depths plumbed, offering surprises which drive the story on from one twist or turn to the next."

The Sinistra Zone went on to become one of most important Hungarian books of the 1990s, ensuring Bodor his place as one of the most celebrated Hungarian authors, alongside Péter Nádas, Péter Esterházy, the 2002 Nobel laureate Imre Kertész, and László Krasznahorkai, winner of the 2015 Man Booker International Prize. The literary art of Bodor and Krasznahorkai even shares certain features, to some extent, only for the differences between them to become, ultimately, more eloquent. Krasznahorkai's novels of the 1980s (*The Melancholy of Resistance*, London: Quartet, and *Satantango*, New York: New Directions, both translated by George Szirtes, in 2008 and 2012 respectively) are also set in isolated areas, the former in a rundown town in the provinces, the latter in a decaying agricultural cooperative, and in both cases the complexity of plot and narrative is amplified by spatial relationships, constricting structures, and networks of repetitions. But while Bodor's narrative is organised around minor details – microstructures, mosaic-like correlations and minimalist sentences – Krasznahorkai, whose books often consist of a single, seemingly endless sentence, relies on forms that are far bigger and – not least – his work has quite a different resonance.

In 1999 Bodor published a larger-scale work: while *The Archbishop's Visitation* does resemble, in some respects, the world of

The Sinistra Zone, it also differs from it in several ways, above all as regards the period in which it is set. The events in this book take place after the fall of communism in 1989, and the eponymous ecclesiastic signifies the return of a familiar operator, in an almost Godot-like coming. However, in some ways the narrative techniques, the episodic building blocks, and the frequent deployment of unusual personal and geographical names are reminiscent of *The Sinistra Zone*, which Hungarian critics regard as his major work. It is all the more necessary to emphasize this, because this was the work that was followed by *The Birds of Verhovina* in 2011. Both readers and critics in Hungary eagerly awaited this work of Bodor's, which bore the telling subtitle *Variations on the End of Days*.

2021 marks the tenth anniversary of the publication of *The Birds of Verhovina*. The intervening decade has certainly witnessed some variations on the end of days. In terms of natural history these ten years do not amount to a fraction of a second, and even on a human scale they are barely more than a moment. And yet: how much more meaningful is it to read today than even a few years ago of frozen rivers and flooded lands, of forests falling silent, and birds that disappear, eventually to return? It is not so much that Bodor is a prophet – he is more a resigned and clear-sighted realist. The fact that in this book we can read of epidemics and quarantines, too, is disturbing yet, in a sense, liberating.

The Bodor Opening

At the end of an introduction there can be no greater indiscretion than retelling the story, giving away the plot's twists and turns, or worse still: offering an analysis of the work. I will therefore confine myself to looking at the opening lines of the work and mentioning a couple of its motifs. Just as great chess-players have their openings, so Ádám Bodor too has a distinctive way of beginning his books. These are the opening lines of *The Birds of Verhovina*:

> *Two weeks before he was arrested my adoptive father, Brigadier Anatol Korkodus, bought me a brand-new Stihl petrol chainsaw. He said he had ordered it from Czernowitz; the parcel had already arrived, and I was to collect it from Edmund Porchiles at the Sign of the Two Queans. I could pick up the present in the morning on my way back from the station.*

A tight, carefully structured beginning: there are precisely timed events (two weeks before he was arrested, the morning after the parcel had arrived), a rather distinctive familial relationship together with a title (my adoptive father, Brigadier Anatol Korkodus), a real place (Czernowitz, today Chernovtsi in Ukraine, the birthplace in an alternative reality of the poet Paul Celan), and a venue in a fictive place (at the Sign of the Two Queans); and to cap it all an ominous event (the arrest of Korkodus) and a surprising gift (the chainsaw). Even if the latter is not the proverbial Chekhovian gun, it nonetheless does crop up later in the book. Now let us consider the opening lines of *The Sinistra Zone*:

> *Two weeks before he died, Colonel Borcan took me with him on reconnaissance to one of the barren heights in the Dobrin forest*

district. He asked me to keep my eyes open, especially on the mountain ash trees, whose clusters of little red berries stood out in the roadside scrub, to see if the waxwings had yet arrived. It was mid-autumn, and the brush was abuzz with unfamiliar sounds.

The similarities are noticeably greater than the differences: taut temporal structures (the death of Colonel Borcan and the events that preceded it two weeks earlier), the name of a person and a place, and a tense, almost thriller-like atmosphere. That this is a wholly deliberate and consciously applied technique is reinforced by the first few lines of *The Archbishop's Visitation*:

A week before St Medard's Day the first customers at the hairdressers' brought news that the sisters Senkowitz had been arrested before sunrise that day. The two spinsters had escaped months earlier from the Izolda quarter's isolation ward for consumptives.

Here the time interval is not two weeks but just one, before St Medard's Day (which falls on 8 June), and here too alarming events are taking place. Is this all some kind of verbal game, a piece of authorial tricksiness? Or a deliberate indication that his works are closely related to each other? This is a question that has indeed been put to Bodor, but in his characteristically laconic way he has always avoided giving a direct answer.

The magic of names and the enigma of languages

The very first paragraph of *The Birds of Verhovina* mentions Czernowitz, while elsewhere there also crop up Lemberg (today Lviv, now likewise Ukraine) and Besztercze (Bistritz, today Romanian Bistriţa). This is the Bodor map: the real overlaid by the imaginary, the mythical. When we read of Yablonska Polyana, we are reminded, even if only subconsciously, of Tolstoy's legendary village, Yasnaya Polyana. In the universe of this narrative the personal names possess as much allure as the place names, defining the protagonists and their relationships as distinctively as their personal odours. There is, for example, Nika Karanika, who "had no papers, only her name could be made out, since following the custom of the southerners down on the coast, she bore it tattooed on the back of her hand: in the land of her birth, the child's name is branded on the back of its hand using a needle when it's still a baby, so that they can't later disown it." (p. 41). It is a particularly ingenious of the writer to have a reduplication within the name (Nika). Others are referred to only by their nicknames, some only by their initials.

It is a commonplace of psychology that one's name is an important part of one's identity. Bodor has spent almost fifty years demonstrating the various ways in which this claim is true. It is a fundamental issue in reading Bodor: how are we to understand his coruscating humour? This is even more difficult to convey in translation, not least because even for Hungarians Bodor's names can be understood only to a very limited extent; on the other hand, for those who also happen to know Romanian they are wholly meaningful. But here too it is worth treading with care. One of *The Sinistra Zone*'s memorable characters is the trucker Mustafa Mukkerman. This is a genuine *nom trouvé*, yet invention was overwritten by reality. Bodor himself tells the story in *The Smell of Prison*: "When we were preparing the German version of *Sinistra*, one of those involved remarked: just a moment, we should be careful. There is no such name as Mukkerman. So much the better, I countered, because there is now. I wouldn't have changed it for the world, since this character surfaced in my imagination inseparably from his name, and by the time that chapter was finished, all around him the Mukkerman universe had taken shape, his character had Mukkermanified the atmosphere, the whole environment had become entirely dependent on Mukkerman. What else could we have named him? These are absolutely fundamental issues, on which no author can yield an inch. But the well-intentioned colleague was mistaken. Not long ago I found a Muckermann in the Berlin telephone directory. For a moment I suddenly wanted to know what he looked like and would have found some excuse to ring his doorbell – his address was there by his phone number – but I'm a very poor actor and find it difficult to play such roles. And perhaps it's better that way, that I play only my own part."

Or consider the Boursin farm and Klara Bursen. Where might this name have come from? Some remote corner of multinational Transylvania? Ádám Bodor's imagination? Or – maybe – the refrigerator? For Boursin is a brand of French cheese, first created in 1957. On the Boursin farm Klara Bursen lives a life "filled with a fantasy of love, awaiting a Hungarian army officer from Beszterce who the clairvoyant had said would soon come for her on horseback, sweep her up into the saddle before him, and ride off with her beyond the mountains, into Trans-Sylvania." (p. 68). At this same point we find the following words of Adam's: "At the lady's request I read to her for an hour from a book in Hungarian on the orography and hydrography, and the world of flora and fauna, in Máramaros county. I picked up a smattering of Hungarian at the reformatory, but I didn't understand a great deal of the text, while I believe Klara Bursen understood none of it. Still, I read out loud, crunching and cracking the unknown words, while the lady pricked up her ears, training them to get used to Hungarian speech." (p. 68). A masterly double metaphor: a book of geography and Hungarian speech. Of course, *The Birds of Verhovina* was written by Bodor in Hungarian, but it does not transpire from the book what language its characters speak: we know only that it is *not* Hungarian. But there is something that we do know, which is that after editions in Polish, French, Italian, and Spanish, we can at last read in English, too, about all the goings-on in this fantastical world.

János Szegő, Budapest.

THE BIRDS OF VERHOVINA

by ÁDÁM BODOR

This translation is dedicated to Julia and Miriam,
sine quibus non

1.

(ANATOL KORKODUS)

Two weeks before he was arrested my adoptive father, Brigadier Anatol Korkodus, bought me a brand-new Stihl petrol chainsaw. He said he had ordered it from Czernowitz; the parcel had already arrived, and I was to collect it from Edmund Pochoriles at the Sign of the Two Queans. I could pick up the present in the morning, on my way back from the station.

It seemed that, even if he had his suspicions, he was dissembling because, as if there were nothing brewing, another of his protégés from the reformatory at Monor Gledin was due and he asked me to meet his train at daybreak and see him to the office. He was intending to keep to his bed that day, so I was to make sure the youngster was fed, to talk to him, and generally keep him entertained until the afternoon, when he would have time to speak to him himself.

Normally it was Balwinder, the office dogsbody, that he despatched to the station when the settlement had a visitor, or indeed a new arrival such as this one, but on this occasion for some reason best known to himself he wouldn't hear of it.

As the timetable here had recently been cancelled and all you could know for certain was that the first train of the day, which comprised chiefly freight cars and just a single decrepit third-class carriage, would arrive before clocking on time at the timber yard, I decided to set out for the railway station well before daybreak, and waited patiently near the exit, huddled on a bench thick with hoarfrost. I put down beside me, in a clearly visible spot, the piece of cardboard on which my old man had written the newcomer's name with a thick, felt-tipped pen, in big letters and bold strokes, so that even in the meagre lighting of the station it should be easy to make out.

His name was Daniel Vandyeluk, which sounded like some seedy sexton reeking of old age, though he was obviously just a delinquent kid off the streets. He had been sent over from the reformatory at Monor Gledin for re-education, to stay at the settlement until he found his feet and learnt to behave.

Anatol Korkodus readily took in young misfits, boys who had gone off the rails, so that here, far from the temptations of the city, amidst rolling mists, sulphurous hot springs, abandoned bunkers and slagheaps, they might revel in untrammelled freedom and find themselves and their own path to a better future. But he never got very far with them. Nor did he delude himself that he did. He called them his birds, knowing that it would always end, one fine day, in their flying away. Some would leave for parts unknown within days of their arrival, disappearing without trace. Many, once their probationary period was over, were sent by Anatol Korkodus back to the reformatory. And there had not so far been a single one who had sought his final resting place in the area and intended when the time came to be buried here, on the slopes of the Paltin.

I had by then spent quite a few years in Verhovina. Many years earlier I, too, had been brought one frosty morning from the same place, by this same rundown local train.

On nights when there is little wind, especially when the valley is covered by a dome of thick cloud, the train can be heard an hour or two before it gets in, as it begins its climb along the Yablonka and clanks its way over the hundred-year-old iron bridges. To the practised ear, just the occasional sound from the far distance is enough to work out exactly where the train might be at any particular time. But today the hollows of the groves, the ditches lined with bushes along both sides of the embankment, were hugged by a blanket of dismal fog that muffled even the barking of the dogs nearby. An indication that somewhere beyond the recesses of the valley the train was indeed getting close came only from the little groans of the sleepers, an occasional creak or rustle that shivered along the rails like an electric current.

Apart from me the only person waiting for the train was Station Master Stetz; it would seem that these days people are no longer inclined to travel by train. A recent rumour had it that the station was about to be closed down and perhaps even the rails taken up and sold, along with the iron bridges, because the Yablonka Valley line, from the ford at Tuverkan Pasha and all the way to the loading bay of the timber yard, was said to have been measured up by persons unknown; some even claimed to have heard that the valley, together with all its extensive hardware, had been bought by a rich foreigner called Bazil Haraklán, supposedly from a far-off, abundant plain beyond the mountains, Coltwildgarden, Holtwildgarden, or some such mythical-sounding place. Apparently even the letters sacking the railwaymen were ready to be sent out; no wonder, then, that the stations were becoming ever more deserted.

So it was that when the first train of the day pulled in, hissing, puffing and wreathed in clouds of steam, from the window of the third-class carriage only a single head, wearing a black-and-yellow striped cap, poked out to inspect the empty platform. Nor did its owner seem in any hurry to make a move, and it was only when he saw the uncoupled engine exhaustedly trundling off by itself in virtual silence towards the engine shed that he realised this was the end of the line, and finally got off and hesitantly made for the exit.

It was immediately apparent that he was not, in fact, wearing a cap on his head; rather, his close-cropped hair had some design daubed on it. Amidst his original dark head of hair gleamed streaks of golden yellow, prominent in the greyish mist. He wore a cheap denim jacket that he had long outgrown, had no luggage, and when he came close enough to be illuminated by the light of the lamps, you could see that he wasn't even wearing shoes. He walked the length of the platform barefoot, making the edges of the frozen puddles crackle on his way. He had no choice but to pass in front of me, so that when, as he came closer, he saw the piece of cardboard on the bench and slowly made out his own name, he came to an uncertain stop.

Hell's teeth! Not waiting for me, are you? I was supposed to be coming tomorrow.

Anatol Korkodus had a feeling you'd be coming today.

And there I was thinking I could take it easy for a while in the station bar, spend my savings, suss out the lie of the land, and then turn up tomorrow. You've ruined my day.

He spoke in a thin, reedy voice; none of his teeth could be seen. He had piercing, bluish-grey eyes, like Edmund Pochoriles's husky at the hostelry. The yellow stripes glaring in his hair gave his head a fluffy bloom.

I looked him up and down: Then come to your senses. Can you see a bar anywhere around here?

The station here consisted of just two buildings: in one, the station master and the traffic controller, a girl, worked in shifts to deal with the freight and other traffic, issuing tickets through a small hatch open to the elements, while at the back, in a more spacious room behind a swing door, lived Station Master Stetz with his family. Back in the old days what was now a ramshackle and dust-laden hut with a tacky metal table and a couple of broken-backed tubular chairs had served as a bar, but that had been shut down long ago.

As there was no bar to be seen, Daniel Vandyeluk turned round and round in his disappointment. Then he stopped in his tracks and took several huge gulps of air.

It stinks here. What the hell is that smell?

I have no idea what you're talking about. You need to have your nose examined.

What he must have detected was the choking smell from the thermal springs in the Paltinsky meadow, which even at break of day clings to the bottom of the valley until dispersed by the welcome winds.

Crossing the square in front of the fuel depot and the timber store, we trudged along Yablonska Polyana's deserted main street, carefully skirting the frozen clods of earth. Only the soles of my boots could be heard tapping on the ground; the barefooted Daniel Vandyeluk lagged a good half-step behind me, negotiating the frozen puddles noiselessly.

What, if I may ask, happened to your shoes?

Threw them away.

You must be joking. Keep a civil tongue in your head when you speak to me.

You heard. I threw them away, like I said.

He halted on the Pissky bridge and stared down into the Yablonka, black and silent as it wound its way between the blanket of ice that covered both its banks. I stood behind him, wondering what he would do. But in the end he just spat into it.

At this I adopted my most withering tone: Don't let me see you doing that again. Spit where you like but not into the water. Best if you just swallow it.

The yellow light from Nyegrutz's bodega spilled out into the fog, and before its open entrance swirled the smell of roasting chestnuts and hot oil. I grasped Daniel Vandyeluk lightly by one elbow and steered him over to the doorway. He had a scrawny little arm, like a child's.

I looked about. The street was deserted.

You will now wait here nicely and talk to no one. If anyone should stare at you wondering who or what you are, you will take no notice. Pretend you're not here. Understood? As if they'd seen a ghost.

And why would they stare?

I looked him up and down again, from the top of his head, aglow with its yellow streaks, down to his bare feet.

They might.

There was no one yet in the bodega. Behind the counter sat Irina Nyegrutz, preparing the dough for the deep-fried lángos in a blue dish covered by a chequered cloth. In a roasting tin on the gas stove lay some hot chestnuts, steaming, their shells burst open. I asked for half a kilo of chestnuts and two lángoses topped with curd cheese. While Irina Nyegrutz rolled out the dough, added the curd cheese and prodded and patted the dough around in the sizzling oil, I walked up and down the empty room, from time to time looking out of the open door and the steamed-up windows. It was exactly six o'clock; behind the looming curtains of fog the sawmill's siren boomed out with a dull sound. The veins of condensation dribbling down the purple glass of the window made the image of my unshaven face quiver, as if I were weeping.

Daniel Vandyeluk stood obediently on the threshold, like a dog tied up by its master in front of a shop, plumes of steam rising from his nostrils, hands in pockets, one bare foot resting on top of the other.

Irina Nyegrutz slipped the lángoses into a paper bag and put the roast chestnuts into another. She peered out of the door.

Who's the other one for?

No one, as you can see.

New kid. I can see he's not up to much. He won't stay long.

We live in hopes.

Daniel Vandyeluk and I continued on our way. After just a couple of steps, he piped up, a touch testily.

Tell me, why did you leave me outside?

Next time you can come in, if you like.

But for some reason this time you left me outside.

I didn't want your smell to irritate Irina Nyegrutz.

I've been on the road since yesterday. I must smell of the train a bit.

I said nothing about smelling of the train. Go on, tell me why you threw away your shoes?

They'd been shat in.

Are you serious? That shouldn't have stopped you putting them on. In case you didn't know, it's lucky. Someone likes you a lot.

Little Zsanett did. Poor thing was ever so angry they let me out.

You may meet again. Be sure you repay her affection in kind.

At the entrance to the Man-Gold courtyard, I once again brought him to a stop by grasping one of his elbows. The sun was coming up, the sky was beginning to acquire a congealed yet translucent look, but in the courtyard, entered through a wide, high archway and enclosed by four single-storey buildings, there still lingered the hemmed-in murk of the departing night, and on the steps of the scone bakery you could make out only the bottles of goat's milk, laid out neatly in four rows. I picked up a couple of the bottles, and when we went on, barely two houses further, but by now on the other side of the road, I knocked on one of the windows of the Augustins' house. Or rather, on a plank that covered up the window.

The window of the Augustins that looked out on the street was nailed over with planks, vertically and horizontally, as well as cross-wise, leaving just a small gap in the crudely knocked up trelliswork to let a hand poke out and take in the odd item, say a bottle of milk. The Augustins were a couple we had been holding under house arrest for many years. As the gaol in Yablonska Polyana had burned down long ago, there was no choice but to keep them locked up in their home.

I put one of the bottles on the windowsill and waited for the window to open. From behind the planks came the voice of Mrs Augustin:

Is it true that Madam Subprefect Vaneliza has made off? And that things are not looking good for Anatol Korkodus either? My husband and I had the same dream again. Because if it's all true, we're being kept here under false pretences. Would you kindly have a word with Constable Hamilcar Nikonuk and have him set us free this very day.

Dream on, you two. Any number of things could be on the cards. But for the moment you are both urgently expected by the examining magistrate in Gledin. You'll have a leash tied round your waists when you're taken before him.

I gripped Daniel Vandyeluk by the arm again, and gave him a meaningful look: They think, in there, behind the planks, that I've nothing better to do than pass the time of day chatting with them.

They done something, or d'you sometimes just lock people up?

That depends. I don't know if you can really take in what I'm about to say. These people hooked some schoolkids up to an electric current. One was seven years old, another eight, the rest eleven. A live electric current, 220 volts.

Experiment, or what?

I waved my hand dismissively. Does it matter?

At the Sign of the Two Queans I made Daniel Vandyeluk stop once more. The petrol chainsaw, still in its original Stihl packaging, a colourful cardboard box secured by metal bands, lay on a bench in Edmund Pochoriles's kitchen. They were just having breakfast: there was my niece Danczura, who was a waitress in the hostelry, and also hovering about was the Lutheran pastor, Lorenz Fabritius. They knew where I'd been and could also see Vandyeluk near the door, which was slightly ajar. He stood there with his head hanging down, steam rising from his nostrils, as from a horse, in two different directions. He doesn't look much to write home about, remarked Edmund Pochoriles.

No, he doesn't, I nodded. I don't know what my old man will make of him.

Fabritius jabbed a finger at the box as I put it under my arm.

Expensive gear. What d'you need it for?

Well, what d'you think. I can take it to the Mute Forest, or I can use it now to cut up firewood in the yard. But if needs must, I can use it to dismember my enemies.

On my way out Pochoriles remarked: It's not as simple as that, you know. It's not so much the bones, but the blood, the flesh, and the innards that clog up the bearings. That makes the motor stall and you have to clean it all out. You're better off with a good axe, or a sharp cleaver.

I had a nice ginger cat, Tatyana. I used to call her Charlotte but when she started to run to fat and a collar of fur began to bulge around her neck, I gave her a new name. She was just short of eight kilos in weight, with stripes and a thick tail, her ears with tufts like a lynx; if a dog met her in the street, it would cross over smartly to the other side. Now she was crouched expectantly on the transom of the gate, but as we approached she jumped off, and though she was not of a friendly disposition, she initially fixed Daniel Vandyeluk with a stare, holding her head up high, then, moving behind him so she could brush his trousers with her tail, slipped slowly between his legs. She sat down facing him again and stared him in the face, looking straight into those piercing eyes. When we got going again, she trailed in our wake, a couple of steps behind, slowly and ruminatively, her head held low.

Yours?

Whose did you think it was?

Why's it wearing a cat collar?

It's not a cat collar, it's her own collar of fur. She does have a cat collar as well, when needed. Should I happen to be afraid on the night shift, say, I take her along on a leash.

Start kissing her goodbye, because I want her. Name your price.

He may have been serious, but inwardly I just laughed.

In the office I asked him to empty his pockets completely and lay out everything in an orderly fashion on Anatol Korkodus's writing desk. Apart from his release slip he had only 32 coupons on him. He could have used these to get at least a pair of slippers or shoes of some sort for the trip and still had enough left over for a change of underwear and a pair of socks. But he had nothing else. When I had thoroughly patted him down and satisfied myself that this was indeed the case, I led him around the courtyard of the water conservancy brigade, at the far end of which I lived, with my old man, in the old Czervensky mansion. This was a bleak courtyard, overgrown with weeds and with bare tracks traced in the frozen mud. In the open-topped granary lay a rusting snowplough, an ancient sandbuggy covered in thick dust, and beside them the clapped-out old Willys jeep belonging to Honorary District Commissioner Hamilcar Nikonuk, its tyres quite flat. Wherever we walked in the courtyard Daniel Vandyeluk left footprints glinting darkly on the frozen ground. He stopped at the privy entrance and asked for permission to relieve himself.

As I waited for him I caught sight of our dusky Balwinder, the office dogsbody, by the open gate. I had no idea how he came to be there, as earlier there was not a living soul to be seen. Without so much as a 'Good Morning', or even a nod in my direction, he was just standing there motionless, squinting into the yard. The yard where there couldn't have been anything for him to see but us. I went over. Something wrong? What on earth are you doing hanging round here?

Why should there be? I'm just looking around. Isn't that allowed?

Well now! It seems to me you're doing this on purpose. Not much point in it, I can tell you.

Perhaps there is.

Phooey! I was so furious that I spat.

Meanwhile Daniel Vandyeluk had come out of the privy.

Is this where I'm staying, too?

Where you're staying tonight is in quarantine. For a full three weeks. That's how we do things around here, as you well know. Because of the germs.

You could see he didn't quite grasp what I said. Perhaps he didn't even know what quarantine was, or what germs were, but since he didn't ask, I didn't explain. I sat him down in the kitchen, laid a piece of old carpet before him, and told him that if he was cold he could cover his bare feet with that. Though it wasn't especially warm indoors either, his features relaxed and his nose began to run; he wiped it on the sleeve of his jacket. He was a pale, thin-skinned, scrawny kid, his frozen, bluish-grey, dog-eyes swivelled back and forth between the walls. On the back of one hand he sported crude inked-in tattoos, mysterious relics of a mysterious, criminal past: dots, lines, crosses.

Earlier Anatol Korkodus had told me to be sure to treat him well and talk to him, and when they brought lunch from the canteen, to get him to eat, and send him in to see him on his sickbed once he had been properly fed. But that morning I was in no mood to make polite conversation. Various conversational topics flashed through my head, and I was about to take a deep breath several times, but whenever I looked at him and my eyes met his, I got cold feet. Rather, what occurred to me was: how much better it would be if it were not Daniel Vandyeluk sitting there but someone else.

Whenever there is a lengthy silence, one that seems to go on and on, it eventually, quite suddenly, finds a voice. It begins with a gentle sigh, like a distant waterfall, then it starts to crackle, and then, when it is going full blast, raging unbearably, all of a sudden, as if spurting right into you, the whole world comes dripping icily in through your ears. Now, for the moment, only the whistling of the oven's flue was audible, then the ticking of the alarm clock, as if somehow borne on the wind from meadows far away, now fading, now becoming more intense.

Eventually my cat Tatyana began to scratch at the door. I opened it for her, but she didn't come in and just turned her head from side to side, gaping open-mouthed and miaowing barely audibly as she took a sniff into the room. She was a mysterious creature, wilful, self-contained, like every animal with ginger fur. I opened two tins of liver and coaxed her over into the back yard. I shut her up in the toolshed, from where she had no means of escape.

In the woodshed next door, I piled a basket high with peat, put some kindling on top, and went back with my load. I wrapped some oily sawdust in newspaper, and lit the fire in the range, then, once the fire began to flare up, I threw some thin sticks of wood and a few chunks of peat on it. I did this in a leisurely, unhurried way, as if just hoping for time to pass. It was still only morning.

Why didn't you let her in, seeing as she was miaowing?

Today the woodshed's the right place for her. We're getting a few guinea pigs, I wouldn't want them to cross paths.

I opened the paper bag with the two curd-cheese lángoses. I shook the hot chestnuts out of the bag onto the greasy oilcloth covering the table. I peeled myself one and as I popped it into my mouth I gestured to Daniel Vandyeluk to help himself without further ado. He first tore off the corner of a lángos, then reached for the chestnuts. He set about this task with reluctance, shelling them slowly, breaking each into small pieces, sticking them in his mouth and sucking on them.

You don't have that many teeth. I say that because I see the chestnuts could have been left to roast for a little longer. What you can't chew feel free to spit out. Into the palm of your hand, I mean.

Keep your hair on. I chew with my gums. Until they grow again.

What do you mean, grow again? What makes you think they will?

The doc gave me some injections, he said that would make them grow again.

We had no idea here that not all's well with you. It would've been helpful to know that kind of thing in advance. You'll have to ask to be put on a special diet in quarantine for the time being. What happened to your teeth?

Give it a rest.

And couldn't you at least tell me something about how you ended up in the institution? Just broad brush, mind.

No way.

You're right, not a word about it to anyone. That reminds me, Anatol Korkodus told me to ask if you're glad they let you out?

Don't know who that is.

I pointed to my old man's door.

He's the one who had the feeling you'd be arriving today rather than tomorrow. When you've had a rest, knock on his door. He'd like a word as soon as possible.

He gave me a suspicious look but seeing the index finger I had put to my lips he didn't ask any questions even if he'd intended to. And to make sure he understood clearly that we wouldn't be discussing Anatol Korkodus, I turned on the radio.

Well, what d'you think? It's Maya. Maya Miklovitz singing. Know her?

He glanced at me, gave a shrug, but didn't deem me worthy of an answer. Still, I pressed on:

Anyway, what do you think, is there such a name? Do you think it's her real name, or one they just made up for her?

Hey, you're just making fun of me.

Sorry. Just asking. Well, I'm going to leave you here for an hour or so. Take it easy, eat, listen to the news.

Off you go if you've things to do. I like my own company.

In the mornings, when I do my rounds, I start with the public wash-house, checking on its state of cleanliness, whether the stone floor has been washed down, the troughs scoured clean, then I open up the hot taps for those who come for free, locals who are less well-off. We get our hot water from the side of the Paltin, the hot springs of Paltinsky meadow, but when the water is left in the pipes overnight, it cools off considerably, and when the taps are turned on first thing in the morning the water coming from them is no more than lukewarm for quite a while, so between eight and ten the use of the wash-house is free. The better-off come with their washing from ten o'clock onwards: they already get hot water and, of course, have to pay. Once I've finished at the wash-house, I drop by the rapid response unit to see if there's any news; if they are in a good mood we have a game of cards or backgammon, and then, finally, it's off to the river bank. The ice started to break up not long ago: I have to check whether the fast-drifting floes of ice have damaged any of the water-level gauges.

So I trekked out to the Yablonka under the bare willows, all the way along the bank to the Czervensky watch-house, then on to the Czervensky jetty, and the ice-bound Czervensky water-mill, to gaze again at the wonder that is Yablonska Polyana.

One late autumn Balwinder, whose duty it had been for many years, forgot to open up the water-mill's sluices in good time, so they froze solid even before winter really set in, and it proved impossible ever to move them again. The ice began to swell, slowly humping up, spilling over the gates, and the water just kept on coming and coming. At first only the millwheel froze in the swell of crystal that later embraced the entire wooden structure, so that enormous icicles, terrifying glinting tusks of winter, hung down even from the shingle roof. As if encased in glass, the mill stands there still, completely pristine. Sometimes Tatyana and I go for our walk there to look at the mice frozen stiff into it as they tried to flee, their enormous eyes, magnified by the ice, staring out into the eternal, endless void.

Around the water-level gauges, where the waters of Spring No. 2 give off clouds of vapour as they gush into the river and, in summer, its eddies churn sluggishly under the thin, glassy crust of ice, there could already be seen, amid the twisting strands of reed-grass, like messages from an unknown, submarine world, iridescent bubbles swirling round and round. The river was just waking up, on its banks the branches of the willows, too, were beginning to acquire a yellow sheen. After a bitter, frosty dawn at winter's end it seemed as if the fragrant breezes were at last wafting over from the direction of the Paltin's slopes, the occasional, unexpected gust already even carrying a hint of the earthy smell of the plains beyond the mountains. Somewhere behind the tufts of the dispersing mist the sun was playing hide-and-seek, as with a gentle tinkling the eaves began to slough off their icicles, glittering as they oozed in thick black streaks down onto the grey of the frozen soil.

The Man-Gold courtyard, too, wore the iridescent yellow mantle of the melting hoarfrost. This had at one time been the site of Man's dry-cleaner's, until Anatol Korkodus took it into his head to have the Paltin hot springs' waters channelled into the disused synagogue, have a series of troughs built along the walls in the shape of an arc, and the whole building fitted out as a public wash-house, where only the better-off had to pay. Gregor Man didn't close down, but sold his washing-machines, dryers and ironing boards to bagmen and, sensing the way things were going in the world, used the money to buy a kneading machine and a scone-baking oven. Here, in winter, you could also take afternoon tea on the steps in front of the open door, where from a steaming urn he served hot, honey-flavoured dittany tea.

I walked round the courtyard, a steaming mug in hand. Mükk the hairdresser was still shuttered, the windows of Isac Gold, too, still gleamed black, but opposite, in the spital-house, all the lights were on, as if they were already open for business. They didn't see patients this early, and on the backless chairs lined up for them there now sat Subprefect Vaneliza Nikonuk, as the little blue-tit demon, Nurse Nika Karanika, busied herself with her hair, comb and scissors in hand. But quite possibly it was not Madame Subprefect herself, but her daughter: it's impossible to tell them apart, they resemble each other in every way. Nika Karanika held the brittle, lustreless hair between her fingers but was only trimming it, making it look boyish and, to be able to cut the more easily, she would from time to time spit on the scissor blades. Although it couldn't yet have been particularly hot indoors, she must have sensed that spring was on its way: under the light blue smock that came down to her knees she was already stockingless, standing there in flip-flops, and when she occasionally limped her way around the chair, there twinkled on her bare feet, among the cut-off locks of the subprefect's or her daughter's hair, her mother-of-pearl-painted toenails.

Nika Karanika had a slight limp, about which numerous pieces of gossip were in circulation, even some that were barely credible. One of these claimed to know of a knife whose blade had penetrated her spine and remains to this day embedded in her vertebrae, inflaming the nerves in her back.

While I was lost in contemplation of her bare feet, purple-veined from her marble knee down to her alabaster ankle, she stopped cutting Vaneliza Nikonuk's hair and began to rub the skin on her head with cottonwool, from her forehead down to her neck. But suddenly she stopped doing even that, came over to the window, and opened it. She leaned out so that no one else should hear her words. The cottonwool that she still held in her hands gave off a smell of paraffin.

Has something happened, Adam?

Not a thing in the world. As you can see, I'm just having some tea.

I had the feeling you were about to say something. I heard you've got a new kid. That he's hardly a sight for sore eyes and walks barefoot even in wintertime.

You're not far wrong. I really wouldn't mind now if I could call it a day. When could I have a word in confidence with the young lady?

Sometime. But for the moment I'd ask you to move on, as the person concerned doesn't like people staring at her while she's being attended to.

In the cellar under the surgery the Tatars' shop was already open for business, and Akimova and Akimofte lay stretched out on the carpet, dozing amidst the goods they had on offer. Honorary District Commissioner Hamilcar Nikonuk had not long ago diagnosed them as suffering from sleeping sickness, but they were simply addicted to the hookah. Whenever they overdosed, they would generally spend a day or two staring at the world languidly, their pupils dilated. In the cellar, mingled with the smell of leatherette, there lingered even now a bitter-sweet whiff of smoke. In addition to bags, belts and straps, they sold mostly identical pairs of glossy black shoes smelling of faux leather, but behind their stock of these an entire shelf was devoted to three rows of blue, green, and black wellingtons. I chose a pair of black ones at random, sort of medium size, and signed for it; the office would pay.

Meanwhile Daniel Vandyeluk had chosen the bench as a place where he could take his ease, and from its position near the stove he'd pulled it over to the window and lain down on it on his back. I threw the boots down before him but he merely gave them a surly glance, as if they weren't meant for him. I asked him to try them on and quickly picked up a couple of footclouts drying on the washing line, but he said he didn't like walking about in rubber boots and anyway they didn't look as if they were his size. I suggested that if they were really too big, he could find some paper sacking among the kindling: if he wanted to line the boots to make them fit, he should tear some off. And should he happen to want something more stylish, he could spend some of his first month's wages on a pair to his liking from the Tatars.

When even this failed to elicit a response, I gestured in the direction of Anataol Korkodus's door.

Been in to see him?

Not yet. You said to go in when I was rested.

Don't keep putting it off. And you didn't answer my previous question. Are you glad you've been let out?

It wasn't so bad inside. But now: my turn to ask you something. Tell me, who are you, what do you do here?

Well, as you can see. I am someone who meets you at the station, who brings you a brand-new pair of rubber boots for your cold feet. Anything else you want to know?

It's just that I'd like to ask for something right away. Before I go in and see him, tell this person, if you have his ear, that I want to be put with the birds at all costs. So that he knows in advance.

What birds do you have in mind?

The bird section. Where you deal with the migratory birds. In the institution I was a regular at the ornithological circle and I also took part in group observations of birds. Chief Instructor Balmos said that if I really wanted to better myself I should ask straight off to be assigned to the bird section. That I would calm down there, and then I wouldn't be much trouble.

He actually said that?

Word for word. That he couldn't imagine anywhere better for me.

Hm. Well, I don't know. I'm not aware of any bird section. There are no birds hereabouts.

You're having me on.

He stood up from the bench and with his hands in his pockets fixed his greyish-blue gaze on me for a long time, while his big toes curled nervously upwards.

What d'you mean, there aren't any? You surely don't know better than those in Monor Gledin?

Take your hands out of your pockets and sit down again, will you. Those may well have been the words Chief Instructor Balmos used, but even he can't be expected to know everything. We have no bird section. Because there are no birds here. There were, once, but when some people came along and started blasting the nests out of the trees with firehoses, they had a premonition and bang in the middle of summer they thought better of it all and flew away. And another thing: since those events at the Brustyina lakes, when fires were lit in the reedbeds for instance, and belched black smoke, even the migratory birds have kept away. That's the cold hard truth.

You're just winding me up. I don't believe a word you say.

You ought to know that birds are sensitive creatures. If they sense people have harmful intentions towards them, they just take off and fly away, it's in their nature. That's what happened. They went away. From the jays to the finches and the redstarts, they've all gone, except for the old crows. But if that's what you really want me to tell Anatol Korkodus, I can, of course. He's a clever man, he's sure to find you something you like.

Daniel Vandyeluk again stretched out on the bench, glancing at me doubtfully from time to time, hoping that by keeping an eye on the lines of my face he might spot when they softened, in case I happened unexpectedly to say something that might, after all, allow him to simply smile at all he had heard.

Although lunchtime was still some way off, I swept the chestnut shells off the table, wiped the oilcloth with a wet rag, and laid the table for two.

Until you've been through quarantine you mustn't appear in any public place, that's why I've ordered lunch today to be brought over from the canteen. Friday is a meatless day, you can choose between cabbage and semolina pasta. I've ordered the cabbage for you, it often has some potatoes in it, but I can fry up a little fatty bacon to go with it, if you like that kind of thing.

He remained silent, as if he hadn't heard a thing I'd said.

I see I'm talking to a brick wall. You have a face like a wet weekend, but you'll see that Anatol Korkodus will find you something to your liking. If you're so keen on them, you might try to think of a way to tempt at least the songbirds back. Because nothing's impossible. For example, regaining their confidence, that would be a start. Here you'll have plenty of time to think.

I wiped the condensation from the window. The weather outside must have eased off, water was dripping from the eaves. Balwinder took shelter and, resting on the seat of the dune buggy, scanned the courtyard from there. Donning the cap of my water conservancy brigade uniform, I went outside.

Now, what the hell's going on? Do you really have nothing better to do today?

I really don't.

Have you perhaps already taken the Augustins their lunch?

Imagine, today they're getting cold cuts.

Even so. I'll make sure Anatol Korkodus gets a detailed report about this.

He'll be delighted.

He even gave a little smirk.

I went in to see Anatol Korkodus. Although he had earlier said he would be keeping to his bed, he now lay on it fully dressed and wearing boots. His hair was unkempt, his brow damp, and his rough beard trembled with every breath he took. Beside him lay a closed copy of Eronim Mox's cookery book. Even now he occupied only one side of the bed, leaving the other empty. Since Roswitha had left him, Anatol Korkodus used only one half of the bed. The other pillow still had a dimple in it where Roswitha had laid her head.

My head's swimming a bit, I said, I'd like a shot of brandy.

My old man swivelled one eye in the direction of the cupboard where he kept his blackberry brandy.

I gave myself a double shot, with my back to Anatol Korkodus, so he wouldn't see my hands trembling. I half-turned towards him:

I have something to tell you. I wonder what you'll think. It's about Balwinder. How d'you feel about him? He's either completely flipped his lid, or he knows something. Something that we don't. He does nothing all day but moon about, wasting time and grinning like an idiot.

Anyone can have an off day, muttered Anatol Korkodus. When his brain is addled by unusual thoughts. Pay no attention. Just yesterday he asked me for a couple of days off.

And you've never seen the like: the kid dyes his hair. In the normal way it would be brown, but he's used something to put yellow streaks in it. I'll fetch him an old cap of some sort and pull it right down over his ears. I'll go to quarantine with him, so no one sees him in that state. Do you really want a word with him, or can we set straight off after I've been to the Boursin farm?

I certainly do want a word. That's why I had him come here. Let him come in as soon as possible.

It was getting on for midday when I heard the gate, followed by the clink of tin bowls on the doorstep. A kid had brought over lunch from the canteen. I picked up the bowls, threw a few sticks of wood and some peat on the fire, then took my jerkin off the hook.

If it's not hot enough, rest it on the edge of the stove for a while. Give it a stir from time to time, so it doesn't get burnt. When it's done, help yourself, because now I must be off. Friday morning belongs to Miss Bursen.

Go, if you have things to do. It doesn't matter much if you're not here.

Tell me, wouldn't you happen to know some Hungarian? Because if you did, even a little, you could give her lessons. She's no spring chicken, but in these dried-up women there's always some hidden spark.

Daniel Vandyeluk said nothing for a long while, repeatedly shooting daggers at me.

Come on now, what's all this about?

As I put on my jerkin, I tried to press on:

You could take my place. It's enough for her if you just read. To have the buzz of foreign words around her, that's all she wants.

But there was no one listening.

For years now, Friday mornings had belonged to Klara Bursen. Miss Bursen felt resentful towards Yablonska Polyana, only visiting the settlement on high days and holidays, so once a week I do her shopping and take it to her on the Boursin farm in a saddlebag. On my way there I would borrow the odd Hungarian-language book from the library of the former Lutheran school and take that as well. She doesn't understand Hungarian, yet she veritably devours books in the language. Once I arrive with the saddlebag, and the book in it, she asks me to take a seat and, while she makes me elderberry-cordial pancakes, asks if I would read her at least a page or two from the book I have brought. While I do that she is careful to make not even the slightest noise with the dishes, so that not a syllable escapes her attention. It's all quite pointless: she doesn't understand a single word, but she listens in awe with her eyelids lowered. Sometimes we make a joint effort to guess what the piece I'd read might be about. But we never get anywhere.

Not long ago she found herself in such distress that she sought out Madame Aliwanka, who told her future from a freshly wept-on handkerchief limp with her tears. That she could see a man in a soldier's uniform, yes, an officer, who was making his way from the Medwaya pass on horseback over the snow-covered crags, looking for her, Miss Klara Bursen, by name. And this army officer spoke only Hungarian. Ever since the spinster had wanted to learn Hungarian by hook or by crook. But few Hungarians had ever lived in Verhovina, and even here in Yablonska Polyana hardly any remained. The only trace of them were a few mouldering Hungarian books, their pages yellow with age.

This morning, too, Klara Bursen immediately snatched from my satchel the book I'd brought and sat me down to read to her as she tossed the pancakes. The first chapter must have been about some Pipó Ozorai, because that name occurred several times in the text. We learned little else about this person, and in any case the reading this morning was not going well. I kept stumbling over the sentences and had to make several attempts before managing some of the words. Afterwards, since it was a Friday, she handed me on a slip of paper the numbers she wanted to play in the weekly lottery, remarking in a chilly tone:

Am I right in thinking that you are a little stressed, somewhat troubled? Though I'm not surprised, as you'll have to come to terms with the idea that soon you'll be left on your own.

You mean me? What would Miss Klara have in mind?

Your uncle, or whoever it is that you're living with. He won't be with us for very much longer. His time is over, soon strangers will come for him and take him away. As they might put it in town: he'll be arrested.

I stared at her, with a degree of sympathy and pity. I was used to her coming out with all kinds of stuff and nonsense. This was another thing she'd made up, she of all people, who hadn't been down to the settlement since Christmas.

Arrested? That's for nobility. It's not how things are done in these parts. Here people are simply kidnapped. Anyone can be carried off. Even a brigadier like Anatol Korkodus.

And in Verhovina whenever they did come for someone secretly, in the dead of night, news of it got out spontaneously and passed from house to house with the dawn breeze, so that by morning everyone knew all about it. As well as the fact that the person would never be seen again. But that anyone should have known about it in advance? Never had such a thing happened.

The previous night Anatol Korkodus had asked me that as I did my chores I should pick up for him from hostelry keeper Edmund Pochoriles a number of guineapigs. As I couldn't deal with them in the morning because I'd been preoccupied with the chainsaw, I decided it was now time once again to drop by the hostelry at the Sign of the Two Queans. I also thought I might have a word or two with my niece, red-headed little Danczura, who had likewise been originally sent here from the reformatory at Gledin and was now waiting tables at Pochoriles's. The hostelry keeper had recently been presented with two dozen guineapigs by District Commissioner Hamilcar Nikonuk and had promised to give six of them to Anatol Korkodus. Since the great fowlpest epidemic in the autumn the birdcages in the back yard had been empty and my old man had already prepared some straw for them there.

In the hostelry Pochoriles also had rooms to let on the floor above the bodega, with windows overlooking the Man-Gold courtyard opposite, from where you had a view of the whole marketplace. Whenever I look that way I see a nightmarish spectre: as if two bald, cowled men were staring out from behind the windows. My question to Pochoriles, as to whether I was seeing aright, seems to fall on deaf ears, and he doesn't answer.

But seamstress Aliwanka knows about them. She can see the world in water, she can even see into the future, all she needs is a little water or some other liquid. Drizzle, rime, dewdrops, or tears, or even the angry, swirling eddies of the Yablonka – any and all of these will do. Though she has not yet actually seen them, she knows of two cowled individuals in pilgrims' garb, who have long intended to pay the settlement a visit. It may be them, their prefiguration, that's quivering behind the window-panes. Their names were Damian and Cosmas, they were monks, and had come to Verhovina to heal the sick. They would take a room here, wouldn't leave the hostelry, and would advertise their presence only on slips of paper posted on fences and left to stream in the wind, announcing that they would be available from morning till nightfall to receive the sick. According to Aliwanka they are pale, malodorous, and clammy-skinned.

Hm. From time to time a hazy exhalation seemed to ripple across the first-floor windows.

I found my niece Danczura in the corridor, amid besoms, pails and floorcloths. I asked her if there was any news, whether as she went about her work she'd heard anything of Roswitha, who had recently disappeared from Anatol Korkodus's house and indeed from Yablonska Polyana.

Roswitha, the tiny, cosseted jewel, the living bauble from whose looks and minuscule size one couldn't tell whether she was really a fully-grown woman or just a little girl, was Anatol Korkodus's household pet. He dressed her, combed her hair, dandled her, cooked for her and read out to her, even though he knew she was deaf and dumb. He guarded her fiercely, as if in her person he awaited some kind of miracle, the great day of truth. This little household pet, golden-fleeced Roswitha, had recently been abducted.

Danczura was just elaborating her theory that Madame Subprefect, or her daughter, had had a hand in the business. Because these two were as one in every way, you couldn't even be sure which of them was the mother and which the daughter.

In the hostelry's back yard, in front of Edmund Pochoriles's summer kitchen, in a clothes basket covered with a net lay six trembling guineapigs. Anatol Korkodus says that from the moment the guineapigs come into the world they expect their own demise and never stop shivering and shaking, for they know they will not die a natural death.

On my way home, with the basket under my arm, I once again drop in at the Man-Gold yard.

In the spital-house the lights were still on. I waited until the last patient had left and knocked on the surgery door. Nika Karanika, seeing that it was not one of her patients wanting her, came out onto the front step, closing the door behind her. She had already taken off her light blue lab coat and was now wearing her little sand-coloured sheepskin jacket with strings of dark blue and black pearls on the collar. The smell of paraffin had also drifted away, and from her collar and the depths of her cleavage there now rose the heady scent of cardamom oil.

I've got wind of something, I said to her quietly and in a confidential tone. There are two people looking for you, staying here, in Edmund Pochoriles's hostelry. In all of Verhovina, it's only you they're interested in, no one else. They claim that they, and they alone, can cure you of your slight limp. That if some small object should have got stuck in there, in your spine, they are the only ones capable of removing it. I beg you, truly beg you, to be careful: if you should run into them, whatever they say, don't believe a word of it.

Nina Karanika gave me a chilly brush-off: I'm not aware of anyone staying in the hostelry. But should it be as you say, then they are bound to seek me out in due course. And who knows, maybe they can indeed winkle it out of there.

Never. They'd only wedge it in tighter than ever. Because that's what they've come here for. I couldn't bear it if something were to happen to you.

Once again, these are strange things that I'm hearing from you today.

Believe me, it may be that I'm just having a bad day. A very bad day.

Adam, why don't you go home? We'll have a proper talk sometime. You understand? Sometime. One summer, at sunset. But tell you what. Today one of my patients gave me a long, thin glass, unless I'm mistaken it's for distinguished drinks, but since I drink only water, I'll let you have it.

From the surgery Nina Karanika brought out a flute glass wrapped in tissue paper and since both my hands were full, she squeezed it into the pocket of my jerkin, above the trembling guineapigs.

Just so that you see: I too think of you.

Then, she stuck out her tongue, touched it with a fingertip, and drew a cool cross on my brow.

The dish with the three portions of cabbage was perched where I had left it, on the edge of the range. Since the fire had gone out, I lit it again, and as soon as it had warmed the dish up again, I helped myself. Daniel Vandyeluk's portion was untouched: he hadn't eaten, you could see he hadn't touched a thing. He still lay stretched out on the chest, staring at the ceiling.

I ate in silence, washed up the plate, unwrapped the little flute glass I had got from Nina Karanika, and only then remarked:

You must have a delicate stomach, seeing as you haven't touched the food. If you didn't feel like the cabbage you could at least have fished out the potatoes. You can't not like potatoes.

I'm not hungry.

Have you been in to see him?

He called me in. He said it wasn't certain I'd have to move into that quarantine thing, as you call it. Even if I do, I'd have a little bit of business to attend to beforehand.

Then set about it double-quick. Meanwhile I'll fill in your registration form and then take you over myself. Are you sure you heard right? That you may not have to be quarantined?

He said it was up to me. That I can decide on the way whether I want to go or not. Because he's sending me off somewhere. He said I should go out to the dam. But as you can see, I haven't gone yet.

All by yourself? To the dam? Even if you set off now you may not get back before dark.

He said that at the dam I should seek out damkeeper Duhovnik. That's his name, he said. Because he's had enough of him. He said he would like something to happen. To the damkeeper.

You sure you heard right? Is that what he said, word for word?

Word for word.

Well then, you'd better be off. But you won't make it back today. On the other hand, you have to be checked into quarantine before they close for the night.

But I tell you, I really may not have to come back here. If I understood the old boy right. He said I can decide on the way, he leaves it up to me. What d'you think?

No use asking me. You're the one who spoke to him. You must know what he wants. I've no idea what he could've had in mind.

Anatol Korkodus was still lying on his bed, fully dressed and with his boots on, his greying locks hanging into his eyes, his bristly beard rather scruffy. Beside him on the covers lay Eronim Mox's book of stories. I sat down opposite him and since I waited in vain for him to look at me, I began.

I've brought the guineapigs over.

Only a deep intake of breath came by way of an answer. After a while I tried to continue:

Two are as black as coal, four are brindled. They're mature specimens, won't grow any bigger, and ready for slaughter any time. I must just make sure Tatyana doesn't set eyes on them.

And then I tried again:

The Subprefect woman has had her hair cut short and had herself doused in paraffin. But it may be her daughter. It seems she has lice. She must be about to go on a trip, or wants to look her best for someone.

As if he hadn't heard me came his response:

Remind me tomorrow to leave a written note concerning what I have already told you all. If I should happen to die, lay me to rest in the bluestone Spring No. 2. Lower me, clothes and all, with pebbles in my pockets. You'll see: I'll be preserved in it for years. If you ever want to see me, on my name day, say, you need only take a walk out to the spring with a slice of milk loaf and a jug of wine and you'll be able to have a look.

I swallowed hard, several times, wondering whether he would say anything more.

But Anatol Korkodus fell silent, his hands giving the occasional jerk, as if trying to make a gesture of resignation. Outside, the sound of the dripping eaves could be heard. From the icy silence of the kitchen came the ticking of the alarm clock. I wiped the condensation from the windows with the palm of my hand and looked out.

I wanted to have this Balwinder brought over to you. But now he's disappeared, I can't find him anywhere. It may well be his day off, but even then I can't see why he has to spend all day loitering by the fence. He just stands in the middle of the yard, staring with a gormless grin on his face. He never did that before. But now he's finally sloped off. He behaves as if he were privy to some knowledge. It would be a good idea if you gave him a piece of your mind.

I coughed lightly and lowered my voice as I continued:

And I don't know if you happen to have noticed, but it's at least two weeks since the phone last rang. We haven't had a single call. The silence is dreadful. It seems that these days no one wants to talk to you.

Even this didn't make Anatol Korkodus look up. This meant that he was not in the least interested in what I had to say or, more likely, that these were all things he already knew. Nor did he look at me when, much later, he did speak up:

Has he gone?

I didn't hear the door. Nor did I see him go. But if I really want to, I do know what's going on behind the scenes. For example, that he went off the moment I came in here to see you.

What do you think: will he do what I asked him to?

I don't know, Anatol Korkodus. I don't know why you ask me such things.

Still. What do you think?

I don't know. I also don't know what the hell you saw in this kid. Why it was him, of all people, that you had to have brought here.

As it happens, I didn't think there was anything special about him. That was the point. He was the sort of nothingy kid I happened to need at the time.

I don't like to hear such things from you.

Come now. Sooner or later you find something out about everyone. Why should we keep trying to hush things up.

I don't know what's got into you. You never did such things before.

Of course I did. You just didn't know about them. Even I didn't know myself. But don't let it bother you now. He's got a bit of money, wherever he ends up he'll manage for a while.

And now that the thaw is upon us it will soon be time for the rainbow trout to spawn. Is there a new damkeeper, a reliable lakemaster to take Duhovnik's place?

No need for anyone up there anymore. Someone, who might just go by the name of Duhovnik, dug a trench as long ago as last autumn to make sure the water drained into the lake from under the slagheaps. There's a solid layer of dead trout beneath the ice. One day you'll go out to the dam with Balwinder and when the sluices have unfrozen you'll open them up and drain all the water from the lake.

Fine. We're ready to go whenever you say. But should you change your mind I could saddle a donkey and catch up with the kid before he finds Duhovnik. I'd bring him back and take him to quarantine.

Don't be silly. You don't understand a thing. That's quite out of the question now.

The fire in the kitchen must have gone out long ago, a draught hummed between the ventilator and the flue; the ticking of the alarm clock occasionally sounded louder, like some bug that had strayed indoors and was flying to and fro as it bounced off the walls. For a while I just rested my elbows on the table, rubbing the itchy corners of my eyes with my fists. If truth be told, I hadn't slept much since the previous evening.

Suddenly I looked up for a moment and my eyes happened to alight on the bare doorpost. Where Tatyana's leash always hung. And indeed, that's where it was hanging when I'd gone in to see Anatol Korkodus. But now it wasn't there. I stood up and went over to examine from close up the spot where the nail stuck out naked from the doorjamb. So: Tatyana was gone, too.

The pair of wellingtons I had bought from the Tatars lay where I had thrown them, in front of the bench. Yet up above, at the dam, the snow was still piled high, melting and slushy on the road leading to it, while the path was covered with a veneer of ice.

Daniel Vandyeluk must have got quite far. He had set off barefoot to find damkeeper Duhovnik.

It had been a wretched day. With my elbows on the table I waited for darkness to descend on us at long last. Very close to my face, with the purple window reflected in its stem, gleamed a slim goblet. The slim little crystal goblet that the blue-tit demon, Nika Karanika, had presented to me earlier in the day. As I stared at it long and hard, at times I would see its outline double before my moist eyes as it shimmered, now coming nearer, now moving farther off, or happening to pulsate with light now and again, setting even the air aquiver. Eventually the waves of sleep drew nearer, washing over me ever so slowly, as if what I had been waiting for all day was just this crystalline sound, a low hum that arose gradually, of its own accord.

2.

(DELFINA)

Hanku went by just one name. You couldn't tell whether it was a family name or a nickname that had stuck to him: it was simply the only name on his papers. He'd come to Yablonska Polyana from the reformatory some time ago and his probationary period was long over when Anatol Korkodus entrusted four sticks of madezite to his care, saying he should take them out to the Mute Forest and hand them to the damkeeper.

Once at the end of March, when hereabouts night and, along with it, the chilling silence of the frost settles upon the houses, Anatol Korkodus was startled awake by the noise of icicles clattering down from the eaves. In the morning, when the sussuration of the melting snow from the slopes could be heard even indoors, he sent a message by pigeon post to the reservoir lake, that damkeeper Duhovnik was to open up the sluices without further ado. Though the pigeon failed to return, Anatol Korkodus nevertheless braved the drizzle and went out in his rain-coloured cape several times over the following two days to the banks of the Yablonka to check on the water-level gauges, keeping a wary eye on the floodwaters ablare with the breaking up of the ice floes. But the streams were only swollen because of the turbid snowmelt streaming down from the nearby slopes. It seems that despite his message, the sluices up above had not been opened.

Despite his message indeed: because damkeeper Duhovnik was by this time long dead. His wind-blasted, crow-pecked body had been dangling since autumn in the vicinity of the dam, on the lowest branch of a mountain maple, at the end of a thin wire rope.

But Anatol Korkodus was unaware of this. It was common knowledge that the damkeeper spent the winter in hibernation by the frozen lake, so he wouldn't have been missed by anyone. It would have been just about time for him to wake up, now that spring had come.

Anatol Korkodus had suspected for some time that the headwaters of the Yablonka had attracted someone's attention, and that this would also be where his own career would come to an end. Soon all his ties to this place would be severed, yet he continued to carry out his activities not as if he were working with that decline and fall in prospect, but for all eternity. At the onset of the thaw the reservoir had to be emptied in good time. Having waited in vain for three days, he knew that something up there was amiss, and imagined that over the long hard winter the sluices must have frozen solid. If that had happened, several days' work on them would be needed, and the damkeeper would require assistance, so someone had to go out to the site.

That was when he thought of this Hanku, and immediately sent him a message that he should get ready, his day had come. He had a sensitive task for him: a few sticks of madezite had to be taken to the dam, in case it proved necesssary for damkeeper Duhovnik to dynamite the ice around the frozen-up sluices. He should help him to sprinkle the salt on the ice and spend two or three days in the forest if need be, until he could see that they had managed to lower the lake to a safe level.

At the same time Anatol Korkodus also sent a message to the communal stables, asking them to saddle up a donkey for Hanku's use. And to lead it out at once to the entrance of the public washhouse, where Hanku had a job as a cleaner, so that he had neither the time nor the inclination to think twice about his mission. Here, apart from the single hack that Anatol Korkodus shared with Deacon Ambrozi, they kept only donkeys. The one they chose for Hanku had neither tail nor mane. Someone had surreptitiously just clipped them off. It had a simple wooden saddle for haulage, uncomfortable to sit on, which was, rather, used for attaching packs and saddlebags.

Nor did Hanku want to sit on it: he set off down the road leading away from the houses holding the donkey by its bridle. His next stop was beyond the Czervensky jetty, close to the rapid response unit, where he was to pick up the madezite. Anatol Korkodus was sitting on the bench in front of the entrance, but when Hanku hove into view he went inside the single-storey, tin-roofed building.

Through the open window Hanku could see him signing various documents, one after the other. They must have been the special authorisations for the explosives and the receipts for the transaction. He saw that the sticks of madezite, factory-sealed and wrapped in greaseproof paper, were counted out again and again, as if there were vast numbers of them, and were then carefully placed in a smallish wooden box padded with sponges, and the lid was bolted down. To the wooden box was attached also an elasticated chain, from the end of which dangled a carabiner and a small lock, should the bearer become concerned and want to lock it, or even attach it to his own body if need be, for security's sake. The whole lot was placed in a fatigue-coloured canvas satchel. Soon, Anatol Korkodus came out of the building, hung the satchel by its loop on the wooden saddle and proceeded to strap it down as well. He also carried another satchel, which he hung on the far side of the saddle. He made Hanku sign two pieces of paper confirming he had received the goods and folded them into the pocket of his greatcoat. He left Hanku two additional copies, to be returned with Duhovnik's signature.

D'you know what madezite is?

I don't.

No matter. Keep it away from heat, don't put it anywhere near a fire, and there's no need to jump up and down on it. Hand it over to Duhovnik, he knows what to do with it.

He warned him that for the first two days the salt should be sprinkled only on the ice, to make sure they didn't damage the dam gates. Hanku should sleep at the sappers' lodge so that he could get to the dam every morning in good time. He would send him some provisions that very evening.

In the other satchel you will find two flasks. The one filled with the gentian root brandy is for Duhovnik. The other also contains alcohol, but the kind that trooping-funnel mushrooms have been soaked in for a year, so you mustn't drink any of it. That's for Delfina, for her skin. Her forehead is covered with virulent pustules.

At the bottom of the slope, at the sappers' Birtz lodge, where there was room in the spacious hall on the ground floor for a smallish canteen, Hanku came to a halt. He called in through the open door, asking for a bed to be made up for the night and, should the provisions promised by Anatol Korkodus fail to arrive, also supper of some kind, as he would be staying overnight. He asked for a tin of beans, opened it, and taking shelter from the light rain under the eaves, spooned it out completely.

As he ate, Master Sapper Dragila made an appearance. He was a rotund, red-cheeked man with a straggly beard and kestrel feathers stuck behind the ribbon of his hunting hat. On his tunic, at the armpits, salty spots of sweat shone grey. His clothing, too, reeked of garlic and louse-powder, which mingled with the smell of paraffin in the room. This was the first time Hanku had met him and he backed away. But the fellow kept coming closer. He had a feel of the canvas satchel on the side of the donkey.

What's in it?

I don't really know. Madezite, they say.

Seriously? Yours? Tell me, what are you going to do with it?

Nothing. I'm supposed to hand it over to Duhovnik.

Hm. Is that so?

Yes, indeed. I'm taking it to him.

I said: is that so.

I heard you.

You could sell it to me.

Hanku looked around.

Why? What will you give me for it?

How many sticks are there?

Sticks, you say. I wouldn't know. If they're sticks, then four, I think.

You'll surely get a thousand for it.

In coupons? Then twelve hundred at least. Duhovnik must get two hundred, so that he signs the papers as if he'd received them.

Hanku took out from his tunic pocket the documents he had received from Anatol Korkodus for Duhovnik to sign. He showed them to Master Sapper Dragila. The sapper gave them a passing glance.

Aha. I see. Well, get him to sign them in due course.

Dragila came out with the money, and counted it out before Hanku, in units of one-hundred coupons. He went back and reappeared with two gobletfuls of brandy. When they had drained these in silence, the master sapper lifted the canvas satchel from the saddle and took it indoors. He brought back the empty satchel, together with the empty wooden box and its chain.

This I don't need.

Hanku took it from him, but then flung it against the wall.

Neither do I.

Before he set off, Hanku asked if he knew anything about the damkeeper: had he seen Duhovnik recently? The master sapper just shrugged his shoulders, saying that lately only his wife Delfina had been down to buy some bacon and maize flour. As for the damkeeper, he hadn't seen him since late autumn.

So that was how things stood. At the sappers' lodge, too, no one knew that the damkeeper was long dead.

The cart track leading to the dammed-up black lake in the forest was full of twists and turns, but as Anatol Korkodus had once or twice before taken Hanku along with him, he knew the short cuts to take. To ensure he returned to the sappers before nightfall, he wanted to get there as soon as possible, so he opted for the steeper track. It began hard by the sappers' lodge, a narrow gully that wound its way steeply through the forest.

Along the track in the odd patches of melting snow it was perhaps still the remains of Delfina Duhovnik's broad footprints that could be seen glinting darkly, from the last time she had headed for the dam with her satchel filled with maize bran. The traces of her footprints had become distended and distorted in the slush, now grey with pine needles. As if earlier a bear had been that way. Sometimes there was a smell, too. Where, between two footprints, a yellow stain indicated that she had squatted down to answer a call of nature, a heavy, feral smell hung in the air. On the branches of the pines tufts of grey hair that had caught on them fluttered aloft, glinting.

Up in the mountains, too, the thaw was well under way, the snowmelt dribbling down the hillsides in turbid rivulets. But in places the channels where the water flowed were still covered by windswept older snow; from under this only the staccato rumble of the melt could be heard. At such points the donkey carefully took a roundabout route by itself, trotting off into the forest among the rotting trunks of the fallen pines. There was no need to goad it, as it knew well the way to the dam. It would periodically stop to rest by itself and stared into space with a donkey-like melancholy.

In the silence that suddenly fell whenever this happened, all that could be heard from under the purple cloak of the mist was the whispering of the thaw, the gentle hum of the melting snow. And from far away, behind the heavy silence of the Mute Forest, like a message from the afterlife, there came from forests unknown an echo of the cuckoo's stoical call. Even to the faraway peaks, spring was coming at last.

Suddenly he found himself on the shores of the black lake. Slushy ice still extended over it, unmoving, covered in pine needles and cones and lichen carried on the wind. But in places, along the shore and around the dam's iron sluices, a little runoff, too, glimmered here and there amidst the blue, brown and green radiance of the Mute Forest.

It had been dubbed the Mute Forest by Anatol Korkodus after the birds had departed Verhovina. At the time, early one summer, persons unknown had tramped through the groves and, before anyone had a chance to ask who they were, used hooked poles and jets of water to knock down the nests. That was their message for the birds and then, like people who had done what they had been told to do, they disappeared without trace.

The birds seemed to understand that what lay ahead was no longer of their world, and moved away. The forest that had fallen mute had ever since been the dominion solely of sombre, sullen crows.

And, of course, of damkeeper Duhovnik and his wife, the ursine Delfina. They had little to do. From time to time they would gather up the boughs that had fallen into the water and the dried-up leaves brought on the wind and, using a long-handled scraper, remove the sludge caked onto the grilles of the reservoir spigots. During the autumn rains and the great spring thaw, whenever the basin filled to the brim, they would open the sluices and let all the water out of the reservoir lake, until its bottom could be seen. With the approach of winter, they took to their bed, covered themselves with tow, twigs and the fallen leaves of autumn and, like gruff bears, slept huddled together in their snowbound hut until spring.

At least, that was the way it had been up to then. But it now transpired that in the course of the winter Delfina had been down more than once to fetch food from the Birtz sappers.

Normally at the pounding of hooves or the braying of a donkey, the damkeeper's dog would come running out at full pelt, while Duhovnik himself would be ready and waiting in the doorway of his hut. This time nothing stirred. The wind had dropped, the muffled noises of the forest had died down, and even the distant call of the cuckoo was swallowed up by the gathering dusk.

Behind the hut's only window, pressing her nose to the glass, stood Delfina, staring out of the hut. Her breath steamed up the glass around her face, making her eyes seem like saucers. She made not the slightest movement, and seemed to be painted onto the glass.

"Duhovnik, or whatever his name is, doesn't seem to be at home," Hanku must have been thinking because, paying no attention to the woman, he tied up his donkey, passed by melting snow in heaps as far as the shore, and walked the length of the ramp leading to the dam. He looked down into the deep. Then he opened the metal cupboard where the boxes of salt and ash were stored and for some quarter of an hour shovelled, reluctantly, throwing a mixture of salt and ashes over the dam's seized-up sluices.

Slowly he loped back to the donkey and looked around. Delfina Duhovnik was still motionless, glued to the windowpane. No point waiting, Hanku gestured to her:

Come on, give me a hand. Let's try and give the sluices a turn.

He unhitched the satchel from the wooden saddle and handed it over to the woman.

This is from Korkodus for the two of you. One has brandy in it, the other some rubbing alcohol for you.

He set off after Delfina, who grumpily padded off towards the part of the dam where you could stand. She trod the mixture of slushy mud and snow barefoot. She wore a grey knitted dress that reached down to her ankles, from under which there emanated the smell of rancid fat. Her unkempt, salt-and-pepper hair swirled around her, melding with the steam of her breath.

Hanku kept clear even of her footprints.

Hey! Has the pigeon been?

The pigeon, you say? Is that what you're asking? It has, for sure. Of course it has.

I only ask because Mr Korkodus says it didn't return.

I'm not surprised, seeing as I ate it.

Listen. I'm told that in the autumn you didn't let the water down from the lake. And now, as the two of you didn't salt it in good time, the sluices are still frozen solid. What's got into you?

How should I know? These days it seems that's what we feel like doing. We must've had something else to do at the time.

And then you go and eat the pigeon. Korkodus has clearly told you in writing that you should immediately let the water down from the lake.

Writing or no writing, I can't read.

And Duhovnik? Whereabouts is he now?

He went for a walk.

Under the closed sluices some water just about managed to trickle out in a thin black stream. The plates had to be moved at all costs. Both ends of the capstan were supplied with a winch and it needed a couple of sturdy folk to release from the grip of the ice the heavy plates down in the depths, half-frozen and hanging at the ends of the chains. When Delfina Duhovnik grasped one of the winches, her shoulders bulged, the muscles and veins on her arms stood out, and the gleaming white of her skin and fat-covered shoulder blades could be seen through the rents in her dress.

On the first day of spring the damkeeper and his wife would normally stagger out after their long hibernation, dazed and having lost a great deal of weight, but now Delfina was in fine fettle and showed no signs of hesitancy. It was hardly her fault that the plates proved impossible to move.

For a while there was just the creak of the rusty chains as they tensed, then quite suddenly the heavy cast-iron plates let out a small groan from the depths, when, thanks to the pressure of the ice, the water began to run slowly through the sluices. But it didn't last. When they tried to give it another turn, the plates wouldn't budge.

There was nothing to be done, so they set off for the hut. Hanku warned Delfina, who was now walking behind him Indian file, that because they would freeze up every night, salt must be scattered continually around the sluices. And the next day, they should try to move the plates first thing, even before Hanku returned to the hut.

Well, now, really, what on earth are you thinking of? I can't do it on my own.

So Duhovnik isn't coming home today?

You said it. Not today, that's for sure. And maybe not tomorrow either.

So where the hell has he gone?

Told you. He went for a walk.

All right. Well, you go back now and shovel some salt around the sluices until nightfall. I'll come up in the morning and then we'll give it another go. Mind you keep the sluices open as long as the thaw's on and the streams are swelling.

The woman looked at him. Pimples festooned her brow like azalea buds.

Will you stay in the forest? 'Cause you can sleep here if you like. I'll make a fire and get washed.

I'm staying at the sappers'. Mr Korkodus is sending a man over there tonight with salami, bread and something to drink.

It rained through the night. Hanku awoke even before daybreak. The donkey, since it wasn't needed, he left in the sappers' stables. He took the carrier bag with the bread, salami and drink that Anatol Korkodus had sent, and set off. This time, being in no hurry, instead of taking the steep, slippery path, he opted for the old cart track on the left bank of the stream. A few plump stars were still blinking in the purple sky, while far in the distance, beyond the glades of the Medwaya, the birds were just waking up. The first to make themselves heard were the cockerels, their cock-a-doodle-doo, like clacking in an empty church, echoing about the tree-trunks of the Mute Forest; next came the mistle-thrushes' dawn chorus, weaving a fabric of sound amidst the distant plains. But the sounds could have easily come from anywhere, perhaps even some other land. Equally, it's possible that it was all just Hanku's imagination.

He was already close to the dam, at the point where the pathway widened a little, when the silence of the forest was disturbed by the sound of cawing. A flock of crows was flying in capricious, zigzagging turns, a living winding sheet rippling above the trees. A lonely maple stood among the pines: its branches were all bare, and from the lowest-lying branch, at the end of a thin wire rope, there dangled damkeeper Duhovnik. As the crows swooped down on him again and again, he swung now this way, now that. Like some jolly scarecrow, that even birds need not fear. Swinging hither and yon, as if taking a look around. Though by then he'd long had no eyes. He could be recognised only by his treasury outfit, because he had been seriously pecked at, very seriously indeed. The rough cloth hung off him in tatters, and in places where his bare, bone-coloured ribs were visible the wind whistled through them. From the same branch, on a thin wire rope of the same kind, dangled the corpse of a black and white dog. Damkeeper Duhovnik and his dog. No question, it was them all right.

Delfina Duhovnik stared out of the damkeeper's hut with her nose glued to the glass window. She had enormous globe-like eyes, like those of saints on old stained-glass windows. Hanku motioned to her.

Over here. We can surely open up a sluice or two.

Delfina came outside. She was now wearing short leather boots, a knee-length woven peasant dress with black and blue stripes; her little white mounds shook in its deep cleavage. During the night that had passed it seemed as if she had lost weight, her padding and her bulges had shrunk somewhat, she had not a bit of that rancid fat smell about her, but rather the scent of oak leaves, while her hair was twisted into a loose bluish-black knot and hung down from her neck. The purple pimples of passion radiated from her brow. As they approached the dam, Hanku kept glancing at her.

I see you were waiting for me. What do you dye your hair with?

Blueberries. Generally I use elderberries, but if we run short, blueberries will do.

They gripped the winch-handles and looked at each other, each expecting the other to give the signal to start. They twisted the capstan until they could hear it give a crack down below, then the sluice plate moved, slowly easing itself free of the ice's grip, and the water, sucking the debris down with it, came crashing down towards the bed of the stream.

The woman tied the winch up with a chain that ended in a hook to make sure the capstan didn't slip, then, as if she was about to say something, licked her lips, and looked Hanku straight in the eye. Nonetheless it was Hanku who was the first to speak:

Tell me, but on your word of honour, when did Duhovnik leave?

In the autumn.

Did he say anything?

Only that he was going for a walk in the forest. That it was fine weather for a walk, it would do him good to stretch his legs. A pleasant young man happened to be passing and invited him to come along.

You might at least have cut him down.

I can't reach.

In that case I'd now like to have some of the brandy intended for him. I'm sure he wouldn't mind. And there's a stick of salami from Mr Korkodus. If you made a fire, you could fry a couple of slices before I go down to the sappers.

I'd rather you didn't go to the sappers.

And did what?

And stayed here.

With that Delfina went inside the hut and brought out the flask of brandy and two tin mugs.

They spent the time until midday drinking in the shade of the woodpile, then Delfina made a fire. In a pan she began to fry a few thick slices of salami, covering them with a layer of dry hominy grits. Hanku sat on a treetrunk facing the door, glancing periodically into the hut. He could see that the woman, when she was not poking the slices of salami, was applying the mushroom alcohol to her brow. Hanku called out to her:

You didn't sleep in the winter.

No. Something made me restless. And I was hungry, hungry all the time.

Were you waiting for him to come home?

No, I wasn't.

When they had eaten, Delfina stayed indoors, Hanku again sat down outside the hut, helping himself liberally to Korkodus's mulberry wine. After a while he leaned back against the woodpile and dozed off.

When quite some time later he opened his eyes, he was staring directly into those of Delfina. She was standing in the doorway as if it was summer, watching him. Her lips were painted red, her teeth glistened with saliva, her eyelids were tinted with shades of sloe. She was watching Hanku with her arms folded under her bosom, which made her mounds stick out. And as Hanku watched her, he could see through the woman's clothes. But perhaps not all that well, because Delfina spoke up:

Come inside, I want to show you something. And bring your cup.

Hanku did not stir. He stared at Delfina. She looked back at him, her arms folded.

Can you tell me your name?

Hanku.

Come inside, Hanku. As I say, I want to show you something.

Hanku got up from the trunk he was sitting on, and while Delfina went into the hut, he patted the trousers he was wearing.

Well I never. They're wet through.

We'll take them off, I'm not having you catch a cold here.

Delfina closed the door, and at once undid the belt at Hanku's waist. She fiddled with his buttons, then pulled the trousers off him.

That's better. And now see why I called you in.

She licked her lips again, took a deep breath, and grasping the hem of her skirt above the knee, slowly, like a curtain revealing some grand surprise, began to raise her skirt, an inch at a time. First just to mid-calf, then, pausing for a moment and looking Hanku straight in the eye, she finally uncovered herself up to the navel. She wore no underwear of any kind. Her thick white thighs were webbed with purple veins, and below her navel, like tiny fleeing bugs, birthmarks lay sprinkled in every direction. In the depths of her little moss-covered nest there glistened a small pink snail of living flesh.

The smell of fresh yeast filled the hut. Hanku knelt down before Delfina, and with eyes closed embraced the white pillows of her buttocks, like someone who had all his life been waiting for just this moment.

Not a word passed between them until dawn, the only thing that could be heard was the scrabbling of the odd mouse among the odds and ends in the hut, and the silken sound of thighs rubbing against each other lusciously. Above them through the night, with its ghostly dull glow of a lover's moon, shimmered the flask of mushroom alcohol. And, on Delfina's brow, the stars of contagion.

As soon as the sun came up, Hanku slipped out from under the covers, ate the slice of cold roast salami that remained in the frying pan, scraping out the fat, too, with the dry hominy grits. He pulled on his trousers and boots. Then Delfina, too, got out of bed and opened the window. They could hear the water gushing out of the sluice gates.

We did a decent day's work.

I knew we would. It was written on your brow.

Hanku looked at his reflection in the open window. His face was rather blotchy and smeared, glistening with rainbow-coloured flakes of congealed saliva. He turned to face the woman.

I still don't get it. If you couldn't reach, how did you manage to drag him up there?

It wasn't easy.

And you had to do the same with the dog.

That's right, I did.

Hanku strolled out to the dam, looked down, and watched for a while as the torrent of fetid water came cascading down. The metal cabinet where the salt, the ash and the equipment were kept, also contained odd lengths of spun metal rope. The kind Duhovnik and his dog had been dangling from since the autumn. He inspected them, picked over a piece or two, in the end choosing a fairly longish one, checked its length, and eventually wound it round his waist.

Delfina was waiting for him in the hut fully dressed. For a while they stared at each other in silence, Delfina sitting on the edge of the bed, Hanku standing in the doorway.

Take one or two things dear to you.

I don't have anything.

Because now you must come with me.

I know.

Well then, off we go.

They chose the more comfortable cart track. They went hand in hand, like newly-weds. When they reached the sappers' Birtz lodge at the bottom of the hill, Hanku led the donkey out of the stables, hitched it up, then thrusting the woman ahead of him, entered the room. Dragila was asleep in a corner. Hanku shook him awake.

I need that chain after all, the one with the carabiner at the end, that I left here. If you still have it. And the box as well.

It's still where you flung it. You'll find it by the wall.

And now I'm also going to return your money. And you should give me back the madezite. The damkeeper couldn't sign for it.

Sorry. It's long gone. I sold it on, the same day.

Pity. Because I really need it now.

Hanku took the wire rope off his waist in the courtyard. He stopped and, facing Defina, proceeded to wind it around her waist. And as he knotted the end so that it didn't come undone, he had to embrace the woman.

Tell me if it's too tight, because I can make it looser.

He took the chain and threaded it under the wire belt. He tied one end to the buckle of his belt with the carabiner. As he did so, he stared at the azalea buds of wanton passion on the woman's brow.

See now, you left that alcoholic lotion of yours in the hut.

So I did. I was a little fuddled.

Yet Mr Korkodus sent it specially for you.

Somehow it slipped my mind.

Tsk, tsk. Pay more attention in future.

Next time round. But when you have the time, you can fetch it yourself.

If I don't forget.

I'm sure you'll find it still on the shelf. And hang on to it. From now on you'll need it, too.

3.

(NIKA KARANIKA)

On the morning of Ascension Day, after his RE class, Pastor Lorenz Fabritius chose seven schoolgirls and sent them out into the fields of the Paltin to pick daisies, carthusian pinks and cornflowers for the festival in the afternoon; they were all to bring one bunch of each. His choice fell on the two Nyegrutz girls, the Augustins' two daughters, and the three Gleznárs, cousins aged eight, nine and eleven. They all perished when the forest chapel of St Vaneliza, which stood forbidding and forsaken in the meadow, was struck by lightning.

That year Pentecost Sunday fell on St Médard's Day, but above the Medwaya the first dark clouds had already begun to gather a week earlier. At first they just drifted about the peaks, then, early that Wednesday afternoon, they suddenly slammed into each other and set off with an angry roar in the direction of Yablonska Polyana.

When the children saw that the valley was suddenly shrouded in crepuscular darkness and rent by lightning flashes the thickness of treetrunks that hurtled off wildly in every direction, and balls of fire started to barrel along the slopes of the Paltin right up to the stone walls, exploding with an earsplitting howl, they sought refuge in the ruined forest chapel, even though it was roofless and had virtually only its walls still standing. That was where they were struck by lightning.

Down in the settlement many people feared a disaster: the fields gave off an ominous hemlock smell of hail, so that even as the rain came pelting down several folk rushed over to the forest chapel. There were the Gleznárs and the Nyegrutzes, among others who were worried, including Nurse Nika Karanika.

Augustin and his wife arrived a little later. They were hard-working locksmiths, and also the only ones here who worked all kinds of metals, the woman doing her share of this to the full; not for the world would some stray rumour make them break off from work. Nor were they troubled by the cloying smell of hail-battered onions, parsley, dill and savory from their vegetable garden that wafted into the cellar where they were busily hammering away. At first they were unwilling even to go outside, and sent their temporary apprentice, a former resident of the reformatory who went by the name of Adam, to scout out the lie of the land – Anatol Korkodus had lent him out for two weeks to help them with an urgent roofing job. It was only when he returned that they came frantically racing out of the workshop on hearing the news that all the children were lying motionless on the stone slabs, as over them hung, shroud-like, a pall of freezing vapour. Though at that point no one had yet had the opportunity to see the children from close to.

While through the window they could see the children lying motionless on the stone floor amidst the bunches of daisies and cornflowers, they couldn't get near them for quite some time. The small cross at the top of the pediment had begun to melt and dribble down the length of the wall, oozing onto the entrance steps. On the oaken door, too, the lock had melted, along with the doorhandle, leaving only a huge ball of molten metal where they had been. In the end – since Augustin and his wife, despite being locksmiths, could make no headway – they had to use sharp-edged rocks to batter the door down.

The seven children lay on the stone floor, and it could be seen from afar that no breath of life remained in them. Among the thin little motionless bodies there were already scavenger beetles scuttling about. If the odd puff of white breath still hovered about their lips, that could have been only their souls departing, because within, behind their bloodless lips, there already glowered darkly the eternal night of the next world.

Nurse Nika Karanika walked around the children as they lay on the ground, bending over them and, like a coroner, touched them on the brow one by one. As she did so, her teardrops happened to fall on two of the little girls – one was the Nyegrutzes', the other the Gleznárs' – and soon they gave a shiver and, with a sudden sharp intake of breath, began to stir and make gentle moaning noises. Then they sat up, while the others, including the Augustins' two girls, remained lying flat on their backs.

Augustin began to urge her: go on, go on, but Nika Karanika couldn't undertand what it was that he wanted.

The teardrops, you mean? Yes, maybe, but she had only those two tears to shed.

The little Nyegrutz girl, together with the Gleznárs', was taken into the spital-house for observation, while the Augustins' two children and the Gleznárs' other two girls, along with the other little Nyegrutz girl, were taken to the mortuary.

In the afternoon, when the storm had passed, at Honorary Constable Hamilcar Nikonuk's insistence, Brigadier Anatol Korkodus had Nika Karanika summoned to the community centre.

You brought two of them back to life, so they say. How in hell's name did you do that?

Nika Karanika shrugged her shoulders. She said not a word as she gazed out of the window.

What about the rest? Didn't you want to?

The nurse continued to gaze out, shrugging, as if to say: it seems that was as much she could do, no one's perfect.

Anatol Korkodus sent her on her way with these parting words: On my watch this kind of thing can happen only once. Promise you won't do it again.

Perhaps Nika Karanika didn't even understand what was being asked of her, or why. Be that as it may, that night she was stabbed in the back. It happened in the courtyard, between the privy and the spital-house, in total darkness as, thanks to the series of lightning strikes, all Verhovina was without electricity. The blade caused only a superficial wound, as it was deflected off the ribs, perhaps just its tip broke off. Nika Karanika staggered back to her room, applying honey to the wound all night with a wooden spoon, so that by daybreak she was even able to stand up on her own. When the electricity came back on, she hobbled over to the sickbeds to see how the children had passed the night.

But they were again no longer among the living. Their bodies were twined about with wire, one strand round their ankles, another about their necks, the ends inserted into the electricity socket. Whoever did this knew what they were doing, and how to do it.

Every Friday morning before setting off for Miss Klara Bursen's, I take Nika Karanika a sour-cream lángos from Nyegrutz's, and since no birds remain in Yablonska Polyana to peck at it, I can leave it for her on the windowsill. It makes me happy if I sometimes also manage to catch a glimpse of her, and through a half-open window inhale her perfume, but if I can't, I simply walk on.

On this day, since on her doorstep I came across thick beads of blood that someone had shed and was simply concentrating on making sure I didn't step in them, she was waiting for me behind the open window and exchanged a few words with me.

It would seem that the mere fact that one exists is enough to expose one to a night-time assault, she said. But there'd be no point quizzing her, she knows nothing, she was attacked from behind and spent all night bathing her wound. There was, though, one thing she could swear to, namely that in the sickroom, around the bed of the two dead children, there hung in the air the kind of heavy, metallic smell found in metalworking premises. It's the kind of smell that continues to cling to your clothes and even your skin for a long time. Wherever the person concerned might go, they leave some trace of it behind; indeed, it remains in the air until a draught of air should whisk it away.

It wasn't hard to guess who she had in mind.

So, when Anatol Korkodus, sitting with Eronim Mox's book of tales and a sheet of paper covered with names before him, asked me to guess on whom suspicion might fall, the evidence was compelling and I had no hesitation in replying that he hadn't far to look: the Augustins were responsible.

He nodded, as if this was just the reply he was expecting. Well then: woe betide them.

4.

(EDMUND POCHORILES)

In Verhovina the first Wednesday in October is celebrated as the Feast of the Waters. It is also the Feast of the Three-Legged Woman, who lives nearby in the Mute Forest and whose statue in the centre of Yablonska Polyana is honoured every year by having one half of a plum inserted overnight between her first and second thighs, while the other half is placed between her second and third.

Early in the morning Brigadier Anatol Korkodus wrote in charcoal on a piece of cardboard, using large, bold letters, that everyone should finish doing their laundry by a quarter to eleven as the taps would be turned off on the hour, and gave the sign to the office dogsbody Balwinder to hang on the public wash-house door, while he sent me over to The Two Queans hostelry to make an evening reservation on his behalf for two curtained- or partitioned-off tables in the section of the restaurant nearest the street, one laid for two, the other for four.

I know from Miss Klara Bursen, to whom I read aloud every Friday morning from various, randomly chosen books in Hungarian, that sometime long ago in the past, in the mists of the Middle Ages, as one frosty night was turning into the dawn of a Wednesday market day, it happened that in the proximity of the lodge, nine hot-water springs suddenly burst forth simultaneously, with sky-high columns of steam whose adamantine coruscations in the light of the full moon woke up even those who were truly sound asleep. By the morning, when Yablonska Polyana's wayside ditches were steaming with the hot water pouring down in thick swathes from the mountainside and everyone was standing around outside open-mouthed, there emerged from the Mute Forest Militzenta, Verhovina's patron saint, who had three legs to enable her to glide above the meadows, and came before the market folk's very eyes to bless the mounds whence the hot waters bubbled forth, and in doing so entrusted the entire region, from the Medwaya to the swamps of Brustyina, all that the naked eye could take in from the slopes of the Paltin, to the care of the Czervenskys for a thousand years.

On first hearing this seemed to be a silly little tale, surely dreamed up by some ingenious Czervensky, to ensure that the headwaters of the Yablonka, this picturesque corner of Verhovina, remained forever undisputed by anyone else, yet there is no question that to this day the crystalline curtains of the nine hot springs hover around the slopes of the Paltin; that the moss-covered stone statue of Three-Legged St Militzenta still stands in the heart of Yablonska Polyana; and that the first Wednesday in October is celebrated throughout all of Verhovina as the Feast of the Waters.

That evening Anatol Korkodus was also in charge of the dinner menu, and as he was concerned that I might not pass the details on accurately, he made me write it down on a squared sheet of paper for hostelry keeper Edmund Pochoriles to copy in coloured crayon onto the slate slabs he was to place in the middle of the tables. The dinner menu was as follows: wild caraway-seed soup with cream and drizzled gnocchi, then grilled trout marinated in curd with thyme and parsley potatoes with a garlic sauce, followed by fried dill and curd pancakes in a cranberry sauce. And Ed Pochoriles, who did the cooking for his guests in his kitchen himself, should make sure he doused the burning embers with sage-grass infused pumpkin seed oil at regular intervals, so that its smoke coated the roasting fish with a fragrant glaze. As at this time of the year, early October, it went dark early, by late afternoon, so everything should be in place by, say, five o'clock to welcome the guests. These would include Captain Mordwinn from the Water Authority, as well as Supervising Commissar Kodrin from Czernowitz, together with his secretary, and maybe even the Suffragan Bishop of Lemberg.

As hostelry keeper Edmund Pochoriles listened to what I had to say, he gazed out of the window facing the courtyard. He went out into the yard himself and said something to my niece Danczura, who served in the hostelry. She sat in the worn-out yellow blouse that on bright days she never took off, sunning herself on the steps of the summer kitchen. She kept snatching at the butterflies that settled on her bosom. The colour yellow attracts butterflies, but because of the vapour that Danczura exuded, as soon as they landed on her they would fall into a swoon and she would then pick them off one at a time and eat them.

As soon as he returned, Edmund Pochoriles took the slip of paper covered in writing from my hand and examined it carefully.

And if by some chance it shouldn't be to their liking, who's going to eat it all?

You must be joking. Why shouldn't they like it? Anatol Korkodus knows his guests well. He of all people must know what to order for them.

Perhaps he doesn't.

Meanwhile Balwinder had returned with the news that someone had whitewashed over every single wall of the public wash-house up to shoulder height and painted human figures on it.

Anatol Korkodus happened to be browsing Eronim Mox's cookery book as he sat behind his writing desk, but when he heard this news he promptly slammed it shut and in seconds we were on our way to see with our own eyes what Balwinder was talking about. No sooner were we out in the street than our eyes were assaulted by the shimmer of gold. The culprit, who had most likely carried out his work in the early hours, hadn't even waited for the undercoat to dry and painted on it a dark blue sky with pink clouds trodden by bearded, barefoot, bug-eyed saints, their heads encircled by wide golden haloes, like rings around some distant giant planet. The haloes had been painted on in some kind of metallic gold paint, so that even now their reflection flashed and flickered on the walls opposite.

Someone who can afford expensive paints is busying himself doing stupid things, said Anatol Korkodus.

He walked around the public wash-house, sometimes putting a finger to the fresh paint and sniffing it, then told Balwinder to scratch everything off with a putty knife and then cover it all in thick acrylic paint and, once it had dried properly, to do it all over again, so that no trace would remain of this act of gross vulgarity.

Yablonska Polyana, together with the nearby Mute Forest, the iron mines, the hot springs, and the frozen peaks of the Medwaya, had been for many generations the property of the Czervenskys, who lived in a galleried mansion in Heyduck Street, behind the statue of the Three-Legged Woman, that looked out onto the silvery draperies shimmering above the hot springs of the Paltin. Until one night, without warning, they unexpectedly upped sticks and, leaving everything behind, disappeared from the settlement.

This, too, I learned from Miss Klara Bursen, the owner of the Boursin farm and the longest-standing inhabitant of Yablonska Polyana, who on Friday mornings, when I read for her, by way of payment makes pancakes for me while she regales me with some ancient tale from Verhovina's past.

Though no one saw them leave, she went on, everyone recalls that perishing cold break of day when they realised that the Czervenskys were no longer there. The first suspicious sign was the sizzling silence given off by the abandoned walls, until suddenly, in a sharp, spontaneous explosion, every single window of the house burst and smashed to smithereens, and in the draught that suddenly arose, amidst the flighty fluttering of the tulle curtains, the cold of the Medwaya came roaring in, making the crystal and the china in the Czervenskys' cupboards shiver so much that their jangling could be heard even in Yablonska Polyana's very last house.

They had gone, leaving behind everything they owned.

They may well have had wind of something. Perhaps they had worked out that the thousand years that St Militzenta had promised them in the Middle Ages were now over, and they had gone so that even the first day after the end of the millenium should not find them here.

Klara Bursen concluded the story thus:

They, the Czervenskys, were the only ones here, amid the slopes of the Medwaya and the Paltin, who sensed something had come to an end. That here, shortly and irrevocably, everything would change.

For decades not only did no one ever darken the Czervenskys' doors again, but it was said that no one dared touch even the handle on the gate, so it soon acquired a coat of thick moss. Until one spring day a traveller came by, a youngish man with flowing locks, a rucksack on his back and binoculars about his neck, leading a pack donkey on a rein, and a brown-skinned fellow with a serious squint trailing in their wake. They did the rounds of the building, then mowed down the waist-high weeds in the yard with their own hands, carried every fragment of shattered glass and china outside, threw it all from the gate down the steps and compacted everything down so that even in the dead of night it should shine brightly for them, providing a pathway. After they had used brooms to shoo away the owls perched on the walls, scratched off the floor the calcified bird-droppings and the feathers stuck in them, and scrubbed the entire place clean, the man with the serious squint, Balwinder by name, stretched transparent onion skin parchment over the window frames, and the young man moved in. The premises were rearranged, only the family bed retained its place in the bedroom, with the bedside table beside it, on which lay a book bound in treebark on a square of spinach-green velvet.

Eronim Mox's cookery book, that was the book's title.

The younger man with the flowing locks opened it and since the writing in it immediately began to glow, he slowly eased himself down on the edge of the bed and read right through the night. At break of day he was found by Balwinder, exhausted and shivering, so he hurriedly made a fire in every tiled stove in the building.

That the former Czervensky house had new inhabitants everyone found out at the same time, when smoke began to rise from its chimneys into the sky.

The new occupant seared into a panel of rough-hewn wood with a red-hot knife the words: Water Conservancy Supervision Brigade and nailed it to the gate.

Ever since that day, the brigade has consisted of just one person, the Brigadier.

The brigadier is Anatol Korkodus, my old man. He was the one who once came to Monor Gledin for me, picked me out of two thousand children, delivered me from the clutches of the reformatory and took me in, so that I might share with him the everyday cares of Verhovina and look after the waters. Since then I too have lived in the former Czervensky mansion, and every night, once the furious snoring of Anatol Korkodus has died down, I can hear the sound of the Czervenskys' shivering china haunting the building.

The following morning Anatol Korkodus sent me over to the hostelry again with the message that Pochoriles was not to concern himself about the wine, because the guests would follow custom in bringing their own, and he would be counting only on the provision of a shot of gentian root brandy to whet their appetite.

I found Edmund Pochoriles in the kitchen, just about to make a full pot of late-ripening Verhovina corn. He listened to what Anatol Korkodus had told me to say, then gazed out into the yard and called out to my niece Danczura, telling her to take a bath in the course of the morning, have her hair done, and make sure she had a clean apron for the evening as well as a starched bonnet. But before doing that, to avoid staining her clean clothes, she should bring over from Hamilcar Nikonuk the half-carcass of a wether that he had ordered from him and chop up its thighs and some of its neck and top shoulder into small pieces for robber stew.

You're also expecting guests who ordered mutton?

Mutton, definitely. Nothing else I can think of, off the cuff.

Seriously? Because, if I may remind you, I passed this way this morning and ordered trout from you for dinner.

We'll know by this evening whether there'll be any trout or not.

It was getting on for midday and I was just preparing for my constitutional with Tatyana to the Czervensky water-mill, when Balwinder came looking for me, pitchfork in hand. He asked if I could accompany him to the public wash-house, as he was very much afraid of foxes, and the big news from the women on their way home from the wash-house was that a tame fox had walked in through the wide-open door, stopped in the middle of the wash-house and tempt him as they might with everything they could think of, would not budge from there.

The square, squat building with its ornate façade and oval windows had been built with Isac Gold's money as a kind of small synagogue, but by the time it was completed both the entire Gold clan and the entire Man clan had converted to Lutheranism. The building stood empty for years, until Anatol Korkodus had it converted into a public wash-house. It was fed by hot water from the slopes of the Paltin's thermal springs. Above the stone troughs set into the walls there ran a conduit with taps carved from oakwood. While the women of Yablonska Polyana do their washing – there is room for 15 to 20 of them side by side – the vast space fills with steam to bursting point and, like cotton-wool, absorbs every sound, but now that the women had departed with their baskets full of laundry, and Balwinder had earlier opened the ventilation windows, the air had cleared, and their steps echoed through the damp walls of the empty, barn-like building. From one corner, as if someone had forgotten to turn a tap off, the sloshing of water and a quiet burbling was audible. The fox stood motionless, with a profoundly melancholy mien, near the draining grille, in the middle of the wash-house. Beside it frothing water gurgled into the sink hole.

Although from the notice displayed at the entrance it should have been clear to all that it was long past closing time, on the pounding bench, in front of one of the stone troughs, there sat

Nika Karanika, the new nurse, the little blue-tit demon, as Anatol Korkodus called her, with water gushing from one of the oakwood taps behind her. Done with her washing, she was now dousing her bare feet with water from a watering can; the water churned frothily towards the drain, near to where the fox had positioned itself.

It was a few months earlier that, without any luggage, wearing only a thin gown on her light dress and shabby galoshes on her bare feet, Nika Karanika had turned up in the settlement. She must have arrived in the dead of night because it was only in the early hours of the morning that the news began to spread that some stranger was sleeping under the Pissky bridge. And that was indeed where we found her, on the riverbank, gazing at the waters of the Yablonka from the shade of the wild rose-bush. She wore her bluish-black hair in a knot, on her dark blue cloak were embroidered songbirds with silver thread, while around her head, as if created by some mirage, there flew the blue tits that were thought to have deserted Verhovina.

She had no papers, only her name could be made out, as following the custom of the southerners down on the coast, she bore it tattooed on the back of her hand – in the land of her birth, the child's name is branded on the back of its hand using a needle when it's still a baby, so that they can't later disown it. She said she had come to fill the job of nurse that had recently fallen vacant. She brought with her a letter of recommendation, too, a sheet of white paper folded double, from which she proceeded to read at the top of her voice. Having patiently heard her out, Anatol Korkodus asked her for the letter and turned it over and over in his hand, and then showed it to me: the sheet of paper was blank. To this my old man said that the position of nurse had indeed become vacant, but he would like to sleep on the matter, as he didn't think it was advisable to entrust the care of the sick to demons. From the first moment he divined in her a common-or-garden demon; nonetheless, after

I had spent days begging him, and after Nika Karanika for her part showed how she could remove in minutes the moles on seamstress Aliwanka's hands by applying the sap of the greater celandine and then just blowing on it, he agreed to engage her for a trial period. Olga Kapustin, the previous nurse, had not long ago run away, and for several weeks already there had been no one in Yablonska Polyana to look after those poor in health.

Now Nika Karanika sat there on the bench, in the semi-darkness, like some gorgeous delicacy, her bare knee shone bright, and she kept dipping her watering can into the stone trough that was still half-full, pouring water over her legs. The water dribbled down into the drain-soak by the fox, touching its tail and even its paws, but the creature paid it no heed.

Let's take a break, I said to Balwinder. You may go now.

Are you going to try and deal with it by yourself?

Take the pitchfork as well. Off you go, and leave the keys with me, I'll lock up.

Meanwhile Nika Karanika, having finished bathing her feet, was attempting to put on her galoshes. It looks rather odd when someone cannot reach their own feet, but she obviously had difficulty bending down. She did in fact walk with something of a limp, since she had allegedly – or so ran the tale she told – once been knifed. She was stabbed in the middle of her back, so that the tip of the blade broke off and shifts about even now between her vertebrae, on occasion making it difficult for her to move.

I walked around the room, using the tilting handle to close one by one the ventilation windows that ran high around the room, and ended up standing before her. She was wearing a blue gown, with birds in flight embroidered on it in shiny thread: finches, linnets, bullfinches and blue tits which, if you narrowed your eyes a little, looked as if they weren't sewn on after all, but hovering about her person. And I'm inclined to think that apart from the gown she wasn't wearing anything else at all. I imagined in the twilight of the silk her smooth, creamy curves, amber navel, the little chalice bubbling beneath her belly, and it all made my mouth water.

Good day to you, she said addressing me. Look, what a sweet little dog, I thought I'd take him home. I'll drop by Akimofte's shop and buy him a lead and a collar.

You know very well it's not a dog, I whispered hoarsely, since from under the gown, melding with the sulphurous-salty smell of the thermal baths, my nose had detected the scent of jasmine and cardamom rising from Nika Karanika's body. Anyhow, it's a feast day, I have to lock up the wash-house. If you are not making headway with your galoshes, I'd be glad to give you a hand.

I wouldn't like that. I'm not used to people touching me.

Though she couldn't do it while she was sitting, now, as she stood up, her feet slipped easily into the footgear. Her scent meanwhile once again wafted my way, this time from her chignon, that salty sea air, mixed with the mist of bittersweet cardamom.

Let's go. And while we're still indoors, I must tell you something. You may not be too pleased to hear it.

Just don't send me away from here, that's all.

It may be even worse than that. I understand that two individuals have come to Polyana, they've put up at the hostelry. They're called Damian and Cosmas, they claim to be monks from an order that ministers to the sick and are on a mission to cure ills. But they don't smell of medicaments, nor of rancid fat, like monks. Rather, they smell of the same seawater that the winds from the south swept into your hair. They spend all day looking out from behind the curtains of the first-floor room of the hostelry. My suspicion is that they're on the lookout for you.

I'm interested to hear what you say. Because I have no sense that anyone is looking at me from any kind of window.

Yet I'm sure they will soon seek you out, but you mustn't talk to them. I wouldn't like you to get into trouble. Because these will be the very people who knifed you that time and still they won't rest. And now we really must go. That Balwinder is keeping a squinting eye on us from over there, and I must lock up the wash-house.

There must be some reason why you have such strange thoughts in your head just now.

Yes, indeed, as you say, there is. And the reason happens to be that you are on my mind every single hour of every single day. Why that should be, I don't know.

At noon Balwinder brought over lunch from the canteen. It was slices of meat fried in oil with steamed sauerkraut, the sauerkraut generously doused in a thick tomato sauce. At this, Anatol Korkodus's brow, as if some evil message had come from the canteen, suddenly darkened and for a while he kept stabbing grumpily at the food with his fork.

Sauerkraut in tomato sauce? Bah! Balwinder should take it back and tell the dinner ladies that I don't think it's at all a good idea. They're not going to make a habit of that if I have anything to do with it.

After he had poked at a small piece of meat he pushed his plate to one side.

Next to him sat the dwarf Roswitha, his little house pet, and he tapped his plate:

Have you ever in your life seen sauerkraut with such tomato snot?

Roswitha gave no reply. She was a mute.

Then my old man, as if somewhat mollified, turned warmly towards me:

Tonight we're going to have our fill of trout. If you don't feel like eating in the restaurant's kitchen with Danczura, I'll tell them to send over a portion to you.

At this I pointed out that in the evening there would also be mutton. Because if at all possible, I'd prefer mutton stew. I hear that Pochoriles is making mutton stew robber-style for dinner.

Fair enough. Let him. For the others he can make what he likes. Just because we happen to be celebrating there, no reason why others can't also drop by for dinner, right? That was another reason I asked for two tables to be reserved by the window. I hope you passed on my message accurately.

At this point Anatol Korkodus leaned over the table very close to my plate:

Now, if I may ask, what happened about the fox?

I locked the wash-house door on it. It will have to be knocked unconscious. We must discuss what's to become of it.

I agree. I don't like blood to flow, not even a fox's. And then what's all this business with the monks?

How do you mean?

The ones you mentioned. Those who are supposed to be staying on the first floor of Pochoriles's hostelry. The ones you know even by name. I'm the only one in the dark about them.

You're not, because I just made them up. I suddenly felt I had to say something important to her at all costs.

It's not up to you to invent visitors to Yablonska Polyana. You should know by now that it is no trifling matter if a stranger should come our way and whether we're aware of his intentions. If you still remember the horse-faced vagabond, you'll know what I mean.

Yes, indeed: Horse-face.

We don't know his real name, only that he came here, visited the nearby slopes, finally he even strutted along the Infantrymen's Street, and then disappeared. We never saw him again. But this surely did not happen by chance. Horse-face could return at any time.

Every year, at the time of the autumn tally, which generally coincided with the bird migration, Captain Dominik "Fowler" Mordwinn, Commissioner for the Water Conservancy, came to spend some time in Yablonska Polyana. He and Anatol Korkodus would walk together the slopes of the Paltin, the little valleys of the Medwaya, making a tally of the glinting rills that veined the slopes, the springs that rose from the sides of the valleys, tallying them over and over again, and though they knew perfectly well that there was little point in doing so, took samples and measured the volume of the flow. But these matters Captain Mordwinn tended to delegate to Anatol Korkodus. Apart from his duties at the autumn tally, Mordwinn had a yen for Miss Klara Bursen, on whose farm he rented a room and who, if not with comparable passion, then at least with undisguised enthusiasm, inquired of him concerning the mysterious world of birds. The captain would generally complete his duties by the early afternoon and from that point on, swathed in blankets in the deckchair on the veranda, he would aim his binoculars at the sky and follow with close attention the autumn migration of the flocks, sketch the formations he observed, nailing these up on the doorposts, in the hope that the mistress of the farm would take an even more active interest in his birds, so that one languorous autumn evening, as they scoured the sky together, she, in her lung-coloured negligee in whose décolleté her blue-veined breasts rested forlornly, would fall dizzily into his arms. Alas, for this moment the captain waited in vain. In the deepest recesses of her wilting heart Klara Bursen awaited a Hungarian officer, who was said to be serving with an infantry regiment in Transylvania, beyond the mountains.

Captain Dom Mordwinn did not take this amiss and continued patiently to make his sketches on the veranda, and he was the first to realise, in the course of one of his final inspections, that he had been waiting and scouring in vain the turquoise skies of the north for several days now and had failed to see a single flock of birds. The flocks of cranes, geese, teals, and specklebellies that had previously arrived in untold numbers had either stayed at home in the far north, or winged their way elsewhere. For some reason the migrating birds kept away from Verhovina.

In the distance meanwhile, as if marking the boundaries of the property, he saw all around columns of smoke rising to the sky and extending right across the firmament beneath the clouds, casting a threatening pall over everything. Even if on occasion a stripe of undulating grey could be discerned – it might even have been a flock of migrating cranes – this no longer meant very much to Captain Mordwinn.

The birds had disappeared, and since Klara Bursen had not yielded to him either, the captain's autumn visits tailed off. When the time came for the autumn tally, Anatol Korkodus would pull on his blue rubber boots and wrap up in his waterproof cape to trudge along and tally the springs all by himself. On occasion, just for the sheer joy of it, he would struggle up to the heights above the Boursin farm, where the smoke belching out from the chimneys and the clouds of steam from the thermal springs no longer obscured the view. From that height one could see all the way to the Brustyina lakes, where once above the reedbeds the honking of the flocks as they circled in cloud-like formations could be heard right up to here, echoing around the slopes of the Paltin.

It was on one such walk that it became clear to Anatol Korkodus that he was not the only one to roam these slopes. On a birch-tree stump, clinging to a knot in the bark and caressed by its peeling silken membrane, there hung a pair of 10 × 30 army binoculars. Someone had left them behind. The brigadier knew that no one in Yablonska Polyana possessed binoculars of this kind.

It was during the first weeks of that autumn that the horse-faced stranger turned up in the area. At first, as if merely toying with people's imaginations, he gave the settlement a wide berth, with just an ungainly shadow settling on the hot springs' carpet of steam at dusk, or the lights of alien fires burning in the evening from the direction of the old mine's abandoned workings, while the nightly growls of barely suppressed disapproval from Gleznár's restive dogs indicated that they detected the smell of something alien in the vicinity. Even hostelry keeper Pochoriles's mute husky was panting agitatedly with his front legs planted high up on the fence. And by the evening of each day everyone was back home in the settlement, where everyone knew everyone else, where everyone knew where everyone went, when they left home and when they came back. There was an alien in the area. And the little signs that the stranger willy-nilly left behind approached ever closer to the fences.

First it was on the frost-laden grass, and then on the edge of the depression on the riverbank that Anatol Korkodus happened upon the alien's footprints. It was the first frosty morning: the ashen membrane of ice formed on it a skin tinged blue from the colour of the sky. The imprint was that of a considerable, 48 or 50 size shoe's ridged rubber sole, like that of an enormous hiking boot. No one in the area had feet this size.

The brigadier knew that sooner or later he would come across him in person. Because, to be sure, that was what the stranger, too, wanted. The brigadier was not happy about the matter, no, not by any means: someone, who had not personally announced himself to him, was coming and going, at will and with self-assurance, prowling the land with intentions unknown.

He'll be some sort of vanguard, I said to the brigadier in the evening. He's come to measure up the area.

Anatol Korkodus stared at me in shock.

The vanguard of who, of what?

I was only joking. You should try to put it out of your mind. Even if there is indeed someone prowling around here, he'll go back the way he came. It'll dawn on him he has no business here.

But the matter continued to exercise Anatol Korkodus. After his discovery of the footprints in the mud, he would sometimes also take me along on his evening walks.

When he had completed his daily duties, Anatol Korkodus would generally set off at dusk for one final inspection on foot. He would begin at the public wash-house, checking if any residue from the slopes' thermal waters remained in the stone troughs, whether the drains were clean, making sure every tap had been turned off and the ventilation windows were in the open position, then he would walk up the bank of the Yablonka as far as the Czervensky jetty, take the water-level readings from the gauges, climb up the slope of the Boursin to the hot springs, walk around all the fences ringed with protective wire mesh, then, walking the length of the abandoned slag-heap embankment, and after giving the distant ridges lost in the purplish haze of dusk a final glance, descend at the far end of settlement in the direction of the houses. Most often he would pause to catch his breath in The Two Queans, Edmund Pochoriles's taproom. Sometimes he would forget himself there and spend a long time staring into space, his gaze misty in the dim light of the lamp. On some such occasions Pochoriles would meanwhile close the bar and go to bed; when this happened Anatol Korkodus would help himself to a drink and put his money under a stone ashtray on the counter and leave the premises through the kitchen.

I was with him when, on one of his evening inspections in the vicinity of the hot springs, through puddles covered with a skin of rainbow-coloured film, he again spotted traces of the rubber footprints. They were quite fresh and water had only just begun to gather in them. Then, leaving me behind, he followed the footprints as he hurriedly climbed up onto the slag-heap embankment.

There, at the far end of the embankment, on a log rolled there for this purpose, sat the stranger. He was staring into the distance, brooding, wholly under the spell of the atmosphere of the twilight and the view, as the distant ridges disappeared into the emptiness of the mournful mist and the approaching night with its purple gloom. One might even have imagined that, having had enough of the hide-and-seek, he was in fact expecting Anatol Korkodus, that he felt the time had come to introduce himself.

But no, he was not in the least minded to introduce himself.

He was the one, Bigfoot, as Anatol Korkodus later dubbed him, the one with the horse face. He was indeed a curious creature: his urban attire – faded green raincoat, brown velveteen trousers – were paired not with hiking boots but enormous moccasins. These had a distinctive pattern on the sole and must have been cut from used motorcycle tyres. Unlike everyone else in these parts he wore no hat, had short, salt-and-pepper hair, a long, saggy face with furrows running down it, and rueful, oily eyes.

The stranger, too, saw Anatol Korkodus approaching, and waited with his head cocked to one side, impassively and with an indifferent face, for him to come over to him.

When Anatol Korkodus stopped before him, demanding to see his papers, he just raised his head a little and stared at him with a surprised grimace:

You've got to be kidding me! Did I ask for yours? Leave me alone. Can't you see I'm in a pensive mood?

That's not a tone I expect from a complete stranger.

Who says we're strangers? Don't you get it? Why should we be?

Very well. Then kindly tell me what your business is here.

As you can see, I'm just looking round. I like the lie of the land. But now you'll leave me in peace, won't you?

Fine. You mustn't imagine I'm prepared to argue with you about numerous matters. If you won't tell me who you are, I don't ever want to see you again in these parts.

He turned around and gestured to me – I had meanwhile caught up with him –that we could go. He set off along the marshy meadow steaming with the hot springs' waters, to descend to the settlement along the fence of the Boursin farm.

Nevertheless, he still seemed to be troubled. He was limping, like someone who had been beaten up.

We generally spent the evenings playing Krik-Krak, but this time we hadn't even completed a single game when he suddenly looked up. I should immediately hurry out to Miss Klara Bursen and ask if she had seen anyone sitting around on the slag-heap embankment before. In future – and this he asks her exceptionally and emphatically – if she ever espies a stranger from her veranda, she should always kindly note down the exact time and place.

It was odd that he should ask her to do this kind of thing, for since a tempestuous card game more than ten years earlier they had not been on speaking terms. But now something impelled him to swallow his pride.

Even in the darkest night it is an easy matter to get to Klara Bursen's, as there are flags fluttering from her house's gables summer and winter. They are silk kerchiefs soaked in the raw sap of monk's head agaric, so that in case the Hungarian officer she awaited came in the dead of night, he would see the fluttering of the ghostly banners and, even in the soot-laden darkness of Verhovina, find the heart that beat only for him.

I woke Klara Bursen while I was still on the veranda with gentle little coughs and a line of Hungarian, "shine out sun, blessed sun", so that she could guess from this straight away who was looking for her, as this or something like it was what I had read to her the previous Friday. Though I knew little Hungarian myself, sometimes I would try to teach the lady by reading out to her from the Lutheran liturgy or from other books, sometimes, for instance, the text under the music in Hungarian songbooks. Klara Bursen did immediately realise who was looking for her, lit a lamp, and to indicate that she was ready to receive me, responded with: "The little lamb in the garden will soon freeze to death".

Once indoors, however, she simply laughed at me. Anatol Korkodus should know her well enough by now to realise she is not in the habit of writing spy reports; to do this it is usual to employ the appropriate people. Be that as it may, does she ever see the vagabond, or anyone else, in these parts? Well, to this her reply is: Yes, of course she does. He would sit around on one of the lonely treestumps on the field of the Paltin, or on the edge of the slag-heap embankment. Why shouldn't he? But on occasion he might put up a hammock between two birch trees and sometimes snooze there all afternoon. He sits around, lazes about, sometimes he reads a little now and then, as if he felt thoroughly at home. It would do no harm if it occurred to the brigadier that it is indeed by no means out of the question that certain people had struck a deal above our heads. This is where we live, yet the earth beneath our feet has long not been ours.

On the next occasion it was the horse-faced vagabond that addressed him. Though the voice came from behind him, Anatol Korkodus knew at once that it was Horse-face.

Hey, brigadier, hold on a moment.

What makes you think I'm a brigadier?

That's what they say. I see you're doing your rounds again. Aren't you bored of it?

It's my job. I see that the world of thievery is taking over in these parts, too. I might also ask you personal questions, like why you're wearing moccasins in the twenty-first century. But I'd rather not.

Pity. I could give you an answer. If you were to stay here, you too would be wearing this kind of gear, because you'd realise that whatever century it is, in this kind of terrain this is the most comfortable footwear. But you're leaving, brigadier, you won't be staying here.

Me? Leaving? Are you serious? Where in sodding hell's name did you get that idea?

You've lived here long enough. Go on, tell us, what's all this about a brigade, this whole setup. But mainly: what on earth you all do here? And make sense, mind. I want to hear it with my own two ears.

We deal with water. There was a time when we dealt with birds, too.

Water. Well, I never. Who would've thought it. I always thought that it flowed of its own accord. It gives me a headache, my brain seizes up, when I hear this kind of thing. Because I have to tell you that it's a waste of time, no one's the least bit interested. As for the birds, as I understand it, the situation is that in the end they always fly away. Well, no matter, you'll soon stop doing whatever it is.

Did someone send you here to say these things to me, or are you making this up here on the spot just to annoy me?

Listen, brigadier. The things you're asking are piffle.

One evening we happened to be on our way back from the Mute Forest, where Anatol Korkodus was showing me Fernybank, Three-Legged Militzenta's secret abode, when he came upon fresh footprints. The old man was very agitated as he clambered up the slag-heap embankment. And of course, there he was, just sitting up there. Horse-face had again forestalled him, and addressed him in a warm, sympathetic tone:

I see there's something that won't let you rest. Or you don't remember what I told you last time and expect me to say it again. Am I right?

You're not. I think we're talking at cross purposes.

All right then, listen! So that you understand, just this once I'll say more than I should. The thing is, some friends of mine and I are intending to come and move over here. But we don't yet know what we should do by way of our line of work. Maybe we'll start a mine, open up the old seams; there is also some money to be made in the forests or, who knows, perhaps we'll rent out one of our cauldrons as a rocket silo. We'll have to see. Don't worry about us, we'll manage somehow. But you should get out of here, get out while you can.

That same evening Horse-face dined in The Two Queans. Like a local, hands in pockets, with easy, loping steps, he simply walked along the Infantrymen's Street. It being the restaurant's day off, he found the main entrance closed, so he went around the courtyard and entered the restaurant through the kitchen, behind Edmund Pochoriles's back. He tapped on an empty glass until the hostelry keeper finally came through and before he asked for the bill of fare he inquired why the hostelry was called The Two Queans. The hostelry keeper didn't say a word about their being closed for their day off, but gladly explained that this was after Zhedu Baba and Brigitta Konuvalov, the two queans, who come here in the afternoons to play Shesh-Besh. Bill of fare? Pochoriles did not run to this kind of thing and would just chalk up the dishes of the day on a board, but they weren't cooking that day, it was their day off. The fellow in the end made do with hominy grits and sour cream, which the hostelry keeper quickly whipped up for him over a gas hob, and which he, in order not to be put to shame, decorated with garlicky slices of tomato and basil leaves.

The stranger enjoyed the fare and was still eating when he called Pochoriles over and, his mouth still full, pointed out of the window:

Is that where he lives? Is that where his office is as well?

Yes.

Is that where he keeps that little collection of his and his papers?

Yes.

Right. I knew that, I just wanted to hear it from you.

And with that he calmly resumed his meal. In the end he licked the spoon clean all round, and after he had used his index finger to scrape out the bowl, he sucked that dry, too. Pochoriles asked him if he could offer him a cigar, or whether perhaps he might like a drink, at which he gave a shiver: brr, God forbid!

I heard the brigadier has set some traps, he noted as he paid. I hope it's not me that he's hoping to trap in them.

They're for the badgers, as recently they've begun to chew through the wire mesh around the thermal springs, in order to wallow in the water. They've grown fond of the hot waters.

You don't say! Fucking little badgers! And the man doesn't allow the poor things to have a swim. At all events, as I understand it, he has written a letter to the Supervisory Commissar and complained about me to the Bishop of Lemberg as well. That there's someone roving about here uninvited in the gardens. A horse-face! Yes, using exactly those words. That description fits me to a T. It's what makes me think he wants to give them my scalp, to shoot me as soon as possible. But he won't, because there won't be anyone to catch. I'm getting out of here, I have business elsewhere.

In the afternoon, in the Hour of Death, when, following a donkey's extended braying, a sultry silence descends on Yablonska Polyana, behind which the passing of time is signalled only by the occasional hum of a late-season wasp and the strangulated churning of the waters, the puttering of a motor could be heard as it trundled up the Infantrymen's Street, weaving its way round the potholes and the boulders.

It's a quad bike, Anatol Korkodus called out from his room, from under his blanket, where every afternoon he would take a nap for half an hour or so, closing his eyes. Take a look out of the window and see who it is.

A kid with a buzzcut, dressed in overalls, sat on the little off-road vehicle, turned into the entrance of The Two Queans, and without turning off the motor, jumped off and like someone who knew his way round went through the courtyard straight into the kitchen. He soon came out, accompanied as far as the gate by Pochoriles. He got back on the quad, noticed that the ground sloped downwards a little, whereupon he switched off the motor, put the vehicle into neutral, and, making the gravel crunch under his wheels, slowly and quietly rolled away between the houses.

Sodding little jerk. Never seen him round here before.

That day the water transporters, who pay us good money for the thermal water, arrived later than usual. It takes a good hour-and-a-half to two hours for the cisterns to fill up and at such times the three tankers with their six horses take up the entire width of the road. Generally this doesn't bother anyone, but this time Anatol Korkodus sent me out several times to check on how the filling up was going, to see if there were any way of hurrying them up, and asked me to clean up the roadway after the filth that the horses had deposited there.

At four in the afternoon he washed his hair and dispatched me to seamstress Aliwanka to fetch his blue-and-white striped silk shirt and his red cravat, items he'd had specially made for this day.

At a quarter past four he donned his water conservancy uniform, edged with blue baize and with the blue brigadier stars on the cuffs, pulled on his boots, fussed with his papers in his office, and at a quarter to five went out to the open gate to await the guests.

As he walked up and down the road, he was approached by Brigitta Konuvalov who flashed her diamond-inlaid teeth wildly at him. She must have noticed him earlier from behind her curtains and watched him for some time in this get-up, which she had not seen him wearing before. They chatted for a few minutes, then Anatol Korkodus obviously sent her away, because as he gave her a long look he could be clearly heard saying:

And I would ask you not to expect me later today, I will be in discussion with important personages late into the night.

He and Brigitte Konuvalov were not on first-name terms, even though they were lovers. The woman must have had some financial assets squirrelled away, because she once returned from Velky Lukanar with her two upper incisors gleaming: she had had diamonds inserted in them, their light flashed about the walls as she spoke. Anatol Korkodus fell for the play of these lights one moonlit night, when he met Brigitta Konuvalov on his way back from his other lover, Zhedu Baba, and in the half-light he could at first make out only two tiny fireflies. However intimate a relationship their encounters deepened into, the brigadier was always capable of remaining silent. Nor did he let her in on his plans for the day this time; it seemed he was expecting some developments from this evening and it was no longer his intention to meet up with her later in the day.

After this I went out to tell him that it seemed as if Yablonska Polyana had been cut off from the world: the telephone in the office had gone dead. I wondered what he would say to that. But Anatol Korkodus said nothing, shrugged his shoulders, and gave a dismissive wave of the hand, like someone incapable of taking an interest: this kind of thing had happened before.

Honorary Constable Hamilcar Nikonuk also went out to see him. His brought news that at the railway station there had stood since daybreak an open truckload of watermelons. Stationmaster Stetz had no idea whose it was or how it came to be there, but whoever it belonged to, when darkness fell he would send a little cart to fetch some.

Anatol Korkodus shrugged and muttered, fuck his fucking melons, or the like, something he would not normally say, so uninterested was he in this piece of news. He was in no mood to talk to the constable.

But at this moment something must have occurred to him, and he hurried back into the house, asking me to stand guard outside the gate and indicate to him if I heard the sound of the railcar approaching from the railway station, or perhaps saw the guests themselves coming into view.

He was indoors only briefly, and soon reappeared on the threshold; beside him stood the little dwarf Roswitha, whose head he was stroking in silence. They stood there for a while, then eventually he left her there and resumed his position before the gate, sending me over to the hostelry to see if I could be of assistance to Pochoriles. In the hostelry there was in fact not much to do, Pochoriles nonetheless set me to wiping down the windows with a wet rag. Anatol Korkodus hung around in front of the brigade's gate right up until a quarter to five, with the sun shining on his back. At a quarter to five the sun sank behind the Medwaya and at once a chill wind from the slopes settled on the walls, so he went indoors.

Going over to the back of the hostelry, partitioned off with curtains, he walked around the two tables, and inspected the place settings. The room was pervaded by the smell of corn-on-the-cob. Pochoriles, who was pottering about in the kitchen, caught sight of him through the serving hatch and called out to him:

I'm having a corn-on-the-cob day. Come over and have a taste, I'm keen to know if it's ready to eat.

Anatol Korkodus strolled over to the serving hatch and took a sniff.

Am I to understand that you are concerning yourself not with the trout but with corn-on-the-cob? And I can't smell the thyme, or the sage, or the garlic. You could at least have rubbed the roast well, in advance.

The soup is ready, and if anyone should happen to ask for fish, well, I'll fry one for them.

I'm talking about the trout I ordered this morning.

So am I. I thought I wouldn't touch a thing until I heard with my own ears that there is someone who has set his heart on having fried trout. If and when I do, I'll bring one up from the pit and fry it. I don't like it when there is left-over fried trout.

You mean to say that it isn't certain there'll be someone to eat it? You think their tastes have changed?

It's not beyond the bounds of possibility. They may want something else tonight.

To this Anatol Korkodus did not reply. He strolled behind the counter and helped himself to a drink. Glass in hand he went outside and stood in front of the window, watching as a horsedrawn carriage approached along the Infantrymen's Street, climbed in a curve up the rough, bumpy road leading towards the Boursin farm, passed the tomb of the Unknown Hungarian Officer, and turned into the marshy meadow of the Paltin. From the distance all one could see was that there were four people seated in it. The carriage passed the garland of the nine thermal springs, though now and then it would be hidden by a clump of birch trees or a cloud of steam from the columns, then it stopped at the end of the meadow beneath the slag-heap embankment. Here the passengers alighted and clambered up onto the embankment. Without turning around, Anatol Korkodus asked me to top up his glass, while he continued to keep his eyes fixed on the barely discernible movement in the distance, standing immobile in front of the window. As he sipped his drink he kept a close eye on the travellers walking up and down the embankment, going to its very end, where they clambered down, crossed the meadow to Spring No. 2, gathered round it, stood there for a while, almost certainly staring at the wild piglet frozen into the blue crystal of the ice, returning in a wide arc. Then the carriage set off across the undulating meadow, among the birches, until they descended, disappearing under the hedgerows towards the banks of the Yablonka, in the direction of the Czervensky jetty. From that distance, no one would have been able to recognise the travellers muffled in their blankets, but when he heard the creak of the swing door and sensed that Pochoriles had stopped behind him, he said:

One of them, to judge by his gait, will be Kodrin, I think. But I don't see Captain Mordwinn among them. The others I don't know. I can't imagine what they could be doing without me on Paltinsky meadow.

Perhaps they were interested only in the miraculous wild piglet.

Everything dropped into Spring No. 2 turns blue and after a while is enveloped in a kind of blue crystal with sharp, spiky thorns. At the bottom of the basin there has for years rested a completely blue, dead wild piglet.

Towards evening, around half past five, Anatol Korkodus went over to the office. As if she had sensed it, Roswitha came out of the kitchen, looked around, and then she too entered the office. In a short while they both came out, my old man with his hard-bound diary under his arm, and they walked hand in hand to the back garden to inspect the guinea pigs. Then Roswitha hurried on ahead, ran up the stairs, motioned to Anatol Korkodus, who was still dithering about the courtyard, then with his hard-bound diary under his arm he returned to the restaurant. He went behind the bar, poured himself a shot of gentian root brandy, and took it with him as he went to take a seat in the hostelry kitchen.

Danczura was busily stirring the mutton stew. Edmund Pochoriles, who had until then been sitting in the corner, suddenly stood up, took a long, hard look into the pot, had a good sniff, then swivelled around.

When you make mutton stew robber-style, do you use thyme, or only garlic and bay leaves, he asked Anatol Korkodus.

The brigadier seemed to ponder for a moment what this might mean. Whether Pochoriles was making a serious inquiry, or if he was truly unsure in the matter of the mutton stew robber-style and hence whether he should reply to him at all, when the whinneying of horses could be heard from outside. Turning almost soundlessly through the gate a rubber-wheeled cart stopped in the courtyard. The cart had two palominos harnessed to it, and copper bells and enormous red tassels dangled from their necks. But the clappers of the bells were wrapped in straw so that they wouldn't make any noise. Down from the cart's sprung seats came four men, one went to hang nosebags round the horses' necks, while the other three went around the street side to enter the restaurant. One looked like Supervisory Commissar Kodrin, but this time he was wearing not his usual priest-like black garb but fawn-coloured street clothes and dark brown patent-leather shoes with pointed toes, of a kind we'd never seen before. The other two were unknown to Anatol Korkodus. The one who remained outside must have been the carter they'd hired the vehicle from.

The brigadier looked at Edmund Pochoriles, wondering what he thought about the whole business. Meanwhile through the serving hatch it could be seen that the guests walked the length of the room, pushed the screen aside, took their coats off behind it, placed them on hangers, and settled themselves around the carefully laid table.

They've arrived, said Edmund Pochoriles.

He took off his apron, donned a waiter's jacket with a brown velvet collar that he wore only on feast days, put a box of the Shesh-Besh game under his arm, and went out into the room. He soon returned, picked up a tray up from the server, put on it a small flask of gentian root brandy, a jug of water, some tumblers and liqueur glasses and finally looked at the brigadier.

I've given you a glass as well, I thought now that they've come, you'll go over to them, he said.

Anatol Korkodus stared out of the serving hatch for a while. At length he shook his head.

You take their drinks out to them, then tell Commissar Kodrin to come over here to me.

Pochoriles took the tray out and set it down on the table. He poured the drinks into the glasses, first from the water jug, then from the brandy flask. Then of a sudden he sat down himself on the chair by the table that remained free, and while the two strangers opened up the Shesh-Besh box and began to lay out the tiles, he chatted away with them. After a while he stood up and even then they continued exchanging a few words. Then he returned to the kitchen and made the fire, pulled the rings out of the middle of the hearth, filled a kettle with water, added some salt and a few drops of oil, and placed it over the hole. While he was at it, he gave the mutton stew a stir as well.

What did he have to say, asked Anatol Korkodus.

Nothing. I haven't spoken to him yet. Shall I pour you a dram, or will you have a drink with them out there?

Pour me one.

It would be better if you went and introduced yourself. I don't know how you imagine that I'd just send them here to you?

Captain Mordwinn isn't with them. I wonder where he could be? And I haven't the faintest idea who Kodrin has brought with him. Because I don't know the other two.

That's exactly why. You were expecting guests, weren't you? Well, here they are. Make yourself known to them.

And I will just tell you once more to just go and send the Commissar out here to me. Whisper in his ear: Brigadier Anatol Korkodus would very kindly like to see you for a couple of minutes, because the brigadier would like to speak to you now, this very minute.

Pochoriles took a look out of the serving hatch into the room.

All right, just this once. But let me tell you, I'm not happy about doing this. And you know what? I'd rather you wrote down on a napkin what you want to say and I'll give that to him on a small salver. But even so. Now you really ought to go out into the room.

While Anatol Korkodus tried to write on the napkin, Pochoriles continued to mumble, as if talking to himself:

Here is the new captain and also the new suffragan bishop, and he won't go out to them. Then, loudly: As I understand it, it was you who invited them. They're your guests.

Nonetheless, the hostelry keeper put the napkin bearing Anatol Korkodus's words on a small salver, with an empty shot glass on it to keep it in place, took it out into the room, and placed it before Commissar Kodrin. He continued to stand for a while by the table, nodding as he listened to Kodrin, then returned to the kitchen, lifted the lid on the mutton stew and gave it another stir.

What did he say? Is he coming?

No, he isn't. Meanwhile Pochoriles peered through the serving hatch into the room. I'd say you shouldn't go in there now either. Mr Kodrin says he can't imagine what you might have to say to him. And anyhow, how can you think of such a thing? Those days are long past.

What days?

You should think back on your life, that's his advice. Yes, those were his exact words: those days are long past. That's his message to you.

Right, I understand. It's all quite clear, then. Anatol Korkodus nodded calmly and thoughtfully, asked for another shot of gentian root brandy, emptied it into a glass of water, then summoned me over.

Quietly he said: I haven't expressed myself clearly. The business is by no means clear.

He sent me over to Brigitta Konuvalov with the message that he did after all have time this evening, and provided she was not going to bed early, and would otherwise be glad to see him, he would shortly be on his way. She could meanwhile run a bath for them both.

That evening we dined at The Two Queans. Once the guests had departed, my niece Danczura cleared the table and laid it again with a fresh tablecloth. At the smaller of the two tables, the two settings that had been laid remained empty: clearly, that would have been the seating for the driver of the railcar and Commissar Kodrin's secretary, but these had for some reason stayed away.

Danczura and I scraped what was left of the robber stew out of the pot, then Pochoriles despatched me to Brigitta Konuvalov with the message that if Anatol Korkodus was really hoping to have trout for dinner, he would gladly fry some for him now, while Danczura braised some potatoes and whipped up the garlic dip.

So late that night, at the table freshly laid for six, there sat Anatol Korkodus, Brigitta Konuvalov, the brigadier's other lover, Zhedu Baba, and the unfrocked Lutheran pastor, Lorenz Fabritius.

As if he had detected the smell of creamed wild caraway soup or the sage-rubbed grilled trout, Honorary Constable Hamilcar Nikonuk also appeared in the doorway. He went over to their table and waited for a while, shifting his weight from one foot to the other, no doubt hoping to be invited to join them on one of the two seats that remained empty, but Anatol Korkodus, realising his objective, dispatched him directly to the far end of the room, claiming that they had confidential matters to discuss, of the kind that he, as a sort of official person, had a duty to observe from a decent distance. Nor did the constable get any trout later, as Edmund Pochoriles placed before him a potful of corn-on-the-cob and, finally, an enormous watermelon cut into quarters. They watched from the table, and Danczura and I watched through the serving hatch, as he stuffed himself. Nine stalks of ravaged corn lay before him by the time he set about the watermelon.

Later, when Danczura also served up the fried dill and curd pancakes, Edmund Pochoriles asked me sit in front of the entrance door and not allow anyone else in. Then he took two flasks of wine out from under the bar and went out to the guests' table and sat down with them.

Some time passed before Anatol Korkodus reached across the table and touched Pochoriles on the hand.

What's up?

Nothing. It's just that all sorts of things are going round my head. Something occurred to me just this minute.

Well?

Anatol Korkodus shook his head, and gave a dismissive wave of his hand.

It seems he must have wanted to say something to them. Then he thought better of it. This kind of thing can happen to people when they are tired.

Later Danczura went over to their table, saying she thought Hamilcar Nikonuk was unwell, and indeed it was not beyond the realms of possibility that he was dying. He was headed for the privy at the far end of the courtyard but hadn't got beyond the kitchen when he collapsed and lay supine on the ground, with his stomach so swollen that his belt had burst open and every single button on his trousers had flown off. Anatol Korkodus should please let Nurse Nika Karanika attend to him, perhaps she could do something.

But as if he hadn't heard her, Anatol Korkodus paid no attention. His hand, which had apparently become damp from the wineglass, but perhaps had only begun to sweat, he wiped on the tablecloth. He again reached across the table, touching the hostelry keeper's hand. He waited for the latter to raise his glance towards him.

Do you remember him? The one with the big feet. We called him the Horse-faced vagabond. He had a meal at your place one afternoon. It was your day off, but you served him anyway.

Day off, you say? I don't recall.

I would appreciate it if you didn't forget.

The things you remember. I don't really know why you are saying these things to me just now.

Because of today. You knew something; for example, what it was that you had to cook for these people tonight.

It's just a matter of intuition. Just intuition, I tell you. A good hostelry keeper trusts his hunches.

Afterwards they stayed drinking quietly for a long time. From beside the entrance, it could be clearly seen that under the table Brigitta Konuvalov was holding hands with Zhedu Baba, and even if she sometimes let go, they would make a grab for each other's thighs. With his shock of hair Anatol Korkodus was like some distant mountain peak shrouded in clouds. Suddenly he took out his hard-backed exercise book, opened it, and began to write. When his right hand got tired, he continued with his left.

He was noting down his observations, which had not, for a long time now, been read by those to whom they were addressed.

The long silence lasted until Balwinder knocked on the window of the entrance door. Balwinder was the office dogsbody, he had to be allowed in, come what may.

The images that he had scraped off with a spacking knife from the public wash-house walls and replaced with two coats of acrylic paint, were once again gracing the walls, and in the same place, too. The haloes of light were once again shimmering above the heads of the bearded elders walking on the pink clouds, and their reflection gleamed yellow all the way along the windows on the Infantrymen's Street.

We drew the curtains aside and looked out.

And it was true: it was barely past midnight, yet from the direction of the public wash-house, behind the statue of the Three-Legged Woman and the thick autumn mist that nightly swathed Verhovina, it seemed that a new day, the golden light of dawn, was about to break over Yablonska Polyana.

5.

(ALIWANKA)

When Brigadier Anatol Korkodus realised that Roswitha had left him, he rent his garments, cut off his beard, shaving off even the stubble that remained, then took out Eronim Mox's cookery book and began to leaf through it, hoping he might fight there an explanation of what had happened. For only the lesser part of the cookery book was devoted to providing instructions for preparing meals, and the recipes for dishes using plants from meadow and garden were generally followed by some gnomic tale from the ever-mysterious history of Verhovina. And for readers who knew the score, in these was hidden wise counsel for interpreting the unexpected. When at any point in the course of his life Anatol Korkodus found himself in difficulties he would secrete himself with the cookery book in the office of the water conservancy brigade, emerging only several hours later, or even the following morning, with his heart greatly uplifted. This time, however, having failed to find a single story in which some explanation for what had happened might have been concealed, he suddenly realised that this event fitted very well into the pattern of events whereby someone was trying to persuade him to give up this whole water conservancy business with the brigade, and leave Yablonska Polyana, and all of Verhovina, for ever and amen.

And should that indeed be the case, then he would not, for that very reason, do that someone's bidding. First of all, he would survive these doleful days. And then he would see the story out to its end, and stay.

Roswitha was Anatol Korkodus's household pet, a little runt of a creature, with blonde curls, in all no more than four foot three inches tall. Every day the brigadier would spend with her an hour and a half or so, feeding her, dressing her, cosseting her, and in the evenings he taught her the game of Trik-Trak, while from spring through to autumn he would take her around sunset for a walk, with her hand in his, in the fragrant gardens. Though they had lunch brought over from the kitchen, when Anatol Korkodus considered the food too fatty, too insipid, or even too spicy, he would do the cooking himself, making her red orach soup with maple syrup, or semolina mash seasoned with nettle or wild garlic. On those days they would go together to seamstress Aliwanka to fetch the maple syrup, or to the Czervensky jetty to pick nettles or wild garlic. On longer walks he would put her on his shoulders and hold her by the ankles while Roswitha clung to his long locks, and as they clambered their way up the steep path by the Boursin farm towards the heights of the Paltin, from a distance only the angelic blonde head of Roswitha could be seen bobbing up and down along the line of the fences. They would go to the shrubby marshland of Paltinsky meadow for thyme and porcini but especially for nuts, and on their way home they would invariably stop at the pool of thermal Spring No. 2. Here Anatol Korkodus would point out to her the drowned wild piglet and the lacanthus beetles.

The waters of thermal Spring No. 2 were not used for any purpose, so strong in them was the concentration of acids: the water stung, making the eyes smart, and the stench, as it bubbled to the surface, destroyed everything in it, apart from the lacanthus beetles. Yes, it was these that offered the chief spectacle: the silver-blue lacanthus beetles that flickered and fluoresced as they made a tinkling sound. And, of course, the magnificent wild piglet, lying in the depths and becoming ever more blue with the passing of the years, thanks to the sulphur deposited on its bristles.

In case anyone is getting any ideas, one thing should be made quite clear: though they shared the same wide family bed, Anatol Korkodus would not have touched Roswitha's more delicate parts even by accident, though when dressing her he sometimes admired her mounds, the apricot-like moons of her tiny, dusky breasts, but just as when looking at jewels he contented himself with merely admiring them, he had lovers whose proportions were in the normal range. In the evenings, before going over to one of the two queans, Zhedu Baba or the mirror-toothed Brigitta Konuvalov, or even to both of them at once, to spend a libidinous night, he put Roswitha to bed, tucked her up, and read her a recipe from Eronim Mox's cookery book. He read to her, even though he knew that Roswitha was totally deaf and understood not a word he said. Be that as it may, the next day he would find the girl with a pot by the stove, fussing with the ingredients of the dish he had described the previous night. Their life consisted of small joys like these, or of a similar kind.

That was all well and good, but something must after all have gone awry, if he had been abandoned by Roswitha.

This happened on the day that Yablonska Polyana was again paid a visit by the procurator, Damasskin Nikolsky. Though it was a Sunday, Anatol Korkodus had since first light been using an enormous wire brush to scrape off the layers of salt deposited in the open conduit through which thermal water reached the public wash-house, when Adam, his right-hand man, startled him with the news that in Edmund Pochoriles's bar in The Two Queans there was a stranger taking tea, a grey man with an egg-shaped head and slicked-down hair, someone who had been here before: Damasskin Nikolsky. He had come by an all-terrain vehicle, hauling a trailer in the form of a cage, with foxes yelping in it. The brigadier registered the news, but did not stop what he was doing. Not even when Balwinder, the office dogsbody, reported that there were wild jackals already gnawing ferociously at the wire mesh that covered the cage. Only much later did he set off to look into the matter more thoroughly, when Adam brought the news that the stranger had left The Two Queans, got on his ATV, and driven off towards the slope leading to the Paltinsky meadow, and when he could drive no further, got out, opened the doors of the cage, and set the foxes free. Of course, by this time it was too late. The foxes – there might have been some half-a-dozen of them – quickly went their separate ways. When Anatol Korkodus went up to the plateau to see what had happened, there wasn't a single one to be seen, only the characteristic smell of fox urine indicated that they had indeed paid a visit there.

On his way back, he ran into seamstress Aliwanka, who barred his way, saying:

Korkodus, you are obsessed with your waters and endlessly walk up hill and down dale; the more important things in life hold no interest for you. Because while you were deep in your drains and rooting after your foxes, your favourite little creature, Roswitha, abandoned you for ever.

At this Anatol Korkodus snarled back:

Look, why don't you let me be? What's all this nonsense? What are you on about now?

Because Anatol Korkodus did not believe Aliwanka. The seamstress constantly had visions and prognosticated purely for her own amusement, telling the future in general and people's futures in particular, sometimes on request, at other times simply stopping people, like the brigadier this time, in their tracks. Aliwanka divined the future chiefly by water: rain, dew, hoarfrost, rime, or the swirling current of a river, or the condensation on windows, or by the clouds scudding past. Or, if it was a matter of sudden, doubtful thoughts about a dear, distant relative, a tear would do, or saliva, or a drop of sweat, or even the fleeting steam of a person's breath. On this occasion it was this last that made Aliwanka prophesy.

Now, what's all this nonsense? Anatol Korkodus repeated, more forcefully. I've told you before to spare me your horrific visions.

But Aliwanka held her ground:

Roswitha has left you for ever, Korkodus. She was sprung by Subprefect Vaneliza, because they are in love. Each with a waterflask under her arm, they are already far away. Their destination is none other than Norway. Best forget all about her.

Ridiculous. Anatol Korkodus looked deep into Aliwanka's eyes as he pressed his index finger into his temple. Then he waved his hand before his brow, and with a dismissive gesture left her standing there.

This happened on Sunday, in the midday hours. On his way home Anatol Korkodus stopped at Edmund Pochoriles's hostelry and as he stood at the bar downed a shot of gentian root brandy, liberally diluted with water. Then he made his way home, though even then he first had a sit-down in his office, which a thin partition and a door separated from the rest of the flat, to write up his notes on the day that the stranger with the slicked-down hair had visited Yablonska Polyana and let foxes loose in the Paltinsky meadow.

As he sat in the office, allowing himself to unwind a little, he was suddenly seized by doubt once more. Because silence sounds different when there is someone in it, and different again when there is not a soul to be found indoors, when even one's breath echoes around the bare walls, failing to encounter the soul of anyone at all in the neighbourhood.

Could it be that, for once, Aliwanka was telling the truth?

Because as he stood up from the table, opened the door and set off for his room, he was knocked sideways by a freezing cold draught with the metallic smell of emptiness. Of the smells of dinner there was no trace, though – Sunday being the kitchen's day off – on that day Roswitha would make them burdock leaf soup and potatoes in their jackets. Now, instead of the pot lid being all aquiver on top of the steam from the herbs of the forest – horse-radish leaves, sorrel, and onion stalks –, all that could be heard in the kitchen was the monotonous sound of the water dripping as it marked the passage of time, and only the stale garlic smell of the previous day's supper wafted over the oilcloth-covered table. The house felt as empty as if even the walls had been stripped of their drawings, photographs and tallies, the flowers removed from their pots, and perhaps even the air before his nose syphoned off, whereas in fact everything was in its proper place. Apart from one particular something. Or one particular someone.

On the bed where early in the morning Anatol Korkodus had left Roswitha still sleeping sweetly like a baby, he found only the impress, long gone cold, of the girl's head. The pillow would no longer assume her actual shape. The most terrifying sign that someone had disappeared thence for ever.

Aliwanka had told the truth.

Anatol Korkodus then ripped the shirt he was wearing off his body with a single jerk, angrily kicked out at the buttons that were sent flying, and after they fell ground them with his heels deep into the carpet. He opened the window, spat outside, mussed up his hair. Then, to ensure it caused him the maximum pain, he used a pair of garden shears to cut off his beard. But even this was not enough: he dug out his straight razor and without further ado, splashing only cold water over his face, had a shave. At this point nothing more that he could do occurred to him, and he remained standing before the mirror, staring at his own bare image, suddenly aged and furrowed with rivulets of blood. He went off the boil as he gradually calmed down in his helplessness and began to pull himself together.

Norway. So, something had undoubtedly ended. But perhaps not quite everything.

As so often in the past, he now reached for Eronim Mox's cookery book. After browsing it for a while in vain, because he could not find any story in it to bring consolation and a balm to soothe his pain, he slowly made his way into the vast treasury of recipes. He seemed to recall a short little paragraph there that he had on previous occasions always skipped over nonchalantly: simple dishes gentle on the stomach for melancholy days that pass only slowly – that was something like the title. That's what he was seeking now.

6.

(AUGUSTIN)

The Augustins' day had finally arrived. I was the one delegated to tell them the news, so Brigadier Anatol Korkodus read me the riot act: I should be brief, gentle and sympathetic. We had been keeping them under house arrest for years, just waiting for the day they'd be taken away. Ever since that grim Whitsuntide when seven schoolchildren were struck by lightning and died in the forest chapel. Now, a few days before the onset of winter, Anatol Korkodus had received word that they would be sent for and at last be brought before the examining magistrate at Monor Gledin.

That day I rose early and reported to the brigadier.

Now, at last, we'll be rid of them, he said. Just in time for someone to come and tell us how we should live and bring in some regulation that lets them go free.

Anatol Korkodus handed me a crowbar to make sure I could get inside one way or another, since in the Augustins' house the doors and windows, as well as the entrance had been boarded up. They had half an hour to get ready. The detail that was to accompany them could be arriving at any moment.

The Augustins' house, with the locksmith's workshop in its courtyard, stood beyond the Pissky bridge, diagonally across from Nyegrutz's bodega, in the Infantrymen's Street. Since a storm in late autumn had left the trees quite bereft of their foliage, it was possible to see through their branches from the brigade veranda all the way to the house, despite the curtain of morning mist. While I gathered my things I kept glancing at the boarded-up windows. In order to look the part of an official, I set off wearing the water conservancy brigade's peaked cap, the one I generally wore only when the dredgers or the water tankers came, or when inspecting the public wash-house and the thermal springs.

I had known the couple for a long time and although they deserved their fate, I wasn't too happy with the task I had been assigned, with the fact that Anatol Korkodus had entrusted me with this particular task. The bearer of bad tidings, in the eyes of the damned, is himself damned; now their final memory of me would be the grim look on my face. From the single sentence they heard from me they would know that from that point on only worse was to come. It was over: just a few more queasy hours and they would never again hear the Yablonka's roar as it flowed past their garden, never again see each other's shining brow, nor Verhovina as it wakens from beneath the mists at autumn's end.

True: they really have only themselves to blame.

Even so.

From Nyegrutz's bodega came a yellow light that lit up the mist swirling about the street, and odours heavy with oil circled before the open door, as here this was the hour of the morning when the pancakes and lángoses were fried. On the damp steps sat Ignat Draganovitz, a child not long since arrived here, on the banks of the Yablonka, from the Gledin reformatory. When I approached him he stood up. I too stopped, to see what he wanted.

Are you perhaps getting ready to do a round of inspections? Or, let's see now, what day is it today? And he eyed the peaked cap on my head.

I coughed lightly: inspections? Well no, no question of that. Far from it. There's something else today, something even more serious.

Is it a secret?

Maybe, maybe not.

Can I come with you?

Hm. You could, indeed. Come.

And with the jemmy in my hand I immediately pointed to the far side of the road, the boarded-up windows and doors of the Augustins' house.

That's where we're going.

Ignat Draganovitz glanced at the crowbar.

You're not letting them out, surely.

Oh no. Let me assure you, by no means. And now I'm going to lend you my hat. We'll go in together and you'll tell them that in the course of the day they'll be taken away. All they can take with them is a change of underwear and a day's provisions.

So the Augustins' day had come. It had almost begun to seem as if the affair had fizzled out and that they had been forgotten, but no: look how in the end their turn has come after all. How could they have imagined they'd get away with it!

Years earlier, at the time of the Whitsuntide storm, seven school-children were struck dead by lightning in the ruined forest chapel, two of whom were brought back to life on the spot – only she knows how – by Nurse Nika Karanika, the little blue-tit demon. But neither of the Augustins' two children was among them. It seemed to be a case of favouritism, a flagrant injustice. As a result, in order to set things right, in the dead of night someone had sneaked into the unguarded spital-house where the resurrected children had been put to bed, and while they slept wound chicken wire round their little ears and toes and stuck the other end of the wire in the electric socket. Most likely they spent a while revelling in the tiny blue and green sparks that, like so many jolly little flashes of lighting, sparkled around them, and then went their way, satisfied with their handiwork. The two children were dead once more.

When Nina Karanika found them early in the morning, all she could say was that in the sickroom she could detect the smell of something like iron filings. This suggested that whoever had been there worked with iron.

And in Yablonska Polyana there were only two such people: the locksmith Augustin and his wife, the plumber.

That was why the examining magistrate was expecting them now in Gledin.

As Yablonska Polyana is a small settlement, so small that it didn't even have its own jail, there was nowhere to lock them up, so in the end they were allowed to remain in their own house. Brigadier Anatol Korkodus and Constable Hamilcar Nikonuk simply had their doors nailed down and their windows boarded up, leaving only enough of a gap for the person on duty – whether me, Ignat Draganovitz, or whoever else it might be – to pass them their daily rations. For instance, today it was Draganovitz's turn to take them their breakfast of two lángoses from Nyegrutz's.

We stopped at the entrance to the Augustins' house.

Should you need to pass wind, do so now, as if that kind of thing were to happen indoors when we have such important news to convey, it would cast us in a poor light.

I levered the planks off the door, knocked on it, even gave it a kick, so that the noise should make one or other of them appear behind the glass pane of the door. But I waited in vain, no one came.

But they must be awake, whispered Draganovitz. I know because I took them their breakfast not long ago myself.

I knocked again on the door, once more to no effect, then I inserted the jemmy into a gap by the lock and – crack – forced it open. For good measure I pushed the door in with my foot.

There was no sign of them, even though earlier Draganovitz had found them awake.

But now, in the semi-darkness, under the patches of light filtering through the planks, they could be seen, dressed in what must have counted as their Sunday best, sitting silently in two armchairs pushed together in the middle of the room, both of them with their heads jerked back, and seemed to be staring directly at us as we entered.

Or perhaps not. Directly at the ceiling. Or not even at that. As if they weren't looking anywhere at all.

On the table nearby, on a paper plate, stiff with an oily sheen, glistened the two zigzag-cut lángoses from Nyegrutz's. Though earlier they had taken in their breakfast through the gap between the planks, as through a serving hatch, they had not, apparently, been inclined to consume it.

The two armchairs in which the Augustins sat had been pushed in front of a closed wardrobe, and the wardrobe itself had been pulled a good three feet away from the wall. We went around it. From its top, down behind its back panel, roughly at waist height and bound with cable, there hung a crate filled with junk of every kind. The cable trailed over the top of the wardrobe, splitting into two separate strands with one coming to an end wound tightly around Augustin's neck, the other around the neck of his wife. A piece of string tied to the bottom of the chest led to the chair under the wardrobe, and lay on the floor, by the foot of the armchair under Augustin's limp hand.

Ignaz Draganovitz let out a low whistle as he walked round and round the wardrobe and kept nodding appreciatively, and even smacking his lips noisily.

Right, now listen, I'm just beginning to piece it all together. They put the chest, filled with all that junk, on top of the wardrobe, then all he had to do was give the string a yank and the chest would come plummeting down. That tightened the nooses around their necks. If you take a good look, it's not that complicated. But you have to give it to them, it took some thinking up.

Augustin was a master metalworker, I said, his wife likewise. These folk are jacks-of-all-trades.

Aha. That's how they'd come by all the iron bits and pieces they put in the chest.

So now I also took a closer look: sleepers, weights, rasps, pliers, hammers, an entire vice, a complete set of scales. A shiny copper mortar and even an iron.

Draganovitz kept spinning the chest dangling from the cable round and round. And look: it's lined with felt at the bottom. Am I seeing right, hey, that's felt, isn't it, or what the hell is it?

Felt it is. You bet.

Because it's properly padded.

They didn't want to make too much noise. They even thought of that. Not even a gentle thud, as it would be heard in the bodega. In case the chest came loose and fell before they were ready. I always knew they were no shrinking violets: they weren't taking any risks this time either, and really thought of everything. Like every piece of work they carried out, this too was carefully thought through.

Maybe. Perhaps they were just getting ready to do some kind of trick. A private performance that…

You're beginning to talk drivel, I said. They knew it was over, they sensed it. They knew very well what they were doing.

Meanwhile my glance kept returning to the lángoses. They had long ago gone cold, tiny bubbles of oil glistened on the tasselled blisters of the crusts. I picked one up. I tore off the crust to get at the insides first, leaving the crispy, crunchy outside to last.

The other's yours, I said to Draganovitz.

Draganovitz was standing with his back to me, yet I knew he barely heard what I said, his glance skittered to and fro between the walls. Meanwhile slowly he kept repeating:

They knew, you say? Oh no, I don't think so. It's not certain, not by any means. No, no. I think it was more like some kind of private game…

I tell you, you're talking drivel.

As I was munching the lángos, Draganovitz went and stood in front of Augustin. For a while he just watched him, sizing him up, then he suddenly reached into both of his pockets at once. Up to his wrists in them, he rooted around with a slightly troubled look. I could sense that from time to time he even cast a glance in my direction. I swallowed hard and stopped chewing.

Did you think that he'd keep what you're thinking of in his pockets?

I thought that at a time like this one would.

One wouldn't. Oh, I really don't know where I stand with you. Now I don't even feel like talking.

Because I would have done, that's for sure.

Really? Well, all right, I believe you. But as you see, his pockets are empty after all. Metalworker Augustin's mind works quite differently, he wouldn't have taken it. It was decent of you to come with me. Now, give me back my cap, and off you go. Get out of here.

That Draganovitz, that Draganovitz. Anatol Korkodus's little wandering bird, time to fly away from here. Somewhere else he might yet amount to something. I watched him crossing the wooden planks and boards in front of the threshold and making his way down the steps and disappearing into the courtyard. There'll certainly be something for me to tell Brigadier Anatol Korkodus.

I sat down. At last I'd come to the crunchy crust of the lángos.

Once I watched as Mrs Nyegrutz rolled out the dough, scored lines at lightning speed round its edges with a greased knife and only then threw it into the boiling oil. Little bubbles form along the stipples at the dough edges, begin to swell up immediately, and then burst as the tiny bubbles acquire the palette of coppery colours that give the zigzag crust of the lángos its distinctive crunchiness. A splendidly huge, boiling hot, crunchy flower of dough, whose calyx gives forth rich, oily aromas. Only Mrs Nyegrutz knows how to do this. From a thousand imitations I could easily pick out a genuine Nyegrutz zigzag lángos.

7.

(JANUSZKY, OR RATHER: ROSWITHA)

On his first day following the statutory three weeks of quarantine Januszky had had virtually no opportunity to take a look around and see where he had landed before Anatol Korkodus put him to the test: he handed him a map and sent him into the Mute Forest, off to the dam, with instructions to tally the springs on his way and classify them according to the volume of water they discharged and the colours of the rocks along the flow. He should stay the night at Balwinder's, who was serving out his punishment in a hut by the dam, then take the longer way back to the settlement, via the sappers' Birtz lodge and along the Yablonka, reading off the water-level gauges on his way and making careful notes on everything in a notebook. Januszky turned up in the evening four days later and when asked where he had been all that time shrugged his shoulders and said he couldn't remember, and to crown it all he'd managed to lose the notebook in which he was supposed to write everything down. Though his clothes were rumpled, he seemed well-rested and without a trace of mud on his gumboots.

I drew him aside and asked him: what did he think we were all about? Because in these parts this wouldn't get him anywhere.

To this he replied that on his way to the lake he had been carried off by some birds and all he could remember was that he had spent some days in their nest.

You're lying, I told him. There are no birds in Verhovina.

Several weeks had passed since then and Anatol Korkodus still had no idea what to do with the fellow. It seemed as if, this once, his instinct had forsaken him when he had picked Januszky and thought it would be easy to make a man of him out here. Because whatever task he was entrusted with, he seemed dumbfounded and stared uncomprehendingly, unable to grasp what we were here for. Namely the water. Even the simple word 'water', the essential element of life that falls from the sky and wells up from the deep, he could understand only when it was explained to him over and over again. From the very first moment the kid hung around with a bored, sleepy look on his face and his hands in his pockets in the courtyard of the public wash-house, where he was temporarily put up in a small chamber, as if he'd landed up with the brigade by mistake. On top of it all, he seemed to have been brought up in a glass bubble and not the reformatory at Gledin, so carefully and delicately did he protect himself from everything that here in Yablonska Polyana formed part of the everyday order of things. As if afraid of the ferocious bolts of lightning at night, well before going to bed he would tie a black kerchief over his eyes, and to protect himself against the sulphurous steam of the hot springs that settled on the backyards when the wind stopped howling in the evenings and seeped into the sleeping quarters through the keyholes and the closed windows, he would stick pads of wetted cotton-wool up his nostrils. The braying of the donkeys, which in the dead hours of the afternoon made the windows shake as at the sound of the last trump, he would muffle with rags soaked in oil that dangled from his ears even at the hour of the vespers. With such a delicate flower in this windswept, cloud-sodden place there really wasn't much to be done.

One day I did bring this up with him: there'll be trouble. If things go on like this Anatol Korkodus will send you back.

This seemed to shock him a little:

Oh no, anything but that!

So something must, after all, have been stirring behind that narrow, prematurely aged brow of his.

This became clear on that bright October day when our benefactor, Brigadier Anatol Korkodus, turned up sitting stark naked on his all-terrain vehicle, the four rubber tyres of which had sheered off, so that it clanked its way along the cobblestones of the Infantrymen's Street. The brigadier was naked as the day he was born, only the fob watch that he wore on a thin chain dangled from his neck. On that day, for a few hours, Januszky came into his own.

It was a Friday, when it is my custom to spend part of the morning hours on Klara Bursen's hillside farm: at the lady's request I read to her for an hour from a book in Hungarian on the orography and hydrography, and the flora and fauna, of Máramaros County. I picked up a smattering of Hungarian at the reformatory, but I understood little of the text and I think Klara Bursen understood none of it. Still, I read aloud, crunching and fracturing the alien words, as the lady pricked up her ears, trying hard to attune them to the sound of Hungarian speech.

Klara Bursen, filled with a fantasy of love, awaited a Hungarian army officer from Beszterce who the clairvoyant had said would soon come to fetch her on horseback, sweep her up into the saddle before him, and ride off with her beyond the mountains, into Transylvania, just as seamstress Aliwanka had foretold.

Aliwanka used threads of wool for divination, balls of yarn, though she could also divine from sand, but especially from water, swirling currents of it, raindrops that spread out ringlike in puddles, from the mist, from the clouds. And, of course, from saliva, beads of sweat, and even from Klara Bursen's teardrops.

So I was just getting ready for my visit to Klara Bursen when I found Januszky stretched out on the office steps, his cap drawn down over his face and his tongue lolling out of his half-open mouth. Now, this was a step too far. He may have been just putting it on to wind me up, but be that as it may I put my foot under his back and tipped him off the steps, saying this was no way to live, things couldn't go on like this. If he really had no idea what to do with himself, he could come along with me to the Boursin farm. To make the point I said again:

Let me repeat that Anatol Korkodus is disappointed in you and therefore plans to send you back to the reformatory in Gledin. It's high time you understood where exactly it is that you're living. Because with that great brain of yours you imagine to be in your head, you are walking in the clouds. You haven't lived up to our expectations of you.

At this he wearily struggled to his feet.

We barely spoke on the way. When I happened to tell him off, he would mumble something, offended. In the end I pointed out:

Pity you don't know even a little Hungarian. Then you too could read aloud to the good lady. You could on occasion take over, take my place. At the end of the hour she'd make you a pancake, then draw her legs up to her chin and sink into the armchair facing you, watch you eating, and let you have a glimpse under her dressing gown.

Januszky gave a lazy yawn.

Hungarian? Who says I don't know any? What makes you all think I don't?

Thus it was that when I finished reading, I sat Januszky down on the footstool opposite the lady and pressed the *Orography and Hydrography of Máramaros County* into his hand. Though Klara Bursen noticed at once that Januszky can't have heard much Hungarian in his life, and was barely, if at all, familiar with the letters of the language, and was only mimicking the reading, we both listened in amazement at how he kept making up word after word. Januszky was reading in a non-existent language and with such fluency that tears began to rise to Klara Bursen's eyes, in surprise and shame at what was being done to her. We were open-mouthed at his audacity: to keep up the pretence he tracked line after line carefully, his head, too, moved slowly from left to right, and from time to time, when he felt that he had come to the end of a page, he turned it over.

Until I spoke up:

That will do for now. Stop at once and apologise to all concerned. You're not going to do this to us. Miss Bursen deserves better.

Perhaps you didn't understand?

You have no idea how to behave, that's your problem. You don't fit in here. I'll bring this up with Anatol Korkodus this very day. It'll be better for you, too, if you got out of here as soon as possible.

I beg of you: just not that, please. I'll pull myself together straight away. I promise that from now on I will try to be like the rest of you.

This happened about midday. No denying it, time was getting on. In Pochoriles's kitchen the donkey sausage was already being fried, since the wind brought the smell of rancid fat from the direction of his hostelry, and there we were, still sitting around in Klara Bursen's farm.

It was indeed a shame.

And that's how it could come about that, as Brigadier Anatol Korkodus had gone off to a give an expert opinion in the nearby settlement of Nikolina, where a new hot spring had apparently burst out of the rocks in the middle of the camp, neither of us happened to be very near the water conservancy's office when it was again visited by Damasskin Nikolsky, the procurator for public health.

As a matter of fact, he was always referred to as D.N., if people dared refer to him at all, no one being happy to utter his full name after his first visit to Verhovina. At that time he he had walked around the heights of Yablonska Polyana in casual shoes, done the rounds of the cemetery and the public wash-house, and then took a first-floor room in Edmund Pochoriles's hostelry, from where he had a direct view of the Man-Gold courtyard, the wash-house, and the brigade's office. He did not stir from the room for four days straight, even having his lunch served there, and merely scrutinised the lie of the land from his window through a spyglass. On the morning of the fifth day he came down and wrote his name in the visitors' book – Damasskin Nikolsky, procurator for public health – paid his bill, and remarked that he liked the place and was therefore keen to return quite soon with his friends; then like someone who had done what he had set out to do, and done it well, moved on. But anyone who saw even once his scrawny, thin figure, with that thinning, slicked-down egg of a head, as it slunk off past the hedgerows would certainly wish he would never come that way ever again.

We were still sitting in Klara Bursen's kitchen when Fabritius, the unfrocked cleric, burst in with the news that the person concerned had again paid a visit, and like someone who knew precisely that he wouldn't find anyone in their proper place, had appeared in the office's courtyard, managed to get hold of the office keys from Duhovnik, the useless office dogsbody, ransacked every drawer, carried the papers, records and tallies out into the middle of the courtyard, placed them in a pile, and then set fire to them at each of the four points of the compass, as if sacking a town. Observations going back 143 years, the notes of Captain Mordwinn and Anatol Korkodus, all the records, every one of them, every last scrap. He waited until the whole lot had turned to ashes and, when the sky above Yablonska Polyana was grey with butterflies of soot, got on his Zündapp combination motorcycle and drove off.

It was early afternoon when Anatol Korkodus returned from Nikolina.

Januszky and I were already on our way home, walking alongside the Boursin manor's fence, descending towards the high street, when we heard the familiar roar of the motor. Down below, on the highway an all-terrain vehicle was approaching the Pissky bridge: we could recognise the figure sitting on it from a long way off, from his mane flying in the wind, but the figure, curiously, seemed to be wearing only a close-fitting, body-coloured T-shirt, the kind stuntmen wear, and hardly suggested the brigadier, whom we had seen leaving in the morning dressed in fatigues. Yet it was him; it was just that he wasn't wearing any clothes. Like a naked angel bringing bad news, he trundled along noisily between the houses, as broadswords of flame came licking from the motor's exhaust.

I knew I wasn't dreaming: regardless of how he happened to look, it was Anatol Korkodus. Januszky too sensed that something had happened, because he stopped dead in his tracks and, as something akin to a smile quivered about his lips, he stared after him with folded arms. We sat down for a moment in Edmund Pochoriles's hostelry and watched from behind the curtains as the brigadier passed unsuspectingly alongside the crumpled heap of still-simmering soot, and pushed the clattering all-terrain vehicle under the lean-to, covered it with a tarpaulin, and with the easy, nonchalant steps that only someone in the nude is capable of, entered the house.

Had he been robbed? If so, why hadn't they taken his watch? No, something else must have happened. But there was no time to keep making guesses.

In the yard, the crumpled pile of papers was still smouldering as it gave off the stench of bygone years. Someone must once have dried some savory among the bundles of paper, for a delicate fragrant pall hung over the yard. Though the glass of the kitchen door had misted over, the naked form of Anatol Korkodus could nonetheless be made out.

He was standing in the middle of the premises in a basin half-filled with water. A fire blazed in the hearth, on the burner water was being heated up in the biggest of the soup cauldrons, and the brigadier kept ladling the water over his body. The room was filled with vapour that smelled strongly of petrol and the brigadier's skin, too, gleamed with mottled, oily patches. Now even his watch no longer hung from his neck.

I should have said something but Januszky unexpectedly got in first:

Hats off, boss, you sure did that trip to Nikolina pretty damn quick. You must have worked up an appetite. I'll have a word with the canteen to send lunch over early. Just don't catch a cold for me before they do.

Anatol Korkodus turned in his direction to check if his ears weren't deceiving him. I too could only stare, my gaze kept meeting my old man's. But Januszky went on:

And tell me, boss, that business with the hot spring, was it for real, or was the whole thing just a hoax, a trick to get you to go there. Someone just wanting to make sure you weren't at home today.

Anatol Korkodus looked at me again, to see if I'd heard what this kid was saying. As if he knew precisely what had had happened. But he managed to control himself, and apparently paying no attention to the kid's attempt to show off he turned to me quietly:

Put on another potful. I got covered in a bit of fuel oil, it'll need at least four or five more cauldrons of hot water to wash it off.

I brought the washtub out from the shed, ran some water into it as I stood with my back to them. Raising my voice over the splashing of the water I said:

Imagine, today Januszky also read to Miss Bursen. Januszky's Hungarian is perfect. Who'd have thought it?

At this Januszky suddenly cut in, just as loudly:

I'll wash your back in a minute, boss. But first I'll get a dry towel to soak up the oil. My mother taught me a thing or two way back: hot water just slicks off oily skin. It just rolls off, so you must first pat it dry.

I looked him up and down: what a fellow! And imagine his mother!

Anatol Korkodus had also taken the measure of the kid and didn't know what to make of him now that he had suddenly sprung into action and become so garrulous. Then he turned towards me once more and asked me to change the water in the bowl. He stepped out onto the floor and I picked up the bowl with its rainbow-coloured scum and went to pour it out. Januszky opened the door for me, I emptied the bowl in the yard, and looked up.

Our office boy, the bungler Duhovnik, the brigade's dogsbody, was just coming through the gate. He had constant access to the courtyard and the barn, and also looked after things around the house. He approached at a steady pace, heading straight for the door. He mounted the three steps, then took off his cap and jammed it firmly under his arm, and at first shading his eyes peered through the glass of the door dripping with pearly droplets of vapour. Everything was distorted in the damp glass of the window, behind which there lurked only the bungler's face, aghast with terror. Januszky went right up to the door.

Well, look now. This fellow's peeping. Has he done this kind of thing before?

At this Anatol Korkodus proceeded to turn towards him and addressed him directly at last. Heaven knows why he suddenly became formal:

You know what, my dear Januszky? You get rid of him. Let me see you do it.

The bungler Duhovnik, since he must have heard what kind of things Anatol Korkodus was saying, continued to press his forehead against the glass and tapped on it, shouting into the room:

It's not good news, I'm afraid, sir.

Anatol Korkodus gave Januszky a look suggesting that he get a move on, whereupon the latter opened the kitchen door, though just a fraction. He staggered back, and suddenly I too was knocked back by the draught. Duhovnik reeked of brandy.

The brigadier has no time now. Come back tomorrow. Put your news on hold; if it proves to be of interest, we'll send for you.

I won't wait!

Lowering his eyelids, and giving a sort of half-smile, Januszky looked at Anatol Korkodus:

He says he won't wait.

The reek of Duhovnik's brandy had by now penetrated through the glass pane of the door. He would not let up and continued from behind the door ever more loudly:

It's a shame that sir was not home. I can say it was a very great shame that you were away from home today. That's why it was possible for what happened to have happened. Someone came here, let me not have to utter his name.

Anatol Korkodus threw Januszky a black look.

Ask him which one. The horse-face, or the other one, the egghead. Tell us, then on your way.

Duhovnik then opened the door, sticking his head through the gap. His nose was red, his eyes ablaze.

Not the horse-faced one, but the one that's like a mouse. I was feeding the guinea pigs behind the house when I heard the gate creak. When I came out the fellow was already walking about the yard. He says to me: he can see that the boss is not at home, but no matter, if he isn't, he isn't, perhaps it's better for him that way. That's what he said. Then he says he doesn't have time to wait for him just now, seeing as he has urgent business elsewhere. With that he reached into my trouser pocket and took out the office keys. Both of them, as they are on the same ring.

Anatol Korkodus quietly remarked:

That's quite enough for now. Not another word. Later, when you have sobered up.

That's what happened, sir. He opened the office door, went in, didn't rummage around for long, carried everything nice and dandy out into the yard, all Mr Korkodus's papers, leaving nothing in the drawers. He stuffed everything into a sack as if he intended to take it all away. But he didn't go anywhere, just as far as the middle of the courtyard, and asked me for a match.

Anatol Korkodus stepped out of the washbowl, wiped the steamed-up window and looked out into the yard, at the smouldering black heap. He stepped back into the bowl that was half-filled with water. At this point his head began to tremble of its own accord, as if he were nodding approvingly. Then he gave a hiccup, took a deep breath, and opened his mouth wide, whereupon a quantity of saliva dribbled down in front of his feet and into the washing bowl. He wiped his mouth with the back of his hand, then gestured briefly to Januszky to shut the door. Then, very quietly, he expressed it in words:

Shut the door, my boy.

Duhovnik remained where he was, behind the door, his red earlobes shining through the glass beaded with vapour.

But in the end the keys remained here, he shouted, Mr Nikolsky didn't take them when he went, he left them in the lock.

Anatol Korkodus began to croak, tears rose to his eyes as his head continued to tremble, but in a voice quite calm and low he said:

Now, Januszky, what would you do? What would you do with this man?

Something to make sure we never had anything more to do with him. I mean never, ever.

Then I leave the matter in your hands. Deal with it, because as you can see, I happen to be otherwise engaged just now.

Though it was the afternoon, the hour of the dead, when the donkeys strike up, Januszky removed the rags from his ears. He opened the door.

You will now go home and pack. You'll gather up your things, but only the absolute essentials, as much as you can fit into a saddlebag, because you're getting out of here.

Me? Where the hell would I go?

You heard what I said. You will now go and pack without further ado, because you're leaving. When you're ready I'll tell you where you're going. A quarter of an hour, that is to say fifteen minutes, that's how long you've got.

Duhovnik had heard what Januszky said but, as if he didn't want to believe it, continued to stamp his feet stubbornly in the doorway. He set off, somewhat uncertainly, only when Januszky opened the door for me to empty the bowl, which the brigadier had meanwhile filled with his saliva. I stood there, as if intending to pour the water over him.

You heard what Mr Januszky said. Do as you've been told.

At this point Anatol Korkodus asked Januszky to bring him a bigger bowl from the shed. When we'd filled it with hot water he climbed into it, asked the kid to hand him the shampoo from the windowsill. The petrol-laden vapour clung obstinately to the glass, but the shambling outline of the bungler Duhovnik was still visible through it as he slunk slowly across the yard with his tail between his legs. Anatol Korkodus now slathered his body with the shampoo, especially his more hirsute regions, then he rubbed himself down with a rough towel soaked in hot water. Then, unexpectedly still dripping wet, he stepped out onto the floor and sat down on the edge of the bunk that I generally slept on. Foamy water dripped all the way down his legs onto the floor. He buried his face in his hands.

At this Januszky said:

You haven't said anything about your trip, boss. Is it really true that hot water came shooting up out of the ground in Nikolina? Can I ask what happened? Will they be doing anything with it?

Anatol Korkodus parted his fingers and peered at Januszky intently.

Off you go after him, Januszky. Go, and see about what I've told you to do.

I thought you might tell us something about how the morning went.

The brigadier just gave a wave of his hand and said nothing more.

It was years later that I found out what had happened. By then it didn't matter.

Ever since trains had stopped serving the valley of the Yablonka, only every other day did a bus that had originally been a lorry trundle its way along the embankment that had become so thoroughly overgrown with blackberries and dwarf birch that, when Anatol Korkodus had been summoned to Nikolina to inspect the hot spring there, he made the trip along the winding, unmade road through the meadows on the little four-wheel-drive all-terrain vehicle he had been given not long before by the suffragan of Czernowitz. The valley of Nikolina was famed for its barbed wire fences, the stink of its manure heaps, and its dairy farms, and especially the women, exiled there because of their debauched pasts, who looked after the animals. And yet in this accursed place one crystalline October day right by the camp fence boiling water sprang forth from between the rocks, enveloping the settlement in steam. Even in the moonlit night, like some beguiling mirage or a message from heaven, a silver veil fluttered above the stables and the barracks of the internees. Madame Chief Constable Isadora, who as well as dealing with the dairy farm was responsible for the welfare of the exiles, had Anatol Korkodus from Yablonska Polyana sent for in short order, since it was a water-related matter. She asked him to pay them a visit as soon as he could, take a sample from the spring, and give his expert opinion as to whether it might be possible in some way to channel the hot water into the cavernous hall where the women had hitherto washed the milk churns in ice-cold water from the stream.

Although the settlement of Nikolina did not fall under the jurisdiction of the Verhovina water management region, Anatol Korkodus accepted the invitation and early in the morning climbed into his four-wheel-drive ATV and set off on the road to the settlement, happily dust-free thanks to the early morning dew, to carry out a survey. Nikolina consisted of two or three quite small peasant houses, the barracks, and chiefly the stables, from where could be heard from the crack of dawn until late into the night the twittering of the dung-eating lesser hoopoe. Anatol Korkodus had just begun his survey when an ancient van arrived at the settlement. In this was Madam Karabiberi, the regional commissar, accompanied by her nuns. Hurriedly they cordoned off the settlement with Red Cross tape, then, after holding a rollcall of the women in the camp, put the whole of Nikolina under quarantine for a full three weeks. The reason for the great urgency was, they said, that they had been informed of an unfortunate state of affairs: the cows were drooling and a number of those in the women's residence, too, were feeling unwell. It seemed that once again a new type of illness had raised its head, the one that in these parts was called autumnal glandular fever, since it begins with excessive salivation and is carried on the back of the gossamer-gleaming lukewarm October winds from the marshy plains of the south. First it knocks the cows off their feet, then it is passed on to those in contact with them. It is accompanied by fever, searing rashes, a discharge from the ears, double vision, and spasms that rack the lower half of the body.

But Doc Schwantz, the vet, who like one of the exiles spent his life within the cordon of the wire fence, in the proximity of the stables and the barracks, and whom Anatol Korkodus immediately grilled on the matter, knew nothing of salivating cows nor of ailing women. Gossamer here, gossamer there, as far as he knew the cows were in fine fettle.

At this point Anatol Korkodus decided that this was not the time for further investigations and broke off his survey, wrote on a sheet of paper torn from his notebook a message of a few lines to Madam Chief Constable Isadora, who was in continuous consultation with her nuns throughout and coming to the conclusion that there was indeed a way forward: if the samples taken from the hot water spring proved favourable, they would secure a few metres of six- or eight-inch cast-iron piping and would need in addition some filters and pipe elbows, and of course a covered conduit to carry the water away, and above all a hydrophore to send the hot water into the hall. So he set off to pick up his ATV which he had left in the square in front of the stables, in order to make his way back to Yablonska Polyana. At this point, however, Madam Karabiberi and her nuns barred his way, preventing him from taking another step. The brigadier tried to go around them, but as they would not yield an inch, he showed them the badge of the water conservancy brigade, the silver brigadier's star that he wore on his wrist, on the lower part of the cuff. To press the point home, he mentioned that he was the brigadier in Yablonska Polyana whose duty it was to be in his office, near his brigade, in the midday hours. But the women just stared at him in wonderment.

What he had to say they found interesting, but they had never in their lives heard of Yablonska Polyana. Nor of the brigade that might have some business there, and least of all of that Brigadier Whatever that he might call himself. But even if they had, contagion is contagion, germs don't pick and choose, they could attack a brigadier just as they could anyone else. So he should go with them for a little bit of disinfecting, because until that happened he shouldn't imagine he could leave the area. They took him to an isolated hut behind the stables, where he was welcomed by sniggers from the weasels and by black shaggy parasol mushrooms that grew from the floor and the beams, and here he was stripped stark bollock naked, rubbed from head to toe with rags soaked in petrol, and had his clothes taken away to be boiled, so they said.

For a few minutes Anatol Korkodus shivered on the edge of the rickety bunk under a blanket riddled with holes, staring through the curtain of spiders' webs splattered with the dried-up bodies of insects that covered the hut's single, tiny window, at the dappled yellow leaves of a turquoise October sky, beneath which swam the silver gossamer, gleaming with the distemper.

Yes, the whole thing took but a few minutes, while his suspicions, along with his circulating blood, traversed his naked body, then all of a sudden he leapt up, threw off the blanket, and stark staring naked as he was, leapt on his quad and, ripping his way through the Red Cross ribbons, drove off. As the ATV's tyres had been slashed meanwhile, in order to make progress Anatol Korkodus drove through meadows degged with the autumn dew and springy thanks to the peat, where he couldn't be followed, and this was one reason why his tyres didn't start sheering off their steel wheel-rims until he was nearing Yablonska Polyana, when he reached the cobblestones of the Infantrymen's Street. Their clatter made the windows rattle, and people stared numbly from behind twitching curtains at the brigadier as he sombrely turned into his courtyard.

But even so, he had arrived far too late.

Duhovnik the bungler lived in the building behind the public washhouse, in the courtyard of the stores. He sat in the doorway in his faux leather jacket, his faux leather cap on his head, an almost empty bottle of elderberry brandy before him and two haversacks behind. When he saw me approaching with Januszky, he staggered to his feet. A red haze hung before his eyes.

I'm glad you're here, I don't think I told you everything. Sit down, let's talk this over. I'd also like a word with the brigadier.

Januszky stood in front of him, arms akimbo:

Duhovnik, you have no time for that now, because you're leaving. And leaving for the Mute Forest to boot, to the dam, to be the damkeeper. You'll find that Balwinder there, and you'll send him back home. Inform him he's been forgiven.

Duhovnik shook his head in disbelief.

By morning the brigadier is sure to have slept it off. I know what he's like, I don't think he was serious.

That was me being serious just now, not the brigadier. So you will kindly move into the damkeeper's hut and won't stir from there but keep an eagle-eyed watch day and night over the dam, the level of the water, the sluices, and everything, but every single thing you notice, you will make a note of. Though once a week you may go as far as the sappers' Birtz lodge, to purchase food from their canteen. On the way, both there and back, you will tally the springs on both sides of the track, and you will write down everything, but every single thing, that you see. If you are bored, you can compare the fresh data with the old figures, and if in doing so you happen upon any oddities, you will try to discover the reasons for the discrepancies. Off you go now, before it gets dark and you lose your way.

This doesn't sound good to me, sir.

Januszky inspected the two haversacks.

And what's all this? One haversack, we said, not two.

I packed two, sir. Since there are two of us. The other is Roswitha's.

Roswitha's, you say? And who might that be?

Duhovnik staggered over to the door of his bedchamber and opened it wide. On the edge of the bunk sat a girl with reddish hair, white skin, and pink eyes, staring at us with the gentle look of a calf. Her head was elongated, and perhaps a little bigger than it should have been. When she saw the door open she suddenly adjusted her hair and stood up. Her face was mature, like a grown-up's, but her body was more like a child's, she didn't even come up to my chest. Ah, yes, that head. She, by the way, under her little white lambskin fleece wore a blue, flower-patterned blouse that stuck damply to her chest. Though my nose was still filled with the smell of petrol from Anatol Korkodus's kitchen, I noticed the yeasty odour coming from the shed. The smell of glossy-lipped, lustful women. Roswitha was on fire.

Januszky too was sniffing, fixing Duhovnik with a stern look.

I asked you: who's this?

As I said, it's Roswitha. We've been together since morning. Some travelling salesmen from Velky Lukanar passed this way with their covered waggon, they were selling her.

The girl on fire, who was called Roswitha and whom Duhovnik had bought from travelling salesmen, wore a little heart-shaped pillow around her neck with her name, Roswitha, embroidered on it in red thread. Januszky circled her, eyeing her as he continued to sniff the air.

Roswitha will, I think, be staying here. How much did you pay for her?

Two thousand and eight hundred coupons. My entire savings.

Then you are in the money again: once again you have two thousand eight hundred coupons to spend in the canteen. Your savings will be in the canteen, all your coupons, to the very last slip. Buy whatever you want, no need to pay. What were you going to do with the kid in the forest?

I've long felt that I was alone. I was thinking of the long winter nights.

Januszky, as if he'd had his say, turned his back on him and bent down to the girl.

You heard! You're not going anywhere, least of all where this man would have taken you.

Roswitha just stared, with unblinking pink eyes, watching Januszky's lips, then, startled, Duhovnik's, looking first at one, now at the other, and then at the two haversacks.

And then Duhovnik declared stubbornly:

She can't hear you, sir. Roswitha is deaf. And she can't speak either.

Roswitha was deaf and dumb. So when Januszky put her in his lap and set off with her, she said not a word. All I could do was to race after them with a parched throat.

So what do you intend to do with her? What the hell do you want with her?

None of your business, said Januszky sternly. You'll see, she'll come in handy for something.

Around the walls of the empty kitchen there still swirled a dank mist of petrol, but Anatol Korkodus was no longer there. I left the door open to let the premises air, and also opened the window. Meanwhile Januszky reached under her arms and lifted Roswitha onto a kitchen stool. Now the girl was the same height as us. She didn't know what was happening around her, as a confused grin came and went across her face, teardrops took aim at the corners of her mouth. Januszky tickled her under the chin, as if she were a dog, and turned her head this way and that. Then, as if he were thoroughly at home, he began to explore the shelf above the tap, where Anatol Korkodus kept his soap, toothbrush, razor, and unguents. He found the brigadier's tortoiseshell comb, dampened it slightly, but he got nowhere with the girl's baize-like curls. He tossed the comb back on the shelf, walked round the girl in a circle, took off her little lambskin gilet, unbuttoned her little peasant blouse, which made the pale brown nipples of her scrawny little breasts stand out and drew the eye to the little heart-shaped pillow, embroidered with her name, Roswitha, that hung between them.

Januszky looked her up and down musingly, with a rictus grin, then suddenly swept her up again, and listened for a moment at Anatol Korkodus's door before knocking on it.

Is that you, Januszky? Stay where you are. Tell me how far you've got.

All sorted, boss. I sent him to the dam, we shan't see him for a while if we don't want to. And, with your permission, that's not all.

And without further ado, Januszky entered the room with Roswitha in his arms.

Anatol Korkodus lay in his bed with the blanket drawn up to his chin, his two bare arms resting on it, his billowing head of hair wrapped in a towel, drying, and not a curl of it visible. On his bedside table lay a bottle of sloe brandy. But the room still smelled of petrol.

Januszky stood with the girl in his arms.

This is for you, boss.

Anatol Korkodus reached for the bottle, took a long slug from it without for a moment taking his eyes off the two of them. Long minutes passed like this, Januszky with the mute girl in his arms, all of them enveloped in a vast silence. Who knows how long, perhaps half an hour passed, or even more. Until finally the brigadier spoke up:

Thank you for thinking of me. It seems I misjudged you, Januszky. Just put down what you have brought over there. And now go and get some rest.

In the morning I was already up when Januszky stepped into the kitchen without knocking. I raised an arm by way of warning.

Stay where you are. In future you will stop in the middle of the yard and wait until you are noticed. Until you hear someone from inside call out the words: What do you want? Or: Go ahead.

Until then you will make no move and just stand in the middle of the yard.

I want to speak to the boss.

And you will now kindly stop all this stuff about "boss" this and "boss" that. In these parts we have no idea what that means. So you can't have any idea either. Now off you go. You'll know in good time should anyone want to see you.

Two days passed before they came for Januszky.

It seems he sensed their coming even in his sleep, but also that it would be late at night and that he wouldn't have time even to open the window. He hurled himself at the closed window to jump out. So that as he was being chased with a dog-catcher's net with tiny slivers of glinting glass sticking out of his body, he pelted along the Infantrymen's Street, until in Kapistranov's Snack Bar, under the coathooks, hidden ridiculously under Brigitta Konuvalov's apron, lying with one foot over the other in a small pool of blood, they finally found him.

When he caught sight of me through the net staring at him with folded arms as he was bundled into the back of a lorry – just a filthy cage covered in dog saliva and strewn with clumps of dog-hair, screwed onto the chassis behind the driver's cab – he began to howl in that non-existent language that had already stunned us once in Klara Bursen's house when he tried to pull the wool over our eyes.

8.

(MISS KLARA BURSEN)

The evening before his arrest Anatol Korkodus trimmed his beard, put on his brand-new dress shirt and bow tie, donned his uniform-like grey, coarse woollen jacket, its collar, cuffs and pockets trimmed with dark green velvet cut-outs, downed a small bottle of home-distilled gentian root brandy, followed by a shot of mulberry wine, and by sunrise, when they came for him, had consumed three and a half guinea pigs roasted whole.

By that time my old man hadn't eaten for several days, but this evening, having divined from a few minute signs and later from a rather trustworthy source, that it was all over, he suddenly became calm and, it seems, his appetite finally returned. Almost certainly he thought of this as a kind of small-scale last supper. Gazing at him systematically stuffing himself for what seemed like hours on end meant that I couldn't get a single bite down myself. Now it really did look as if I would be left on my own. My old man had come to the end of his road.

The water conservation zone over which Brigadier Anatol Korkodus held sway at the instance of distant powers-that-be, extending from the Brustyina lakelands, through the former Czervensky holdings and as far as the forests of Mentelina, suddenly became the scene of several kinds of activity. For a start, in the very first week of summer, at the height of the most intoxicating murmurings, the forest fell silent and the brook dried up. Persons unknown had tramped the length of the Yablonka and, using poles and, where they couldn't reach, jets of water to bring down the birds' nests, sprayed the foliage with some kind of rank liquid and spread tar over the resting places of the migratory birds, whereupon the birds left the district overnight, so that apart from the taciturn crows not one of them remained.

It was reasonable to suspect that that was only the beginning. Whoever had dreamt this up was unlikely to stop at this.

Anatol Korkodus therefore sent a report on the event to the landscape protection HQ in Monor Gledin and another to the gendarmerie, and also wrote to the Bishop of Lemberg. He waited and waited, for weeks on end, but no response was forthcoming from any of these authorities.

Next, it was the turn of the bees. One autumn night in the gardens of Yablonska Polyana, heavy with the smell of ripe fruit, every single beehive, together with the plum trees around them, burnt to the ground – there was no wind at the time – so comprehensively that even days later the smell of caramel lingered on amid the treacly ashes. At this point Anatol Korkodus decided to go over to Monor Gledin in person, but as he failed to find anyone to hear him out – some said the Captain was receiving a delegation, others claimed he was out in the field on a special mission – he deposited a further written report in the various offices, while to the Bishop he sent a telegram more than a hundred words in length giving his account of the events. He returned home and waited, and waited, but to none of his submissions did he receive any response.

Then, just before the onset of winter, as the ditch carefully dug under the slagheaps discharged into the river some sticky, foul-smelling liquid in heady colours of purple, green and russet, so that even at night, in the haze hovering above the riverbanks and in the gases discharged by the dead trout, bullheads, toadstools, and a variety of other decomposing matter that blanketed the surface of the water, there glimmered the silvery glow of some captivating mirage. Anatol Korkodus determined to prepare yet another report. In an account that went into considerable detail he enlarged on his recent experiences in the region, requesting the various relevant authorities to urgently carry out an investigation into what had happened. But as soon as he had completed his report, hand-written on numbered pages over an entire afternoon with a ballpoint pen in several copies using carbon paper, and read it over one final time, he proceeded to tear all the sheets into tiny shreds, keeping just a single copy. As if it had suddenly dawned on him that even his earlier reports he should not have committed to paper.

One day towards the end of winter, a time when there's not a great deal to do in the settlement, it occurred to Anatol Korkodus to make a trip to Monor Gledin, visit the reformatory, ask for the personal details and photographs of those about to be set free, and if someone's file happened to catch his eye, he would invite him to start a new life under his aegis in the settlement. This was not the first time he had invited youths to the settlement: every three years or so he would make an effort with some street kid or other. So he went to the station early one morning, with a completed form for a complimentary ticket, ready for Stationmaster Stetz to validate it for that day's train with his signature and stamp. The train was ready to depart but the stationmaster wouldn't accept his form, instead motioning with his head that he should follow him. Stationmaster Stetz lived in the station building, and now they went to his one-room service flat in the back. Inside the stationmaster took off his cap: his head gleamed, as he was completely bald.

Now, listen to me. If you're set on going, try another way of getting out of here.

But I can see the train is in, ready to depart.

I can't give you a stamp. I can't let you on the train. You can take a seat on it if you like, but the inspectors will take you off at Tuverkan Ford. That's about as much as I can tell you.

In that case, I won't ask you for a thing.

In any event, soon there won't be a railway here. Up the line they say foreign workers have arrived to dismantle the railway bridges. They're bound to take up the rails, too.

I should have known.

With that Anatol Korkodus turned to leave the flat, but before doing so he said to the stationmaster.

And what's happened to your hair?

It's been cut.

I can see that. And you thought winter was the best time to do it?

The questions you come up with. Two people came in, asked what kind of hairstyle did I call that, was I in my right mind, and shaved it all off. Did I hell ask for it.

And when did this happen?

Today, first thing.

Who were they?

How should I know?

A few days after this, late in the day, my old man was sought out by Lorenz Fabritius the local ex-Lutheran pastor; they ensconced themselves in the office and spoke for a short time, nine or ten minutes, so quietly that not a sound filtered out. The ex-pastor, following the demise of Yablonska Polyana's Lutherans, had nothing to do but catalogue the school library's stock for the bonfire, and to make ends meet he worked as a simple clerk in Hamilcar Nikonuk's gendarmerie office. A clerk like this, who scribbles away quietly, or even noisily pounds a typewriter, is well-placed to know a great deal.

As soon as the pastor left, Anatol Korkodus rang for me.

I'd be glad if you left here now. I'll give you a few addresses where you will be welcome.

If I don't have to, I'd rather stay. I'm getting quite used to being here.

You'll soon leave of your own accord.

That very evening, before closing time, he visited Madam Aliwanka in her lingerie sewing shop. Most people visited Aliwanka because she told fortunes for her acquaintances or those referred to her; she did this out of the kindness of her heart, since she was the repository of unusual powers. But on this occasion Anatol Korkodus merely took her a yard and a half of light grey poplin, to ask that she use it to make him a dress shirt. He was most particular that she should use silver-white silk thread to embroider the monogram A.K. on the pockets and the two wings of the collar, and to let the cuffs be half a span longer so they hung out of the sleeves of the jacket. In general, Aliwanka tried to see immediate or far-off events that remain a mystery to others by means of water or some other liquid, or something wet, and now, too, having measured up Anatol Korkodus, she was compulsively scrutinising the pearl-drops on his snow-slicked cape. But my old man caught her in the nick of time.

I beg you, no. Even if there is something that you can see, just this once it'll be best if you keep it to yourself.

When the shirt was ready, he sent me to fetch it and also asked me to order, on my way back, from the hairdresser Anka Vaczulika three stems of artificial red flowers that should, if possible, resemble roses, with silk petals varnished with nail polish and with leaves of taffeta, and to have them wrapped in cellophane and tied with a silver-coloured ribbon.

That same day, at midday, he was also there to receive the water trucks. He stood in silence by the tanks until they filled up and when they were done he turned off the taps with his own hands. In the afternoon he washed his hair, put on his new shirt, and, with the cellophane-wrapped bouquet in his hand, trekked over the snow-covered Boursin vineyards to the Boursin farm, to Miss Klara Bursen, in order to beg her forgiveness after nineteen years of stubborn rancour. A long time ago they had had a difference of opinion in the course of a game of Trik-Trak, but as Anatol Korkodus, in a fit of blind fury, had poured a bottle of walnut liqueur over the lady's head, they both swore that their anger would this time last not for a week but until the end of their lives. Apparently Anatol Korkodus sensed that he had reached the end of his.

Klara Bursen was born a cheerful old maid, but with the passing of the years the last traces of her cheer had evaporated: she went about in worn blouses, her gaze had lost its lustre, she became like an old muff shedding its fur. Her brow was dull, her posture frail, her kitchen smelled strongly of cats. But now, catching sight of Anatol Korkodus with bouquet in hand and already inside the fence, at the grave of the Hungarian officer, coming up the garden path that led directly to her front door, she hurriedly let down her thinning hair and awaited him wrapped in a soft woollen shawl. Once the initial ardour of their meeting had cooled, she made some pancakes, opened a small flask of home-made walnut liqueur, and just as in the old days they stayed up till dawn in the cold kitchen playing klaberjass.

That's how I found them, sleepless and red-eyed, when I knocked on her door early in the morning. Since the public wash-house's keys had remained in my old man's pocket the previous day, I had no choice but to disturb him so that they could open up at the usual time of eight in the morning. My old man then began to gather his things. They said their goodbyes somewhat awkwardly. As if clinging on to him, the woman grabbed a button on Anatol Korkodus's jacket.

I know why you have come to see me.

You do? So why would I, as I'm curious to know, too.

It's that the two of us, Korkodus, will never meet again.

Anatol Korkodus gave her a knowing wink, and nodded:

That could very well be.

At these words Klara Bursen, instead of looking up at him with a melancholy glance by way of farewell, reached for his hand and angrily bit it.

That evening Anatol Korkodus, having let his hand bleed copiously and bound it with a damp kerchief, tried feverishly to find the sole copy of the torn-up report that had remained intact, perhaps in order to tear that one to shreds as well, or possibly to hide it in some even more secret place, or – what would be safest of all– to eat it up; but he couldn't find it. It wasn't where he had put it. It was nowhere to be found.

After much reflection he fired up the kitchen range, stuffed it full of hard kindling and when the plate was red-hot, he emptied his drawers and burnt all his papers, including all his personal documents. Only the Augustins' file was left on his table, lent to him only for his perusal by Constable Hamilcar Nikonuk on the occasion of their confession ten years earlier that they had electrocuted the children of the Nyegrutzes and the Gleznárs. Every other document, including the annual tallies and reports, every single of them, was consigned to oblivion. The only thing he didn't touch was the coffer with the coupons in it and the reports on the organisation's accounts going back many years. At the very end, he also began burning some of his old clothes, shirts, jackets, and finally he even stuffed his service uniform into the range to join the burning sheaves of curling paper. He stood before the open door of the range, amid the choking fumes, to make sure everything was completely destroyed, waiting until the sooty embers finally sank from the touch of the draught. Then he poured a cauldron of water over the lot. Though our wordless glances would sometimes meet, there was nothing for us to talk about. The evening passed in silence.

Since the priest's visit, I had practically not seen him eat. As soon as lunch was brought in from the canteen, even the smell of the lunch tins made him back away and hole up in his room, and he pored over Eronim Mox's book of tales as if it were manna in his hands. Though he once did send me to fetch some goat's milk from the Man-Gold yard, and spent the afternoon sipping it unboiled. Meanwhile, as if expecting someone, he stared stiffly out into the yard from behind the curtains, looking beyond the fence, at the street lined with piles of slushy snow, and frowned whenever the wind happened to grab one half of the gate. But no one came looking for him.

And indeed: no one did, because the someone whose coming he was expecting generally arrives at night. That's when he emerges from the impenetrable gloom, from the depths of the deepest silence imaginable, out of the void, as it were, and comes knocking on the door. Or he doesn't even knock but simply walks in. He's suddenly there. To take him along.

On that last day a number of other curious things happened. In the morning, when I brought him news that in the communal stables someone had shorn the donkeys the previous night, every single one of them without exception, he nodded approvingly. Yes, that may well be so, he said, that's a sign of mourning, of pain, one can count on that happening at a time like this. The loss of someone, of a loved one, may prompt people of profound sensitivity to carry out such actions. Someone was being mourned.

And late in the afternoon, as he dozed off at his empty desk, Subprefect Vaneliza Nikonuk's daughter made an appearance, and slapped down on the table the two hundred coupons that barely a week earlier she had asked if she might borrow from petty cash, pleading with pearls of tears glistening in the corners of her eyes that she had a dreadful problem: she needed to secretly abort her foetus. My old man, though he was surely incapable even of imagining how this wizened, prematurely aged, nondescript girl with the face of a badger could have been impregnated by anyone, proceeded to give her two hundred coupons for the secret abortion. Now the girl stood before him, arms akimbo, as if she were not herself but rather her mother, the freckles on her pale face pullulating, her dry, lacklustre hair sticking out at wild angles and giving off tiny electric sparks. Anatol Korkodus, seeing the money flung down on the table, shrugged his shoulders as he returned to her the receipt for the loan, whereupon the subprefect's daughter, with those badger-like lines aquiver around her nose, angrily crumpled it up. As if she had been forced to accept the aid she had originally sought, as if she had been implicated in some murky transaction, she began to hiss. That next time Anatol Korkodus should be more careful about whom and, especially, for what purpose he offers loans from public funds, because in case he didn't know, procuring an abortion was forbidden, a crime against the state. And he should admit, once and for all, that she didn't need anyone's help, least of all the water conservancy brigade's, since she was comfortably off and had no need of money. It was obvious from her bearing that she had recently been practising in front of a looking-glass what she would say and how she would say it. As soon as she had said her piece, her simulated anger seemed to dissipate, her freckles subsided, her hair flopped down, and her face turned red with shame. With a bewildered smile of doubt and fear in her tiny badger eyes, she rushed off, as if she was urgently expected elsewhere. It never became clear what all this fuss was about.

She left in her wake a bitter, icy blast of air, the kind that comes on parched afternoons borne on the wind from distant, ice-bound meadows, betokening the approach of a storm.

But it was still winter, outside the snow fell evenly and quietly, on their way to the gate the subprefect's daughter's footprints glittered blue. I wanted to say something, for example that it was a pity to let her go without her revealing who had sent her, but I saw in time Anatol Korkodus's index finger planted across his lips. There was nothing to talk about.

Yet this silly business must have continued to rankle with him somewhat afterwards. He locked up the office, got dressed, and sinking his face in his raised collar walked in slow circles around the yard spitting substantial gobs of saliva in the footsteps of the subprefect's daughter, and kept on walking until there was nothing left around him but the gleam of the snow. Meanwhile, after many weeks' silence, as if the sound were borne on the bitterly cold stream of air, the telephone in the office rang. Though my old man did hear it, and in fact tiptoed as far as the door, listening to it in a curious way, his head cocked to one side, as if wanting to decipher what message the ringing betokened, yet he did not open the door to pick up the receiver.

It's a trick. They just want to know if I'm in.

Who he had in mind, he didn't say.

Later he came indoors and eyed me up suspiciously, as if trying to establish from my outward appearance whether I was worthy of hearing what he was about to say. At length he spoke.

You've noticed, haven't you, that it's snowing quietly outside.

Of course I have. In fact, ever since the water truckers were here.

Indeed so. No sooner had the water truckers left than there came a cloud from the direction of the peaks of the Medwaya in the shape of a letter N. Exactly the kind I had dreamt about. That's what brings us such fine snow.

I didn't see that. And you'll forgive me if I've never seen an N-shaped cloud, and can't imagine what an N-shaped cloud might look like.

Well, it's like a big letter N with ragged fringes in the sky. It means: Nikita.

Nikita, in Eronim Mox's book of stories, and in all of Verhovina, is the name of death.

And as if all this were not enough, without anyone calling him, amid the biggest fall of snow, the boss-eyed Balwinder turned up, the dogsbody of all the local offices. On other occasions when he came without being summoned, he would knock politely, and wait cap in hand on the threshold for the door to be opened for him. Now he behaved as if he were in his own home and simply walked into the kitchen drenched to the skin and stopped in front of the table to shake off the snow.

When Anatol Korkodus asked to what we owed the pleasure, what had happened, all he said in a flat voice was that it was his heart that had brought him here. He came only to say farewell, to say good evening, seeing as night was approaching, soon the day would be done, and he wanted to see Anatol Korkodus just one final time. And now he would ask only that, whatever happened, he should not think of him in anger.

With that he turned on his heels and walked off.

Now Anatol Korkodus set about polishing his boots, trimming his beard, having a wash, sprinkling Cendar talcum powder in his armpits, and withdrew for one last time to his room. It was getting late when he rang for me. By this time he was waiting for me in his office, having got changed, with a dark red, silver-speckled bow tie under his chin, one he had never worn before, with the Birtz order of merit on his chest, which he had hitherto kept in the depths of his drawer in a fancy box.

He kept other items in his drawer, too, in particular a plain little pine chest, reinforced with metal bands. He proceeded to take this out and hand me the key to it.

Open it.

It was full of coupons in one-hundred units. There appeared to be many, a great many, as the draught made the banknotes flutter like butterflies' wings. I closed it hurriedly, turning the key in the lock to make sure they didn't fly away.

What am I to do with it?

You'll need it.

Why? Where are you going?

I don't know. Wherever they take me.

And when will you return?

Never.

But tell me a little more, so I can understand.

By way of reply he just waved his hand. Though he added in a low voice: Later on, browse Eronim Mox's cookery book. And that reminds me, it would be good to have supper today.

With that he sent me over to The Two Queans, to Edmund Pochoriles's hostelry, for a tankard of blackberry wine and asked me, while he made a fire and until the range heated up properly, to skin four or five guinea pigs for him.

Four or five?

That's right. I'm hungry.

We kept a few that my old man had received from District Commissioner Hamilcar Nikonuk in the chicken coops. They were supposedly the South American variety, easy to look after, resistant to the cold, and eating little, yet with the most delicate flesh. My old man had so far been loath to slaughter them. But now their time had come: seemingly they too had been affected by the evening's rather bitter, icy blast, because as soon as I reached the garden gate, they huddled together terrified in the corner of the coop and began twittering like birds.

By the time I had done with them, and after gutting, skinning, washing and spicing them, coating them in thyme- and coriander-infused pumpkin seed oil, and I had placed them all, interlarded with slices of dried wild pear, in a roasting tin that I put in the oven, Anatol Korkodus was already sitting in his ceremonial outfit in his usual place at the head of the table. First, he drank some brandy, offering me some as well, then poured himself some blackberry wine, at the same time beginning to write in large, curlicued letters in a yellowing notebook that had up until then lain empty on his bedside table. He used his left hand, as his right, despite the wet compress, had swollen up enormously. He paused only when, two and a half hours later – that was roughly how long it takes, with continuous basting, for a young guinea pig to roast to a crisp – I laid the table for him and served. At first, he only poked and picked at it with bad grace, then he speared pieces of various sizes on his fork and chewed away steadily for several hours. He ate the guinea pigs one after the other, until only about one and a half remained in the roasting tin, now cold and gelled into the fat. Then, as he took sips of the blackberry wine, he resumed writing. He put the date separately at the bottom of every page, added his signature, and stopped only just as day was breaking.

Before daybreak, in the final hours of the night, he heard the gate creak as it opened and then closed, and soon saw that it was Balwinder, the office dogsbody on the doorstep in his spattered, patched-up grey greatcoat, looked into the room boss-eyed and then, opening the door and without a word, with just a crooked index finger, beckoned him to come.

As he did not stir, Balwinder addressed him:

Let's not make a fuss about it, sir, but may it please you to get up now and come with me.

With you?

With me. You are awaited outside. They say you are under arrest.

Aha! Well, in that case, you Balwinder are also in on the business.

Balwinder gave a slight cough, and blinked in agreement.

Yes, sir, I am. But that's hardly the point just now. Come along, we're in a hurry.

Anatol Korkodus glanced at me, and even seemed to give me one last wink, as if to say: well, he knew the score, his preparations had not been in vain. That, lo and behold, we have come to the end of the story.

So the moment had come, the moment that he had been secretly expecting for some time. He rose from the table, wiped his beard carefully with the napkin, adjusted his bow tie, and slowly, measuredly, without showing the slightest sign of being upset or unwell, as if putting a full stop at the end of the story, vomited into his plate. He bent down, and now wiped his mouth and beard on the edge of the tablecloth, then reached for the half-filled notebook, wanting to take it with him. But Balwinder, who kept glancing out into the yard to see if they happened to be keeping an eye out for him, indicated with a raised index finger that he shouldn't, and took it from his hand. He leafed through it officiously and when he began to grasp what the rapidly written, spidery, childishly officious lines of block capitals were about, he immediately closed it and threw it back on the table. He again looked out into the dark, whence it was possible to see and hear what was happening inside through the open door.

All water under the bridge! These are small fry, we don't concern ourselves with piddling stuff. Who the hell cares what happened to your madezite, you could have eaten it even, right? Yes, indeed, no one's interested in these things. In Delfina Duhovnik's cunt least of all.

And with that he led Anatol Korkodus, who now bade me farewell only with a last, confused glance and a vague, uncertain movement of the hand, out into the yard. He left the door ajar for a moment, so that I would see the outline of my old man melting into the void and feel for a second the damp cold of the approaching dawn, and then he closed the door behind him.

So my old man, Anatol Korkodus, was gone. Only his full plate remained. From the spines and thorns that stuck out of it, I could see that he had eaten the guinea pigs virtually without chewing them, bones and all.

As day broke a lukewarm wind arose from somewhere in the south: it must have come from the passes of the Medwaya. The smell of rain and sodden soil seeped in through the keyholes and the cracks in the windows. The snow, with its palm-sized flakes visible even in the dark, had continued to fall into the small hours, when it turned into gentle, warm rain, and as it suddenly started to thaw, the eaves began to tinkle. When the smell of the thaw mingles with the aroma of the fresh pastries from the direction of Man's scone bakery, you know that morning has arrived in Yablonska Polyana.

In the morning, as always, Balwinder, the local offices' dogsbody, came in. He opened up the office, aired the rooms, swept the floors, watered the houseplants. He finished off with a bit of dusting and, as if we were expecting visitors, rubbed the windows down with wet newspaper.

When he stopped in front of the door with a basketful of kindling, and knocked on the door cap in hand, I let him into the kitchen.

Good morning, sir. When I am done here, and if you let me have the keys, I'll go and open up the public wash-house.

They are hanging where they always are. Take them.

He did two turns between the kitchen and the woodpile, scraped the ashes from the range, took them outside and scattered them in the yard. Finally, he made a fire.

When he had completed his duties, he stood in the middle of the kitchen, rattling the wash-house keys and tried to look out pensively through the condensation on the windows.

Is sir not at home?

I've not yet seen him today.

Because just now, as I was eating my cabbage lángos in Nyegrutz's bodega, I heard people saying that they saw sir leaving here in the middle of the night.

Leaving here, you say? Could be. As I say, I haven't yet seen him today.

They say a snowmobile, with its lights turned off, came for him. It had tiny silver snakes and bats painted on it, these were all that lit up the dark. It took but a moment for them to speed off into the night. But the rumbling of the engine could be heard well after the break of day.

That may well be so. I too seem to have heard the rumble of an engine, but I thought I was just dreaming. A snowmobile, you say?

That's right. A fine, big snowmobile, the people said.

Because I'd have liked to have seen that. That's something that if I had the wherewithal I'd buy for myself. A Firecat, or even better, a Bearcat, forty-eight horsepower.

Balwinder nodded, gazing blankly out of the window.

Expensive stuff. Not something for the likes of us. They say it can glide over not just snow but also mud. Who knows, perhaps even through the air. That's what the folk say in the bodega. That it must have been quite far away, the snow must have melted under it long since, but somewhere from the clouds the rumble of the snowmobile could still be heard.

In that case, it would seem he really has gone. But he might have told us. He might have mentioned it to us, too.

True. There he goes, off with some people. Without a word to anyone. In that case he may never come back.

If he's gone, he's gone. So please, next time you're passing the canteen, let them know that from today it's just lunch for one.

9.

(DOC SCHWANTZ, THE VET)

Radoj supposedly understood a little Hungarian, having picked up a smattering in the reformatory at Gledin; he could, or so they said, at least read it with a passable accent, almost fluently. And so it happened that one Friday morning found him heading off to Klara Bursen's hillside farm with a book of Hungarian poetry in his knapsack to read to her. Years ago, seamstress Aliwanka had prognosticated to her from a tear-sodden handkerchief that a Hungarian officer would come for her from beyond the mountains to propose marriage, so she was attuning her ears in anticipation to the strange and enigmatic sounds of the many é, ő and ű letters in the language. It was Adam from the water conservancy brigade who was her regular reader, but on occasion, when he had better things to do, or if he happened not to feel like it, he sent Radoj in his stead. At such times – Friday mornings, by mutual agreement – the kid would smuggle out in his knapsack a book taken at random from those stored in the public wash-house's woodshed, destined to be used for kindling or even a proper fire, go out to the farm and, following Adam's instructions, read to Klara Bursen for an hour or two, and by way of recompense she would offer him elderberry tea with honey and, if she was in the mood, also make him a lángos.

Radoj was just jogging along by the farm fence when from its far end the hoarse voice of the laryngitic Balwinder, the water conservancy brigade's office dogsbody and bungler, caught up with him.

He should turn back at once. Hostelry keeper Edmund Pochoriles begs him to rush at once to the railway station, where he will find Deacon Ambrozi sitting on a bench. Radoj should take his ticket and bag and make the journey to Kolina in his stead, there seek out doc Schwantz, the vet, and bring back as much as he could carry of the trout that had been ordered from him earlier. Adam, who belonged to the same brigade as Radoj, knew all about the matter, so he may rest assured that he was departing on his mission with his permission. Certain reasons prevented the deacon, who was supposed to have brought the fish, from being able to travel that day, whereas the trout had at all costs to be here by morning. The ice in the cellar was already melting, the ice that the iceman had brought from the frozen gorges of the Medwaya specially to keep the fish fresh.

In short, Deacon Ambrozi could not travel that day. Radoj on the other hand, who in return for carrying out minor tasks in the hostelry kitchen – chopping wood, sweeping the floor, washing up – received a modest lunch, and already owed them work equivalent to nine bowls of soup, had no choice but to go. His knapsack, a gift from seamstress Aliwanka a few days earlier, together with the book of poetry in it, he left on a hanger in the hostelry and, since the ragged clouds on the mountain peaks were beginning to gather and he was bare-headed, before leaving he asked in the kitchen for a nylon carrier bag to put on his head in case it started to rain.

Early in the afternoon of the previous day, during the hour of death, when neither train nor bus halts in Yablonska Polyana and everyone is asleep and only the gelatinous silence of the settlement quivers above the housetops, a stranger had appeared at the reception desk of The Two Queans, wishing to take a room for two days, a room looking out onto the square. He had thinning, slicked-down hair, combed straight back, and under his grey coat he wore a creased, mouse-grey suit which hung off him as if made for someone of a different build. His haggard, pallid face and large, translucent, bare ears in fact made him appear somewhat mousy grey overall. He carried only a battered briefcase.

Edmund Pochoriles said later that he had a strange feeling from the moment he first set eyes on him: he seemed to recall this person having visited him before. And that his clothes, like that last time, gave off a vinegary smell, as if he'd spent all day in an office heated with an oil stove. Before handing him the registration form, he asked if he could examine with a magnifying glass the stamp on his identity card, but he found it was in order. The fellow was left-handed, and as he signed his name the form was completely obscured, so Pochoriles could make out his details only after they'd been passed over to him when he'd signed in. His name was Damasskin Nikolsky and, as for his occupation, in the relevant column he had written: procurator episcopal. Who knows what that might have meant.

The hostelry keeper hurried over with the news to the Lutheran pastor, Fabritius. He stuttered and jabbered in his confusion as he tried to describe the visitor. Though he hadn't even mentioned his name, the unfrocked pastor immediately suspected it was the same man as last time, the procurator for public health. The latter had visited the settlement before, when he'd brought three pairs of foxes in a covered trailer and set them free on the field of the Paltin.

Supposedly in order to destroy the myximatosis-ridden rabbits that had overrun the area. It soon transpired that the two procurators not only resembled each other but even their names were identical.

The stranger bearing the name Damasskin Nikolsky went up to the room he had booked and never stirred thence, even asking for his dinner to be served there. At most, a twitching curtain in his window indicated that from time to time he would look out onto the square, desolate in the light of dusk, the old folks playing draughts around the statue of the Three-Legged Woman, the melancholic dogs panting with their tongues lolling out.

On this morning Deacon Ambrozi received a summons from this person, the procurator episcopal. But by then he was no longer at home.

Radoj knew the deacon well and had even seen him a little earlier that morning, trudging to the railway station under the slivers of dispersing fog, lugging his enormous green-and-black striped holdall. In Yablonska Polyana there lived only Lutherans, there were no Old Believers, so he had chosen the settlement only as his temporary residence. It was from here that he travelled twice a week, on Mondays and Fridays, to the nearby settlement of Kolina, to confess the exiled women and carry out spiritual exercises: in his words, to comfort the sluttish souls of the damned.

Since someone had years before poisoned the upper reaches of the Yablonka and the fish had died out, while downstream the waters of the hot springs flowing into the river were sulphurous and salty, Pochoriles the hostelry keeper sometimes had trout brought over from Kolina, where it was still worth fishing the pristine headwaters of the streams.

On its return journey the train did not pass through Kolina until sometime around dawn, so the deacon spent the better part of the night playing draughts at the home of Schwantz, the vet. There were occasions when they passed the time fishing on the banks of the Yablonitska, the branch of the river where the doc lived. Sometimes Ambrozi's green-and-black striped holdall was stuffed with as many as a score of Danubian salmon, bullheads and trout for Pochoriles's kitchen. It was said that they put an electric wire in the brook to stun the fish, so that they might pick them up from under the rocks with their bare hands.

The only daily train service, which consisted chiefly of freight cars carrying ore and timber and had just a single, soot-laden carriage for passengers, did not operate according to a regular timetable, but rather departed whenever they finished loading at the slagheap's silos, so for anyone wanting to take the train it was best to get on it early in the morning and settle back on the seats to await its departure.

Radoj found the deacon, just as they said he would, sitting on a station bench, with his green-and-black striped holdall reeking of fish beside him. He hadn't quite reached him but already started rattling off the news that he had come to take his place, since the deacon could not travel to Nikolina that day. Ambrozi listened thunderstruck, but as soon as the kid came near, sprang to his feet.

You saw him too? What does he look like? Sure he's looking for me? What in the name of God's fucking prick can he want?

Radoj smirked: get a move on, he looks like someone important. And he wants to see you urgently.

He asked him for his ticket, took his holdall, and got on the train.

Ambrozi shouted after him:

You'd be well advised to take care. Don't forget, the train doesn't stop at Nikolina.

Nikolina was the second station along the Yablonka, a good half-hour away. Since the women's penal colony had been transferred there, the train didn't stop and only slowed down as it passed through the station. But the train driver would usually apply the brakes sufficiently for any passengers intending to alight to jump off from the end of the last carriage onto the platform, these days thickly covered with weeds.

It was the first warmish day of spring. For a time the cloying smell of splurge laurel filtered in even through the closed windows of the sooty carriage, as the lights too flashed past, but later, as the train moved beyond the mountain pass towards the gentler slopes, the sky clouded over completely, and soon icy rain began to patter against the windows. Blankets of brown smoke began to gather under the balefully looming clouds and the carriage, too, filled with fumes that had a bitter, stinging smell. Like when they are burning dung somewhere.

In Kolina, they mainly kept animals: the exiled women looked after not only cows but also a small herd of sheep, some goats, and a few pigs. The settlement consisted of a dozen or so hovels, a pen, a couple of barracks and, notably, stables steaming with manure: above the valley hung a gelatinous murk filled with lowing and bleating and grey with flies. Kolina was the haunt of dumb animals and fallen women. Fallen women, who had ended up here because of their reckless way of life, insatiable libido, and sinful lecherousness of every kind.

When Radoj arrived it appeared to have been raining for a week, everything glistened under a grey glaze sodden with water. Doc Schwantz, the vet, was a broad-shouldered man with a bullet head, a trim black moustache, and tiny, wire-rimmed glasses. He was sitting in his yard by the stream, under a tarpaulin ringed by a wickerwork fence, at work in his shirt sleeves, up to his wrists in blood.

Since the pen was packed with animals, entering it was impossible, so Radoj shouted that he had come from Yablonska Polyana at the instance of Edmund Pochoriles, the hostelry keeper, to see him about the fish. The vet carried on with his work, though he turned round several times to take a good look at Radoj, who was wearing the nylon carrier bag on his head. He was completely surrounded by goats and sheep agitatedly bleating and baaing, as a woman wearing a full-length knitted grey dress and an ancient, broad-brimmed hat more suited to a lady from the city herded them, prodding them with a stick to get them to line up for doc Schwantz's knife. After they had dealt with the groggy animals, a girl in a shift led them into the adjoining pen. The creatures left a trail of blood as they passed along the rain-soaked track.

It was spring, castrating time. After he spooned the testicles out of the animals' scrotums, the doc threw them one at a time without a backward glance over the fence, where plump cats with gleaming whiskers were waiting for them. The few testicles that bounced back off the fence shone out in the mud. Nonetheless the doc kept some of the better-looking ones for himself, collecting them on a small tin tray. When he was done and the pen was empty, he stood up and that's when Radoj noticed that he had a rough-hewn artificial leg. He was drenched in blood up to the elbows, and a grey shroud of flies hummed about him. He sized up Radoj sombrely, taking his time.

Tell me again, who are you?

I'm Radoj from Yablonska Polyana. I used to work for the brigadier who got killed. Now innkeeper Pochoriles has sent me for the fish.

The deacon couldn't make it?

He couldn't. I've come instead.

The doc hobbled across the muddy yard, the colour of rust from all the blood. A number of cats perched on top of the fence were already eyeing the testicles embedded in the mud. By the wall was a pile of firewood, beside it another pile, of compacted manure. In the corner of the yard, by a metal butt filled with water, stood the woman in the broad-brimmed hat, ladling water over the doc's blood-soaked arms, wiping them dry with a rag that already had quite a few rust-stained blotches. As she did this the doc continued to cast the occasional backward glance, and looked Radoj up and down, again and again.

What the hell is that thing on your head?

It's raining.

You sure you've come only for the fish?

As I told you. It's an urgent matter for the hostelry keeper, the ice that he had specially brought from the mountains is melting. And the deacon couldn't make it.

Because it would be best if you came right out with it now, if you had some other reason for coming. The holdall seems familiar, but about you I know nothing. Wouldn't you be suspicious?

Radoj shrugged. I don't know.

We live in strange times. Something has stirred hereabouts. I wouldn't be best pleased if I happened to find something out about you later.

I was just sent for the fish. I'd have had better things to do. I was told that once I'd introduced myself, I should simply address the gentleman as 'doc'.

Really? Is that what they said? How nice of them. All right, in the evening we'll see if we can find anything in the water.

In the afternoon Doc Schwantz donned an apron, chopped some onions and garlic, put them in a soot-stained brass pot and left them to stew in a little fat on the stove. Just as the onions were beginning to brown, he took the dish of blood-tinged aspic with the sheep's testicles that he had previously soaked for several hours in salt and vinegar, added a generous dash of pepper, then poured it into the boiling pot, sprinkled it with crushed peppergrass, and then covered the dish.

If you stir-fry it, two or three minutes is enough. But if you want to eat something really delicious, it needs three or four hours to become really tender, he said.

While dinner was being prepared the doc took out the wooden box of draughts, the Shesh-Besh game as it was known there. He opened it and emptied the pieces and the dice out onto the table.

Know how to play?

Radoj shrugged.

They played, meanwhile the doc sipped his gooseberry wine. He offered Radoj some, but the boy declined. I know what it's like, it tastes a bit like mice.

From time to time the doc would stand up, hobble over to the stove, put a piece of wood or a chunk of compacted manure on the fire and give the food a stir, basting it with a little water. He smelled like a stale rubber gown.

So, Ambrozi couldn't come.

No.

Is he ill?

He's not ill. It's just that I came instead.

Yes, we've been there. And you don't know why?

He had no time. He had something better to do.

Pity. I'd have had something to tell him.

He'd set off intending to see you, but he was persuaded to stay.

If you should see him, be sure to tell him that some people were here not long ago. Madam Karabiberi from the constabulary, and some others. They had a word with the women. Those here in the settlement. You know, the deacon would visit them in the camp to confess them. And do some other things.

All right, I'll tell him.

Heaven knows what they wanted. It may be better if the deacon asks to be relieved of his duties and doesn't come this way for a while.

By the evening the rain had stopped. They had a bite to eat, then went out to the banks of the little stream, the Yablonitska. A battery lamp hung from doc Schwantz's neck, and he pushed ahead of him in the mud a two-wheeled wheelbarrow knocked together from metal, which rattled a great deal. It carried a battered little generator, covered in mud, which when they came to the bank of the stream, immediately surged into life at a pull of the string. He drew out some wires, tying up their ends, or just dangled them in the water, and hobbled up and down the bank in silence. He let the motor run for a while, then switched it off and sat down. He motioned to Radoj. There were two sturdy stakes in the ground, with a rough-hewn plank across them, which here served as a place to rest. They sat for a long time in silence. Radoj sometimes got up, stepped out of the arc cast by the doc's battery lamp, and walked off into the dark as if into some enclosed, intimate little space. He retched each time.

Best stick a finger down your throat and spew it all up in one go. You didn't even hint that you didn't like it. Perhaps it needed more pepper.

I've never eaten this kind of thing. But I don't regret it. My brigadier used to say you must try everything in life at least once.

I never knew the brigadier.

They took him away. But then he died, seeing as they killed him. We found him one morning on a cart in front of the house, lying in the straw. He was already stone cold.

Well, fancy. I didn't know the fellow.

Of course you did. You know very well who he was. You just don't want to talk about him.

They went back indoors and sat down again to their game of Shesh-Besh. They moved the pieces by the light of the oil lamp.

Don't forget her name: Madame Karabiberi, from the constabulary. It'll be enough to say that. That'll tell him what they're up to.

It's a difficult name. I wouldn't mind if you repeated it a few more times before I leave.

Kara-bibe-ri. Just so he knows what's up. That not long ago a few of the prostitutes were interrogated. Some 10 to 15 of them. Personally, by Madam Karabiberi of the constabulary. And the prostitutes all said exactly the same thing to her, every last one of them.

Seriously? You think that'll be enough for the deacon to know what the wenches said?

Absolutely. Very much so. He is not stupid, he'll know what to expect.

Quite some time later they went out once more, the doc switched on the motor again and let it run for a little longer. After that they went and sat on the bench again in silence. In due course, doc Schwantz pulled a gumboot on his good leg, rolled the trouser leg up above his knee, and with his worklamp round his neck waded into the water. He must have been familiar with the place, even with his wooden leg he moved as if he were thoroughly at home. The lamp around his neck lit up a wide arc around him. He first had a feel under the bank, and then, where the water surged past very rapidly, he reached down to the bottom of the rocks as well. Whenever he straightened up he had a motionless fish in his hand. He turned it this way and that, and then threw it out onto the bank. The fish was stiff, as if frozen. The whole thing took no more than 10-15 minutes perhaps, then suddenly Doc Schwantz stopped, struggled to keep his balance, then hobbled out onto the bank of the stream. The bag was scarcely a quarter full.

There's no more, it's been a thin day. Though they do like the rain. Still, that's the lot for today.

His wooden leg housed a small drawer, which he now proceeded to open. It contained miniature instruments of a murderous nature: scissors, scalpels, sharp-pointed irons. He took out a long needle, and before throwing the fish into the holdall, stabbed each of them in the head. They were mostly trout, but there was the odd sullen-looking tufted bullhead among them.

That's the way. Otherwise they come round and don't understand what's happened to them. They start thrashing about and will try anything to get out of the holdall. You wouldn't have a moment's peace on the way home. It's not easy to die. I'm a doctor, I should know.

They went indoors. The doc poured himself a shot, and took a sip or two.

You've plenty of time until the train. If you don't feel like a game, have a lie down. Ambrozi could never control himself, he'd always go and visit the women again.

And just wake them up?

Doc Schwantz stared out into the darkness, aglow with the eyes of several cats tempted by the vast quantities of blood and the smell of fish.

Those that the deacon was going to visit were awake. He went to confess them even at night. You can tell him he'd do well to bear in mind that the women all testified against him.

If I get the drift, he has something of a problem.

He does indeed. It's his fault entirely. Like a machine, he was, once he got going, he couldn't stop, if you get my meaning.

I don't, doc.

Really? Well, I have to tell you that the deacon has four testicles.

Radoj's head jerked upwards and he belched. He stood up suddenly and went out to the front of the house. He returned, wiping his mouth.

I've never heard anything like that in my life.

Four. Don't you think that's too many?

Four! I just don't believe it. You really can't tell. Though I'm sure he can deal with them.

Well, I'm not so sure. He produces an enormous amount of semen. He can't control himself. That's what landed him in trouble.

Let me guess: that was why those people came here.

You got it in one. Someone must have ratted on him. Told them what he gets up to in the confessional. Because, I'll have you know, the bottom half of the booth's dividing wall was sawn off.

And I thought he was queer: honest to God I thought he was a proper homo. The deacon doesn't give the women of Yablonska Polyana a second glance. Though it's true they're mostly old and wizened.

Those here aren't exactly in their first blush either. But that eternal desire, blazing in their eyes, scorches you so you don't even notice that you suddenly want them. Because they're on fire, permanently on fire, and Ambrozi got wind of that and from then on there was no stopping him. Well, let's leave it there. If you wish, you can have a little lie-down till the train leaves.

I'm not sleepy.

You threw up your dinner. I've nothing else to offer. So it would be better for you to have a rest, because you'll have to run alongside the train. Fortunately, the track here goes uphill and the train slows down, so even a child can jump on. You first throw on the holdall, then you leap on after it. And don't try doing it anywhere but the very last carriage. So there's not the slightest danger of the wheels being behind you. I'll see you that far.

Meanwhile a large ginger cat came in through the open door, and when it had sniffed its way round the holdall, settled down beside it. The doc motioned towards it with his artificial leg:

That's Paraskiva. She moved in one overcast day. Someone once claimed to recognise her, that she'd escaped from Yablonska Polyana. But I think she came straight from the wild. If you look at its ears and tail, you'll see I'm right. Nine and a half kilos, I weighed her. By the way, she's a nasty piece of work, a heartless devil. I've told her to go several times, but she won't. Pretends she doesn't understand. I don't know what to do with her. My Hippocratic oath forbids me from harming her.

You serious? She's Paraskiva, you say? I'd prefer to call her Charlotte.

You're being stupid. Where did you get that from?

Seeing as she's so yellowish, and plump, and soft.

You're talking though your hat. But how about it, would you like to have her? I'll give her to you if you like. I'm never going to forgive her, ever. Come for her sometime and you can take her with you. You can't just now, because of the fish.

As he promised, Doc Schwantz saw Radoj to the train. It was a clear, moonless night, beneath the stars the slushy, rain-sodden landscape glittered black as tar. Though the train was still far away, it could be heard in the distance, as sometimes the rails would begin to thrum of their own accord. Somewhere, from distant arbours, there suddenly came the sound of blackcocks. Then, from nearby, quite unexpectedly, that of magpies as well. They sensed the coming of the new day as they warbled gently above the bare crowns of the bowers.

Do you have any birds here?

Good question. Perhaps where you live you don't.

Not one. A couple of years ago, but maybe even longer, they all flew away in high summer. These will, too, you'll see.

The stupid things you say. So, anyway, don't forget: I'll say it again, Madam Karabiberi. She is sure to be looking for him, the deacon.

Radoj blinked repeatedly, head tilted to one side: the deacon knows the score, if he tells them how many balls he has, perhaps they'll let him off.

Not that lot. The balls are, er, in his court. Does he intend to live with four testicles till kingdom come? Knowing him as I do, one would be enough.

He should be left with just one, you mean? That he'd manage with just one?

I see you're getting the idea. Just a single one, as you say. Or not even one. And I could help him. High time he did something to show his good intentions.

As I say, I've never noticed anything about him. And it's not the kind of thing I could bring up.

You'll have to. He's in deep trouble. Tell him, he can count on me, I'll always be glad to help him out. As you've seen, I'm pretty handy, I work quickly and cleanly.

Well, I don't know.

Doc Schwantz's glasses glinted in the light.

You can tell him what you've seen. I mean, how you saw me, at work, understand? I'll do it as a favour to him, for free. Don't forget to tell him.

Radoj ran alongside the train, clambered on, and was already standing on the carriage steps when the doc shouted after him once more.

And don't forget to come for your cat sometime.

The Two Queans, Edmund Pochoriles' hostelry, was still closed when Radoj arrived there early in the morning. He went round the building and entered the kitchen from the courtyard. In front of the range Pochoriles was stirring the ingredients of an omelette in a dish. The serving hatch towards the dining area was open and Radoj caught sight of the visitor called Damasskin Nikolsky sitting at a table, while facing him sat Deacon Ambrozi. They were silent.

Radoj put the holdall with the fish down on a chair, gave a slight cough, which made the hostelry keeper turn around.

You've done a good job. From now on you'll always be the one I ask. And remind me to wipe the price of two days' soup from your tab.

Fine.

I'm just making them some tea, you can have some too. And aren't you sleepy? If you have nothing more to do, you could lie down for a bit in the shed.

Thank you. I'm getting ready to read to Miss Klara. I'll have a bite to eat there.

Radoj went out into the room, to lift his knapsack with the book of poetry in it off the hook he had hung it on, but it wasn't there. At one of the tables sat a man who looked like a pale mouse, the procurator episcopal, Damasskin Nikolsky, with Deacon Ambrozi opposite him. They sat in silence, their features tired and joyless. Both their faces were drained of colour, like those of people who have been up all night.

Radoj returned to the kitchen. He sat down on a backless chair, watching Pochoriles use a fork to spread the omelette-to-be in the bubbling fat.

But that's where I hung it. The book was in it too, the one I should be reading from.

Who the hell could have done it? Pochoriles kept shrugging his shoulders. He peered out into the room through the serving hatch. Adam has that Mox book of stories, if you can find nothing else, ask if you can borrow it.

Radoj ran his fingers through his hair, then gave a resigned wave: he thinks it contains all the wisdom of Verhovina, he'd never lend it out.

If it's any use, I have an annual from last year.

A book is a book, I suppose. Miss Klara has books too. It's all the same what I read to her, she doesn't understand it anyway. But I'm sorry to lose the knapsack. It was made of waterproof canvas.

Pochoriles moved a step closer to Radoj.

I'll have Aliwanka sew you another. And tell me. Didn't the doc have a message for Ambrozi?

You mean for the deacon? What message would that have been? It was just the fish, no? Here they are, I've brought them.

Nothing? Nothing at all?

As I say, you know very well you sent me to Kolina for the fish. I've brought everything the doc caught.

But now Radoj set off, in a bit of a daze and with somewhat unsteady steps, hurrying awkwardly. Passing by the gardens, he took the winding path directly to Miss Klara Bursen's farm. On the way he picked a few stems of saffron, some anemones in bud, as well as a fragrant daphne that he found by the fence. He shook them free of their droplets of water. He would beg Miss Klara's pardon at once for having kept her waiting like this, for he was a whole day late for the week's usual reading session.

10.

(BALWINDER)

It was three or four days after Easter when the unfrocked pastor Fabritius knocked on my window at first light saying that Madam Constable Karabiberi from Velky Lukanar was expecting me at the community centre. I asked him what her business with me was, but he wouldn't say.

Though he did add sotto voce: it's best if you don't tell her anything. She has no business meddling in our affairs, does she? Whatever she asks you, just shrug your shoulders.

In the cold light of dawn the madam constable sat alone in a corner of the room behind a small table, her cape buttoned up to the chin. Not a soul to be seen; perhaps she had spoken with others earlier, but apparently she was now waiting just for me. When I stopped before her, she offered no word of greeting and asked without further ado whether I recognised any of the objects displayed on the table before her. Whether I had seen any of them before.

There was a mud-spattered briefcase, black and battered, with sharp corners and one side of it ripped off, a large woven knapsack, also black but covered in rusty brown stains, and a single black male boot, with its sole completely burnt off.

I said nothing. Madame Constable repeated:

Tell me, Adam, on your word of honour, whether you have ever seen these objects before?

No, I said. I've never seen them before.

Are you quite sure? And are you sure you don't know anyone who might have seen them recently?

I'm quite sure. I haven't the faintest idea why you're asking me such things at the crack of dawn.

Just to get you to try and recall the last few days.

I think we had much the same day in mind.

One of the last few days would be Easter Monday, for example.

About midday on Easter Monday, Edmund Pochoriles the hostelry keeper asks me to take Balwinder's dinner over to him. This is a task he usually delegates to my niece Danczura, but recently Danczura has been unable to bear even the smell of food and feels nauseous all the time, so this isn't something she can be asked to do nowadays.

Balwinder is unwell. For years he has been claiming that he was ill, just to avoid having to work; he is laid up in bed all day and hasn't left the house since the autumn. It really does seem that he hasn't much time left. Malingering will be the death of him.

Pochoriles has a generous heart, so he sends a bowl of thin gruel over to him every day. The gruel is thin because we have already eaten the carrots, the millet and the egg barley it had in it. Today Balwinder gets nettle soup that is also thin, not quite ready and without any spices in it, because Edmund Pochoriles would add the dumplings, the batter, and the scrambled eggs to our own bowls only when he served the four of us. It is Easter Monday, a holy day, when as on other feast days, a few of us would eat together: the hostel keeper Edmund Pochoriles, my niece Danczura, and

Fabritius the unfrocked pastor. It's still only Easter but the nettles by the sun-baked fence, along the path to the privy, have already sprouted.

So I take his lunch over to Balwinder, set it down on the stool by his bed, and stay standing there while he spoons the soup from his bowl. As he slurps it down, his grungy, yellowish-grey locks dangle into the dish, while with his enormous squinting eyes he keeps casting suspicious glances in my direction. This time, too, I wait for the final clink of the spoon, so I can take the empty dish back, but as I am about to go, I see him raise a tired arm. He asks me to stay.

Why not have a game of draughts? he asks.

We had a game the day before yesterday. Have you forgotten? Or do you now want to play every day? You should have learnt to read. Then I could have brought you fine stories from one of the books intended for the bonfire. Miss Klara, too, is unwell, but she manages to read. In several languages, to boot.

I was thinking of only two or three rounds. I hear today's a feast day.

I put the bowl down on the ground by the door, to make sure I don't forget it, and wait for Balwinder to take the box with the pieces and the dice in it out from under his pillow. I sit down on the side of his bed.

All right, three games, then. But no more than three.

We play, but I keep glancing out of the window all the while. Over the road, on The Two Queans hostelry's chimney-stack, there has been a seagull resting for the past two days. It's as big as a goose and has a hooked beak, like an eagle. The kids throw stones at it, sometimes managing to hit it, but even then it doesn't move. My niece Danczura stares out into the street, her mouth half-open, leaning against the fence; she must be feeling nauseous again.

She scans the length of the Infantrymen's Street, as if waiting for someone. But above the paved road, which is slowly being taken over by weeds, marigolds and primroses, there flutter only the first butterflies of spring.

Balwinder is an unhurried player, he shakes the dice in his hands for a good thirty seconds before throwing them. He shuffles the pieces along reluctantly. I let him win, to make sure he doesn't ask for more than three games. We are getting towards the end of the second game when he unexpectedly pipes up:

I have a favour to ask.

Go ahead. Let's hear it.

I would very kindly ask you, sir, to jack me off.

I stare at him: he just blinks repeatedly as he stares back. I gaze out of the window:

I thought we were having a game of draughts.

I can attend to that at the same time. I mean, I thought we could still carry on with the game.

That's what you thought, did you? You're a strange creature. Because I, for example, can do only one thing at a time.

No matter. Would you?

Come on, Balwinder. You're a bit old for that kind of thing. But if that's what you want, deal with it yourself. The game is nearly over. We can stop now if you like. I'll be off, and you can do with yourself whatever you want.

It's not the same. Is it so much to ask of you on a feast day like this? I feel I don't have much time left, this would be my last wish.

Nice try. But no, not even then. No, Balwinder, feast day or no, I won't. Anyhow, what does Easter have to do with your darkest desires? I've told you, no. You know best how you like it. I'm not touching you.

Balwinder leans forward and sighs:

I'm completely winded. I don't have enough strength in my hands. Imagine, just before you brought me lunch, I nodded off and dreamt of Zhedu Buba. That we were together. Now I just want to feel good one last time. While sir does it for me, I'll think of Zhedu Buba.

Not Buba, Baba. Zhedu Baba. You don't even know what her name is. You might at least get her name right if you're dreaming of her.

All right, Baba then.

You and Zhedu Baba? That's news to me. I'm very surprised, because, if I remember right, she was never that keen on you. Only you know what you and Zhedu Baba did in your dreams. Fondle yourself the way you like it. One thing's for sure, I'm not going to touch you.

Quite enough of this. I get up from the side of his bed.

You leaving?

I am. You've made me very angry. And you know what? If I were you, I'd call for a priest. You'd have plenty to say to him. You were a bad man, Balwinder, and even now, at the end of your days, you're concerned with your cock, of all things. Instead of telling a priest all you have done.

You think that would do me more good?

No, he doesn't understand. I must leave him. Despite what would have been his last wish.

Easter, bright sunlight: when the sulphurous smell of the hot springs is dispersed by the breeze the fragrant smells of the awakening meadows come rolling down the slopes of the Paltin. As does the smell of nettle soup from Pochoriles's kitchen.

As lunchtime approaches Fabritius the unfrocked Lutheran pastor goes over to The Two Queans, taking with him the young deacon who turned up in Yablonska Polyana only a few days ago. He came carrying a black briefcase and a black woven knapsack, in which he must have kept his musty clothes that smelled of bugs. He claimed that Anatol Korkodus had picked him out in the reformatory and sent him to a seminary, so that he could later come to Verhovina to proselytise. He was obviously lying, as Anatol Korkodus was a Seventh Day Adventist, and avoided people with yellow eyes. One thing's for sure: no one had invited this fellow to come here. For a while he knocked about near the moss-encrusted statue of the Three-Legged Woman, then he went off to see Fabritius. A thin young man with a straggly beard and big, yellow eyes. He wears hulking big black boots.

They take a seat at one of the tables near the bar. On the deacon's jacket, at chest level, gleams a great big silvery letter N, or maybe it was just the play of the light on it. He studies the bottles on the shelves bearing various labels, as if finding it difficult to decide which one to choose, though the bottles have long contained only tea, of various colours. For years hostelry keeper Pochoriles has offered his guests only vinegary wine, pinkish in colour, the kind that the travelling salesmen from Velky Lukanar bring him in plastic barrels, and occasionally, if they are willing to pay, some of his own brandy. The best of his old wines he now reserves for himself.

Pochoriles, as if detecting an alien smell in the room, comes out of the kitchen. He walks around the table where the unfrocked pastor Fabritius is sitting with the deacon.

You might introduce yourself, he says, walking off.

The deacon leans back louchely in his seat:

I am a servant of God.

At this Pochoriles suddenly swivels round as he is departing and asks Fabritius:

Perhaps you know his actual name. Anyhow, today I've cooked only for four.

He says his name is Kotzofan, says Fabritius quietly.

Kotzofan? That begins with the letter K. A capital K. But what I see now on his clothing is a big letter N.

A letter N? On me? Where? I haven't even noticed.

Definitely. N means Nikita. And Nikita in these parts is the name of death. I can tell you it's unfortunate you haven't read Eronim Mox's book of recipes. When you can make out on someone's chest or near their shoulder blade a capital letter N, looking like a fleecy cloud or as if made of birds' feathers, that's the last day of his life.

The priest squirms uneasily in his seat, holding his hands up defensively and spreading his fingers wide, so that his long dirty nails shimmer in the light.

But I'm not about to die. I'm only twenty-seven years old.

Oh, I'd never have known, says the hostelry keeper, with a shake of his head, and gives Fabritius a dig in the ribs. Tell him, that's a ripe old age. And if you continue your conversation, you can also tell him there are no Old Believers here, because everyone has turned Lutheran. Tell him he should know he's wasting his time.

I'll pray for them, and then they'll return to our fold, says the priest by way of response.

At this Pochoriles suddenly turns sarcastic.

Maybe. Who knows. But by then your eminence will be long gone.

Edmund Pochoriles kicks in the swing door ahead of him and disappears into the kitchen. After a time he is followed by Fabritius. The strangulated voice of the hostelry keeper can be heard from the kitchen.

No, I'm not at all happy to serve him. Now that you've brought him in here and, for reasons best known to yourself, are palling up with him, you can damn well drink the wine of the Velky Lukanar travelling salesmen. That's if you really feel like sitting down with him. And you really can't smell him? It's unpleasant to imagine where his clothes might have picked it up. And his body as well. You could do with having a better sense of smell.

Finally, Fabritius nonetheless comes back from the kitchen with two glasses of brandy filled to the brim, taking very careful steps.

Edmund Pochoriles remains in the kitchen, I can hear him whipping up the omelette. As I mentioned, for Easter Monday he is making nettle soup with garlic; only an omelette of that sort will go with that. We all love it, this is a red letter day. The tender shoots of the nettle: the most delicious of all.

The two clerics, that is to say, the deacon Kotzofan and the unfrocked Lutheran pastor Fabritius, are drinking at the table by the bar, while my niece Danczura is laying another table for four. There is no setting for Deacon Kotzofan.

Danczura brings the soup tureen from the kitchen. She is followed by Pochoriles; she serves and begins to dish out the small dumplings that go with the nettle soup, as well as pieces of the omelette, and adds a generous spoonful of garlic and sour cream batter to each bowl.

Before we start eating, I stand up and go over to the table where the pastor is drinking with the deacon. I turn to Deacon Kotzofan:

I see you're not taking lunch. I know it's not the custom on feast days, but I have a small task for you now. If you have the time, go and see Balwinder. He wants to have a word. He is in a bad way, really bad.

Balwinder? Who's that? I don't think I know him.

You can get to know him now. He lives opposite, in the public wash-house's courtyard. He was once the office dogsbody. As for his religion, I understand he's an Old Believer. Or something of the sort. He wants to talk to you.

Me in particular? Would you happen to know what about?

As I say, he's in a bad way. He's not at all well, I'm sure he wants to unburden himself. This is a very sinful man, feast day or no feast day, and you must give him a chance to do so.

Fine, I'll go over. But I see that you are well aware that we don't confess on feast days.

The priest gets ready, though with bad grace. While donning his black soutane, and adjusting the round black hat on his head, he looks at me suspiciously several times. Finally, he leaves. I watch him as he crosses the street with the silver swirl of a capital letter N on his back, moving ever more slowly, then stopping and glancing back, as if to ask whether he was headed the right way. I don't take my eyes off him until he disappears in the courtyard of the public wash-house.

We slurp Pochoriles' nettle soup in silence, from time to time looking at one another in satisfying inarticulacy. Finally, the hostelry keeper turns sternly to Fabritius:

You've taken in a spy. Do something so I never have to set eyes on him again. I really expected better of you.

Fabritius, his nose in the soup, sniffs its aroma:

Every morning I tell him to go and leave us in peace, because there's nothing for him here and never will be. But no, no, he won't. A spy, you say? That didn't occur to me. I'll pray he leaves here as soon as possible.

The afternoon sees the two queans come in: Zhedu Baba and Brigitta Konuvalov. At one time they were both paramours of Brigadier Anatol Korkodus's, but it ended with the two women falling in love with each other. Though they are somewhat wilted, even now they stick fragrant leaves of pennyroyal or strong-scented lily of the valley under their plump arms, and in their hair wear daisies cut from plastic chocolate boxes, and walk about arm in arm, like an engaged couple. Goodness knows where they get their money from, but every afternoon they down several shots of the hard stuff, Pochoriles's sloe brandy, while they play rummy at the corner table until the lamps are lit.

Now they invite me and Fabritius over to their table. It's a feast day, they say, so let's do a jigsaw, the four of us. Zhedu Baba repeats several times:

Today you're our guests! Order whatever you want from Pochoriles's under-the-counter stash.

Fabritius shifts uncomfortably in his seat:

I'm not alone. You know I have someone with me.

Ah! We'll have none of him. Out of the question. The invitation is for the two of you, as friends, since it's a feast day. Anyway, rummy is for a maximum of four.

Pochoriles's stock is fast diminishing and apart from his own brandies that he makes every year and the plonk in the plastic barrels, he keeps barely a few dozen bottles of wine in the cellar. He says that when that too runs out, he will shut up shop. That's when he'll show us where he wants to be buried. As if he himself could hardly wait for that day.

Pochoriles now stops behind our table, then walks round in a circle and takes a look at every board, one at a time. He doesn't sit down, but leaning against a pillar watches in astonishment how we are playing. Until Deacon Kotzofan unexpectedly returns.

Ahem, he begins. I'd like to say something to the gentlemen.

Pochoriles gestures towards us, indicating to Kotzofan that he should not disturb us, we're playing. He places his index finger across his lips: psst, later, when the game is over.

But it's important!

I said: Psst!

But I really must show the gentlemen something at once. That's why you must come over with me. The person who sent for me to visit him is, I believe, no longer alive.

Balwinder is covered by a blanket drawn up to his chin, his brow gleams, while above his mouth there circle Easter flies. The draughts set is on the stool by the bed. Silence, and the smell of a dead man.

Pochoriles bends over him.

Was he like this when you found him?

Not quite. He asked if we might have a game of draughts.

Pochoriles sees Balwinder's outspread arms, takes a long look at the uncreased blanket, carefully smoothed down, as if pulled over a lifeless body. Then he suddenly lifts it up. The lower half of the dead bungler's grey body is completely naked, covered in dried-up specks and encrustations.

You touched him.

Me? No, not me.

Yes, you did. I see what I see.

He asked me to.

Aha. Well, come on, this way.

There are no guests in The Two Queans hostelry, but Edmund Pochoriles looks round before going behind the bar. He places two brandy shot glasses before him, reaches under the counter and takes out his most precious gentian root brandy. He fills the shot glasses and slides one towards the deacon.

You must be very upset, I imagine. Swallow this quickly, then you'll get another. You're a filthy homo. You were willing to reach under his blanket.

I tell you, he asked me to. At first he just wanted us to play draughts, then he wanted me to do something for him. So he might feel a little pleasure.

You're a filthy homo, I tell you. What does a man's life matter to you! I knew from the off the kind of man you were. As soon as I got a whiff of that bug smell of yours. All three of us, the men here, find you repulsive.

He said I should treat it as his last wish.

Extreme unction indeed. All right. I promised you one more shot. Drink up and then get your things together. Be gone by sundown.

Pochoriles would be off, heading for the kitchen, but the deacon, like a pleading child, blocks his way hopefully.

Whoever would deliver punishment on me for this, whatever it might be, I would like to atone for it here and now, in the presence of you all.

I can well believe you would. But you won't. Just go back nicely to those who threw you out. They'll know what to do with you. Your first job will be to tell them everything.

The deacon now turns to Fabritius, standing silently by the bar.

Please say something. Tell him not to make me leave.

At this Pochoriles:

You want Mr Fabritius to speak to me? That's a good one. And what should he say to me? Go on, off with you. This kid, and he points to me, will see you as far as the border of the settlement. Go and don't look back.

Come now, let's go, says Fabritius to him quietly.

Now they finally set off.

Fabritius lives nearby. But even so perhaps as much as an hour passes and dusk is well and truly falling by the time I spot them slowly trudging towards the hostelry. The pastor is wearing an outsize pair of black boots, on his back the black woven knapsack, in his hand the black briefcase. As soon as they reach the hostelry, Fabritius gives him a farewell slap on the back as I catch up with him.

We trek along the Infantrymen's Street. From time to time the priest turns his head towards me and gives me a long and hard look, but I pretend not to notice. At length he pipes up:

Is there really nowhere for me to sleep around here?

No, there isn't.

Really? It will be dark soon.

A servant of God is not afraid of the dark.

But he is.

I'm sorry. Be glad you can leave a free man. You killed Balwinder.

With its shattered windows and grafitti-sprayed walls the abandoned old station is the last building in Yablonska Polyana. It's now home only to a few screech owls. It marks the settlement boundary. It was as far as I had to stay with him. I could now go back if I wanted to.

This way, I say to him.

I lead him along the track overgrown with weeds and thorns. Beside the ramp to the store are lined up empty bogies and the side-dump cars only slightly bigger in size. In the old days, when there was still some mining going on, this was where they transferred the debris to the wider-gauge trucks.

Listen to me, Kotzofan. See these little trucks? No one would dream of using them anymore, you can unhitch one if you like. You'll find axle grease in a tub behind the building and there's a spade to go with it. When you have given it a thorough greasing, you can go and take a seat in it, and since the track slopes quite a bit, you can roll down in it almost as far as Velky Lukanar. To stop it speeding up, you'll have to apply the brake. In that case you have a choice: you could stand directly on the axle, but it's better to stick your foot between the wheels and the chassis and keep it there. Best leave it there all the way, until the slope bottoms out. Then the car will come to a stop by itself.

I wait for him to decouple one of those little side-dump cars, grease the axles and climb up into it. This kind of side-dump car is not all that comfortable to travel in and Kotzofan can't really settle down in it properly. He grasps it with both hands, awkwardly, as he tries to put his feet between the wheels and the chassis. As the truck can't start of its own accord, I give it a shove. I put my shoulder to it and push it until it finally starts to move, creaking.

Stop, Adam, stop! Not just yet, please!

Dammit, now he's even trying to make friends with me, but with all the effort I'm putting in and the creaking of the wheels I can barely hear him; I just keep on pushing. I nudge it over the rusted-up points clogged with weeds, then break into a run as far as the open track, where the slope begins. There I give it one last big shove. Now it's rolling by itself. As it accelerates and disappears, as if into a tunnel, into the mist of the approaching night, the track begins to sing and hum all around me. Even the tin roof of the station rings out and continues to reverberate as I trek back along the Infantrymen's Street, an organ being played in the vault of the sky above.

In the evening we play rummy in the hostelry. Pochoriles the hostelry keeper, my niece Danczura, and Fabritius, the ex-pastor. It's a feast day, we are drinking gentian root bandy topped up with spring water. The wind seems to be rising and the swell of an organ repeatedly swoops past the windows. Or it could be just my imagination.

Madam Constable Karabiberi asks:

What's your name again?

Adam.

For the last time of asking, Adam, have you seen these objects anywhere before? The person that they belonged to I can't show you.

The boot, with its burnt-off sole, the knapsack covered in reddish splotches and reeking of bugs, the black briefcase, muddy and ripped. I circled the table, shrugging my shoulders as I surveyed the objects on display.

And if I had seen them, what then?

11.

(NIKITA)

It's St Urban's Day, the last day of the ice saints. In the past Anatol Korkodus would send Balwinder over to the public wash-house at the crack of dawn, to toll the bell bidding farewell to winter. But Anatol Korkodus is no more, nor is Balwinder in the land of the living, and the wash-house tower has collapsed. It was no longer to the sound of bells but that of Gleznár's dogs that people awakened. These were barking at the white slopes of the Medwaya as they emerged from the ragged fragments of the departing snowclouds enveloping them.

Hereabouts, though the meadows might turn green earlier amid the primrose paths of May, a doleful cloud would come from the frozen night of the north, settling with sluggish wings on the heights, and a few days later, lift lightly and drift off in a south-easterly direction, allowing the slopes to once again array the courtyards in white from top to toe. Now snow covers the steeply descending ditches, too, as far as the gardens. There's something up there making the dogs restless.

As I'm making the fire in the morning, my niece Danczura taps on the window, wanting to say something. The door is not locked, she stumbles in and sits down on the edge of my bed. Her belly, like a sack of flour, hangs down between her two scrawny legs. Who knows what there is in it.

For a good while she watches me as I do my chores. She reaches under her breasts, cups them in her palms, glancing down now at one, now at the other, and waits for me to catch her eye. Her butterfly-catcher blouse of yellow hemp is all damp and her large, liver-coloured nipples are showing through. She points to them, wondering what I think: is that milk or what? Because she is fit to burst and the kid still shows no sign of coming out. Even Pochoriles the hostelry keeper wrote to her not long ago that there wasn't much point in expecting just yet, since in Verhovina the period of gestation is two years.

I tell her this hadn't struck me before. But where does Pochoriles scribble that kind of stuff?

In a notebook, she says. They haven't been on speaking terms for weeks, but Pochoriles has a notebook he uses when he has something to say, and she replies the same way.

That hereabouts winters are long, summers short, and the embryo spends more than twenty-three months inside, in the warmth of the womb.

I shrug my shoulders: it's news to me, but if Pochoriles says so, it must be true. And if her milk really has come after all, she should try expressing it. Or let the hostelry keeper suckle. Write him a letter in his notebook.

Danczura shakes her head, she doesn't think it would work: the hostelry keeper doesn't drink milk.

Danczura is not my niece, though everyone here, even Danczura herself, believes that she is. Years ago I was visiting the reformatory in Gledin with Anatol Korkodus to help him choose a new kid to set on the straight and narrow in the settlement, when it occurred to me that we might, just this once, opt for a girl. And when I happened upon a berry-eyed tomboy with a razor-cut, I persuaded my old man to let the insitution assign her to me, so that I might at last have someone of my own. She was a bit grubby, with dirt under her fingernails, but her nose was like dew, her look wistful and filled with longing, and when she noticed that I was pointing at her, asking her to take a step out of the line and show herself off from the back as well, she began to pant and tremble with excitement.

But when, after several years, the request was approved and Anatol Korkodus was informed that the girl had been let go, and I went out to pick her up from the stopping train: as soon as she was illuminated by the crystalline lights of Verhovina, I said to myself, Adam, you've been bloody well had.

She wasn't the girl I'd picked out.

But by then there was nothing to be done, and she has lived here, in our midst, ever since. Her hair is as dry as weedstalks, her eyes are frosted glass, her face pullulates with freckles and pimples, and the veins show through her prickly, white skin.

Yet she just waited and waited. One sultry afternoon, in the hour of the dead, while I was dozing woozily, she sidled up to me and let her saliva dribble into my mouth. When she saw that even this failed to arouse me, she asked:

Then why did you have me brought here, to live among foxes, badgers and bats?

To this I replied: just so I had a relative. Don't you know that you're my niece? You surely didn't imagine I'd lay a hand on you.

I made the whole thing up on the spur of the moment. She was a mere spasm, a sticky little wind-blasted, spider-webbed burdock plant. Yet there was something about her that appealed to Edmund Pochoriles, the hostelry keeper.

And now it's come to this: she comes to me with her milk. I leave her, stroll over to the public wash-house, and turn on the taps. All of them at the same time, letting all the water straight into the empty stone troughs. I keep at it for a good quarter of an hour, while the room fills with choking, sulphurous fumes. Very few people still come here to do their laundry, so to ensure that the salt and the harsh residues don't settle and block the pipes carrying the hot spring water from the mountainside, I rinse out the conduits every day.

Meanwhile the barking of the dogs can be heard even above the gushing of the water. These two dogs were the only ones remaining in Yablonska Polyana, the rest had fallen victim to the foxes, the lynxes and the bats. Oh, and Edmund Pochoriles's husky. But that can't bark.

I amble back, take Anatol Korkodus's old spyglass off the hook, and stand outside on the threshold to scour the slopes. The first thing I can see, on the hostelry's chimney stack, is an enormous seagull, like a fat duck, with a hooked beak like an eagle's.

The wind is now beginning to whip up the clouds; beneath them the slopes that were still green the day before yesterday now glisten a blinding white. But up in the heights, on the steep slopes covered in fresh snow, footprints in the form of a Z, zigzagging from side to side, glower darkly. They are the footprints of the person the dogs have been yelping at since dawn. The footprints become more frequent, but appear isolated: they emerge from the snow at regular intervals, one black splodge after another, only the person leaving them behind can't be seen. He's quite invisible, casting only a stray shadow across the snow, yet the dogs can sense his presence from afar.

The spectre vanishes as the invisible person emerges from the steep, snow-covered slopes onto the tussocky area near the thermal springs, where no snow remains on the somewhat warmed-up soil. There, of a sudden, he is visible: he is white all over, as if made of solid snow and ice. Keeping clear of the nut bushes, dwarf birches, and the columns of steam rising from the thermal springs, he takes stumbling steps as he slowly descends, heading straight for the settlement.

Danczura is still sitting on the edge of the bed. Her blouse glistens damply. And as the place warms up, the smell of milk becomes increasingly pungent. Her glassy eyes harbour a hesitant expectancy.

I open the door for her, she can go. I repeat: write to Pochoriles, this is his doing, so he should go ahead and suckle. Every three to four hours, as is the custom.

I no longer need the spyglass, the man in white head-to-toe is now at the bottom of the slope, near the Czervensky water-mill encased in glass. He is half-hidden by the fencing, only between the gaps does his snow-white form flash by, the moment he gets to the houses he is out of sight for a while. By the time he surfaces again he is quite close, by Nadja Kapustin's veranda, walking in the middle of the road along the deserted street.

A stocky figure, lurching a little from side to side, he nevertheless makes an effort to walk with a strutting gait, and, as if in a place he knows well, looking neither to the left nor to the right. Though he has left the grim, ice-bound heights far behind, he remains solid snow, ice and rime from top to toe. He wears a sort of cape that reaches down to his ankles and there's a battered shako on his head.

He must at some point have had a horse, because he is approaching along the Infantrymen's Street lugging a saddle over one shoulder. Although there is really no one to tell him which way to go, he is heading straight for the entrance to Edmund Pochoriles's hostelry, at the Sign of the Two Queans.

Nowadays, as visitors are few and far between, Ed Pochoriles mostly spends his days reading, buried in the former Lutheran school's books before he uses them for kindling. If one of us should happen to want a drink while he's lost in his reading matter beneath his blanket until late in the day, we simply help ourselves in the bar, chalking up what we have consumed on the menu board.

Since Danczura began to balloon up, hostelry keeper Pochoriles has become sullen and reclusive. He's stopped cooking, eats hardly anything, doesn't respond when you ask him something, and drinks from the early afternoon until late into the night. Not long ago he took stock of the wine in his cellar, the wine he kept solely for his own use, and on a piece of torn cardboard drew as many flasks as still awaited him on the shelves down below. Every time he opens one, he puts a cross on one of the flasks. The wine stock is diminishing, the day will come when there will be only one left. He says that's when it'll be over: he will lie down, cover himself up to the chin, and fold his arms across his chest.

If only it were that simple.

The snow-white stranger is by now standing uncertainly before the entrance to the hostelry, as if trying to make out the battered, sun-scorched, rain-soaked inn sign. At length he walks into the hallway, takes the saddle off his shoulder and throws it into a corner, and without shaking off the snow frozen onto him, disappears behind the door of the empty room.

Not much later I see Edmund Pochoriles leaving through the garden gate. He is wearing creased track suit bottoms, the kind he usually slouches around in, a tattered short-sleeved top, and his peaked cap, pulled right down over his brow. He crosses over the road hurriedly, and stops under my window. Though I call out to him, he doesn't enter. He speaks rather quietly, the words tumble from his mouth as if steeped in some kind of embrocation. He asks if I would hurry over to the unfrocked pastor Lorenz Fabritius and tell him to come to the hostelry without delay; if he should be asleep I am to wake him up. He has a visitor from the next world, someone emanating an icy draught: wrapped in a cloud of vapour he is staggering around the room as blasts of steam in many colours flicker about him. At the same time Pochoriles can't understand a word he's saying and has no idea what he wants, because he is speaking Hungarian. Fabritius should quickly put on something decent, and hurry over to get him to reveal what he wants.

Edmund Pochoriles just keeps staring inquisitively from under his cap. He says:

I think this person was sent by Anatol Korkodus to hound me.

Anatol Korkodus? How in hell? Anatol Korkodus is long dead.

Well, from the other side. It looks as if he's now sent someone to fetch me, too.

Pochoriles pulls his cap down even further and, tilting his head back a little, eyes him from under its shade.

I should take a good look, he says, at the footprints on the snow-covered slope: the way they approach along the steep incline, going now to the right, now to the left, alternately on the hillside, an entire series of letter Ns, in an endless wreath. The letter stands for Nikita. And Nikita is the name of death. That was also the sign that Anatol Korkodus saw before they did for him.

I scan the sun-lit, snow-covered mountainside, the Z-shaped marks as they descend from the steep slopes. If I make a real effort, and tilt my head slightly to one side, they could, I suppose, be letter Ns lined up one after the other. But even if so, what's this all about, really?

That Anatol Korkodus, too, saw large letter Ns in his dreams.

Stuff and nonsense. He shouldn't have buried himself in Eronim Mox's book of recipes day and night. To the point where his visions turned into reality.

In the small hours of the day when people in a snowmobile came for him at dawn, Anatol Korkodus had a dream. In it he was approached by a faceless, saint-like figure dressed in white from top to toe, who had come without a word, just with the proximity of his presence and a hand raised to his brow by way of warning, to forewarn him of his death. Above his light, white puffy woollen cape covered with the dull sheen of hoarfrost, embroidered in barely visible silver silk thread as if in curls of steam, there flickered a translucent letter N. Anatol Korkodus had no trouble immediately interpreting his dream: the letter N stood for Nikita, and Nikita in Verhovina was the name of death. If anyone, whether in his sleep, or even in broad daylight, even as a momentary flash, whether nearby or in the sky between the clouds, ever saw this sign flicker, a goodly prayer should pass his lips, because that is his end, his time has come. He would have at most a few hours' grace to prepare for his departure.

We thought the brigadier had lost his mind. But no. The next day he was no longer among us. At dawn on the third day a horse and cart came to a halt in the courtyard of the water conservancy brigade. The horses seemed to have unharnessed themselves and cantered off quietly, leaving the cart standing where it was. In it, covered with straw, lay a dead man with a big nose: the brigadier. Anatol Korkodus.

Still, I ask Pochoriles whether anyone else knows anything about this faddish business with the letter N.

That doesn't matter in the least, he says, what he knows is enough for him. Once he knows something and feels it to be true, he needs no explanations: in that case it's curtains for him either way.

I tell him: Fine. In that case, I have just one question: if you see your letter N upside down, so that its left-hand stroke begins at the top and the right hand one ends at the bottom, and not at the top as it's usually written, does it still mean the same thing?

He says he doesn't know. Anatol Korkodus's dream involved a normal letter N.

Because there is here in the courtyard a large letter N of that kind, I continue, as it happens, in the privy. The day procurator Damasskin Nikolsky was here, and everyone had a bout of diarrhoea when they caught sight of him, someone daubed an inverted letter N with a finger dipped in shit on the wooden wall of the privy. The way illiterates draw it, with the left-hand stroke beginning at the top. So what do you make of that? What's that inverted N about?

Pochoriles reflects on this for moment:

Maybe upside down it doesn't mean anything.

But the question continues to trouble him and having given it further thought he shakes his head and remarks: if you look at it from the inside of the wall it is, indeed, a proper letter N.

As Pochoriles and I waited for Fabritius, we peered out of the kitchen through the serving hatch into the room. The stranger, whom the hostelry keeper alleges to be death's messenger, is shedding his armour plating of large chunks of snow, ice and rime. As he turns round and round by one of the tables, looking for his seat in the far corner of the room, he notices us peering out through the opening and nods in our direction while touching his ice-covered shako with his right hand. As he takes it off he gives it a shake to get rid of the frozen snow on it and hangs it up, and then makes strenuous efforts to divest himself of his cape, which has frozen solid onto him and taken on his shape, and is now, thanks to the heat in the room, giving off a silken, vapoury steam. He tries to hang it up, but soon gives up, standing it in the corner like some headless puppet. At times he is unsteady on his feet, hiccups, and his features fade into the shimmer of the cloud of vapour. He gives big yawns and, having no handkerchief, blows his nose into the palms of his hands, trumpeting hard and long, as if about to give up the ghost. The crown of his head gleams bright, there's just a little bit of hair gleaming white in frozen tufts around his ears. From his moustache, his eyebrows, and all the way to the bristle under his chin, the hoarfrost hangs down in bunches, and even his ears drip snowmelt.

Now that he is beginning to slough off the frozen crust that had also, until then, hidden the holes in his clothes, his smell, too, is becoming perceptible. It's that of a vagrant who hasn't washed for months.

That's what Gleznár's dogs had detected from afar.

The unfrocked pastor Lorenz Fabritius enters the kitchen from the yard and before going into the room, he too first peers cautiously through the serving hatch. He is wearing his long-abandoned pastor's garb, with its extended neck and reeking of musty patches, which must have lain creased in a chest for years, and has a yellowing dog-collar under it, but his trousers were the frayed, tattered and wax-stained ones he wore day in, day out. After studying the visitor from a distance, Fabritius flings open the swing door before him, ambles to the end of the room, where the stranger is being fidgety. He stands there for a short while, as if intending to introduce himself, then sits down beside him. From the kitchen it looks as if they are already deep in conversation.

Danczura appears and puts on her apron. The apron's strings can barely contain her enormous sack of a belly. She takes out a clean tablecloth, shuffles over with it to the far end of the room, and lays the table.

She brings with her a cold blast of air and the smell of corpses on her return.

Lorenz Fabritius glances frequently in the direction of the serving hatch, eventually raising a hand and gesturing to Pochoriles:

Come out of the kitchen, get behind the bar, so that things look right, like in a proper restaurant. And let them have something to drink, because they're cold. By the way, the gentleman is looking for the miss: what should he say to her then?

Pochoriles stares out into the room, terrified, from under the visor of his cap. He kicks in the swing door before him and makes loud clinking noises behind the bar as he roots about among the bottles. He straightens up:

What miss would that be?

Fabritius stands up and then repeats: Our miss. Don't imagine that the gentleman has come here in error. He came straight here over the mountains, map in hand. He's carrying a piece of paper with the name of Miss Klara Bursen written on it in nice big letters. What should I to say to her?

Just tell her how things stand. If it makes you feel awkward, drawing a cross by the lady's name would do.

I will hell draw anything. I don't even have a pencil on me.

Then it's best if you tell her. So he knows straight off he'll get nowhere with that fairytale. I wonder what he'll come up with next.

Because he'll try to keep the real reason secret, that's for sure. Or he doesn't know it himself.

Even so, Pochoriles makes up a tray, covers it with a checked napkin, takes out two liqueur glasses that serve as optics, uses one to pour a measure of gentian root brandy in the bottom of a tumbler, adds a few drops of blackberry syrup, then tops it up with water to three-quarters of the glass. He puts it out on the bar, but meanwhile writes a message in his notebook to Danczura: before she takes the drinks out to them, she should mop up the floor, placing the dishcloth under the stranger's feet where the snowmelt is dripping.

The wind blew some snow even under the stranger's cape, and chunks of ice keep dropping out of its creases. He is wearing some kind of officer's uniform, without markings, quite worn and faded, greenish-grey, the material here and there shiny with wear, with darker marks on its collar where there had once been pips.

Fabritius calls out from the far end of the room, loudly so that we can hear: Miss Bursen was the traveller's last hope. Now that it has turned to ashes the world has ended for him, there is no way back. To cap it all, he was robbed by birds on his way here, they even ripped out the little money he had sewn into his collar.

Pochoriles stares out stiffly from behind the bar. It's poignant. But he had known what he knows since the morning. For him that was enough. The story is of no interest to him, whoever it might be. If there is no way back, well, there it is: the only thing you can do is put a full stop at the end. He will receive a decent burial, no question. Alongside Miss Klara, if he wants.

Pochoriles takes off his cap: his brow is beaded in sweat and he keeps wiping it with the sleeve of his t-shirt. Then he bends down, peers through the serving hatch, turns around to look out of the kitchen window as well, taking in the mountainside beyond the fence. Even now on the sun-lit slopes the traveller's footprints glisten darkly. He bends down, takes a bottle of wine from under the counter, one of those reserved for him alone, removes the cork, and pours himself a generous amount into a tumbler. He takes a sip, meanwhile pulling his cap down over his eyes again, and from under its shade scours the far end of the room, where Fabritius is sitting with the stranger. He swills the liquid round his mouth for a while, then spits it out into the sink. What's left in the glass, too, he pours down the plughole. He looks at me stiffly, asks me what I'm staring at, it's his wine, to do with as he wishes.

Again Fabritius signals from the room, with a raised hand. He says he can't stand it, we should open a window.

The hostelry keeper shakes his head: you must be aware that the windows are nailed down. If he can't stand it, he should go outside for a breath of air.

Yet a little air would also do the guest some good. He has become profoundly lethargic; the unfortunate fellow is hiccuping and his head is shaking, he's in a state of utter confusion.

Is there really no other way? Because he says that never in his life has such a thing occurred to him.

Pochoriles makes a dismissive gesture: then he's lying. It's something that crosses everyone's mind. You just have to find a way of doing it.

With that, like one who has said what he had to say, he returns to the kitchen, and from there continues to the yard, lifting his eyes heavenward. Then with uncertain steps he goes back into the kitchen. It seems he has suddenly detected the smell of milk, because he starts to eye Danczura, who is sitting stiffly on a kitchen stool. He circles her as he gestures to me to come over. He points to the girl: I ought to tell them that his stomach churns every time he catches sight of them. That is to say, of Danczura and her belly.

He speaks of the girl in the plural. And says they must leave here at once. They can go where they like, to Velky Lukanar, for instance, where Madame Karabiberi's nuns are sure to take them in.

While I'm telling Danczura what she has already heard clearly, that Mr Pochoriles can't stand the sight of her and she should leave at once, the hostelry keeper goes over to the bar and leans on his elbows as he peers into the room. Meanwhile, though, I can see he's on the alert to hear whether I'm passing on the message. He pours himself another, sniffs the glass, and takes a sip or two. Again he just spits it out, pouring the rest into the sink. Then he takes the whole bottle, gives it a shake, and pours its contents down the plughole, to the last drop.

Eventually he turns towards me, eyes me up and down long and hard, studying me with some surprise, but also inquisitively and suspiciously, as if trying to decide whether to send me to Velky Lukanar as well. But he doesn't, and touches my arm in an intimate gesture.

He says he thinks he's unwell. The world is now in Danczura's belly and he has no wish to see this world, but rather that other one. And he's already feeling queer, he can't swallow, even his own spittle doesn't taste good to him, he can't breathe properly, because even outdoors he can now detect that terrifying smell of the end of days. I should go and stand behind the bar, because he was now off to lie down.

Edmund Pochoriles stops at the sink, above which hangs a battered mirror. In the past its purpose was to let whoever was working at the kitchen table see at a glance what was happening behind them in the room. Later the kitchen was rearranged, the worktop was replaced by the sink, but the mirror stayed where it was. Pochoriles stands there now, looking at himself, takes off his cap, and as if bidding himself farewell raises it to his image in the mirror. He is overjoyed to see that it bids him farewell back. Then he goes out, walks through the yard to the summerhouse, where after lunch he always takes his afternoon nap.

I go out into the room, positioning myself behind the counter. The stranger, who Pochoriles claims is the harbinger of his death, is shaking and shivering with cold. I ask Fabritius: is he sure the traveller has understood Pochoriles's message?

He has, says Fabritius, he has understood. In fact, he asks whether it is the custom in these parts?

Yes, you can tell him it is. Hereabouts people know how long something lasts, what the limit is, where the story ends. Then everyone does it their own way, according to their taste. Round our way, while we had a pastor, he would bury those, too, properly. There's no better place for your last goodbye than Yablonska Polyana.

I watch as Fabritius, leaning over the table, quietly explains something to the other. The other's head is shivering so much with cold that his features are a blur. Fabritius looks at me again:

He says Pochoriles is right, that's also the way he sees it, it's just that he doesn't yet know the means.

If the hostelry keeper gets up, I say, he is sure to be able to say something sensible to him.

He has rather lost his bearings and has no gun, though he would like to get it over with quickly.

That I can believe. But there are other ways.

But you can also see, can't you, that he is shivering. We might at least give him a bowl of soup.

We won't, as that'll make him sleepy. A person who's sleepy needs to sleep and isn't capable of rational thought, of concerning himself with serious matters.

Every week Brigitta Konuvalov bakes two tins of shortbread, and always brings over a plateful to the hostelry. So now I put a few slices out on a small plate, with a spoonful of honey and a spoonful of salt, so everyone can eat it the way they like. I take it all out to the room and put it down in front of the traveller.

Fabritius asks me to sit down and stay, perhaps the time will pass better as a threesome, and he too would like occasionally to take a little air and this way the visitor wouldn't have to be left on his own.

He'll be fine on his own. And tell me, do you believe what Edmund Pochoriles says?

Why, what does Pochoriles say?

That stuff about the letter N. That this personage, because I don't know what to call him, has been sent by Anatol Korkodus to fetch him over.

He said nothing to me. But Anatol Korkodus may well have sent him. How would we know things of that kind.

I leave them, because I can see Nadja Kapustin standing by the doorway, her washing in a nylon sack over her shoulder. We stroll over to the laundry, I open a hot water tap above one of the stone troughs. It really shouldn't be necessary but I keep her company, sitting down on a bench behind her. She's not wearing any stockings, as she moves about around the trough, I can see her white calves under her clothes. I watch her for several minutes, perhaps for a quarter of an hour, and many things go through my head. I stand up and make for her. The splashing of the water prevents Nadja Kapustin from hearing me, and I get down on all fours and kiss the back of her knees, those mysterious little hollows. At this she straightens up.

Not again. Leave me alone, Adam, I'm having a bad day.

Mine is no better. But what's the problem? Sometimes I seriously think you're another homo.

What's one of those?

That you allow only women to caress you in that way.

That's indeed so.

Still, I wait for her to finish her washing. She will dry the clothes at home, for the moment stuffing them, wet as they are, back into her nylon sack. A first-time visitor to Yablonska Polyana will say that here freshly washed clothes smell worse than they did before they were washed. Because of the salty, turbid water of the springs. But that's something we don't notice.

Now Danczura is sitting on a chest in the corner. I stop in front of her and say I hope what Pochoriles said, and what I repeated to her clearly, has penetrated her thick skull. That she's out of here. To this she says she's never been to Velky Lukanar. It would be good if someone went with her.

You shouldn't count on it.

Around midday, the two queans Zhedu Baba and Brigitta Konuvalov, turn up at the restaurant. They take their seats in their usual place near the bar and ask for the rummy box. They take off their slippers and play footsie with each other's bare legs under the table. Meanwhile they position the boards in front of them, pile up the tiles, shuffle the cards, but it takes them a long time to start to play. They gaze at the far end of the room, where Fabritius is sitting with the stranger. At length Zhedu Baba pipes up and asks me if I would kindly tell the hostelry keeper that today is a feast day and, exceptionally, they would like some wine.

Pochoriles is asleep, I tell them, I'm serving today, but they must know I have no access to the cellar. And what frigging feast day are they talking about?

She believes it's St Bernard's Day, and they'd like to have something to eat as well. They saw the hostelry keeper moving about in the kitchen, he must have made something for the visitor.

He hasn't. What St Bernard's Day? That's news to me.

They smile and shrug their shoulders. All right, in that case they'll just have their usual gentian root brandy. But what kind of queer fellow is he that they aren't cooking for him?

Wrong question. He hasn't come here to eat but to be buried alongside Miss Klara, in the Boursin garden.

He's going to die?

He is.

I measure out the yellow gentian root brandy into the bottom of the tumbler, adding a drop or two of blackberry cordial. I take it out to them, then I again go to the back of the room, where Fabritius is sitting with the stranger.

Time's getting on, I say to them. Have you and this personage come to some agreement? Because he can't stay shivering here for ever. Pochoriles will wake up soon. He's obviously beginning to lose his marbles. He is tipping out his wine and going to bed in broad daylight. I bet you he'll shut up shop today.

But Fabritius pays me no attention, he is fidgeting, shifting about in his chair, listening to the visitor's ramblings. He snatches at the hem of my jacket and pulls me close.

The soldier is glad you have come over. Imagine, he's saying that there are four of us men here, we could play a game of tarot.

Tell him we are three. Mr Pochoriles is asleep.

It's late afternoon, the yellowish-orange of the slopes lights up the kitchen, the yellowish-orange snow shows traces of violet-coloured footsteps. Danczura is sitting on the chest, with her back to the wall.

Brigitta Konuvalov and Zhedu Baba finish their game early that day. Whenever this happens, I open up the box and check if they have put the tiles back properly, in rows, so you can see at once if even one of them is missing. I ask why they are in a hurry, to which they say Nadja Kapustin also has a pack for playing rummy and they would continue there in a threesome. And that today they can smell something strange here and, anyway, they were expecting a holiday atmosphere.

I tell them: by the way, if you must know, today is St Urban's Day, not St Bernard's.

It seems he was only waiting for them to go, because Pochoriles appears from the summerhouse wearing a clean, freshly ironed shirt under his jacket, velveteen trousers, and a deerstalker on his head. He enters the kitchen and rubs his hands, peering out through the serving hatch.

Hm, I see that the fellow is eating. And I didn't give him anything. What's he munching on?

A biscuit.

He doesn't give Danczura even a passing glance, as if she were no longer there, but he suddenly grabs my arm and drags me out into the room. We don't sit down, he pulls me over towards the little entrance lobby:

I think I must have nodded off. You won't guess who came to mind. I'll tell you: while I was half-asleep, I was thinking about Anatol Korkodus all the time.

The deerstalker has no visor, he can now look me straight in the eye. He pauses:

He was betrayed. The more I think about it, the more certain I am. What do you think?

I agree.

It would have been good to know in good time who was responsible.

I always thought it was you, Pochoriles. Tell me if I'm wrong.

So, that's what you think. Why did you never mention it to me?

I thought: why should I, you must surely know.

Now that this fellow has come here, it's brought it all back. Because you do this and that, time passes, and you forget about things. Then one day it suddenly all comes back. Now that this fellow is here. Today is Nikita's day, I tell you.

Even so, I say to him, at least you had a few years when you didn't think about it all. Surely it was worth it.

It wasn't. You see, at some point, in the end, you remember it all again. And then you wish: if only you didn't live to see the morning.

I'm sure you're right. But I don't want to talk about this kind of thing now.

You can always die, if you really want to. But it takes a while. If you want it to happen as soon as possible, you must take active steps. I'm telling you this now, so that you'll know, when your time comes. It doesn't happen at the touch of a button.

That's for sure. Are you about to go somewhere?

Not far, only somewhere nearby. Tell them it would be a good idea to finish their chat, because we're off. The personage will come with me. We'll go out to Miss Klara's on the hillside, to the Boursin farm.

I give Lorenz Fabritius a shout:

That's it, closing time. Tell him to get ready, you can see him out.

Edmund Pochoriles goes out into the yard and can be heard pottering about in the shed, rummaging around and finally coming back with a home-made rucksack of shabby, stained canvas, which was used by Balwinder when he was alive to bring diesel oil from the railway station. Now it contains a smallish gas canister and he is holding the can of diesel oil in one hand. In the other there is a little woven sack: when he touches it, something in it tinkles, like pearls, sounding just like silken starlings. Without going into the kitchen, he gestures from the doorway towards Danczura, who is crouching in the corner, as he presses the bag into my hands.

I see she is still here. So give her this.

What shall I say is in it.

If she wants to, she can unwrap it and see.

You aren't wearing even a pullover, I say to him. You'll catch your death.

He swills the can of diesel oil round in his hands. He swings the sack with the gas canister in it in the air.

I don't think I will.

Fabritius enters the kitchen. The visitor is reluctant to go, he says, and asks whether he must do so right away? And today for sure?

Pochoriles nods: the sun is going down, the day will soon be over. Tonight he can share Miss Klara's bed. With that he goes out into the street, waits by the entrance until Fabritius appears in the doorway, pushing the traveller ahead of him.

They set off.

Since they can't be seen from the kitchen window, or through the restaurant's steamed up windows, I go out onto the steps out front and watch from there as they pass in front of the Man-Gold yard, then go slowly past the public wash-house, and are soon climbing up along the line of the fences towards the Boursin farm.

Fabritius is standing beside me. We wait until they disappear behind the palisades.

Now he will get into Miss Klara's bed. He's got what he wanted. I don't dare imagine who has the infinite wisdom to deal so sensibly with such matters.

I nod in agreement: better never to think of that again.

Suddenly Danczura hops down onto the wooden chest in the corner of the kitchen behind the fireplace and starts blinking rapidly, terrified. Some kind of turbid liquid has started to stream out of her. It comes cascading down noisily from her, making the hem of her skirt sway.

I'll mop it up in a minute, she says. I think I've peed myself.

You know about such things, asks Fabritius.

No idea what you mean. I take Fabritius by the arm and step out with him into the entrance lobby. We've not had anything to eat today, I say. How about having a bite? I'll go over and have a scout around the scullery. I'll call you when it's ready.

We might as well wait for Pochoriles, says Fabritius somewhat uncertainly, I don't think he's had anything to eat today either.

Pochoriles won't be coming back, I tell him.

I go over, make the fire, put a few peeled potatoes on the hob. I fry some onions in chicken fat, open a tin of luncheon meat from the larder, a leftover from the brigade's former supplies, scrape the meat out of it, empty it over the onions, and putting a lid on the pan I steam them together for a little longer. When the potatoes have become soft as well, I add them, then I beat up two hen's eggs in a plate, adding a pinch of salt and pepper. I am about to pour it over the meat and the potatoes so they fry up together, when Lorenz Fabritius makes an appearance.

He tells me to hurry over to take a look at Danczura, she's my niece after all. He even clutches at my shirt above my chest: imagine, it seems her waters have broken, in fact its head is half out. He's got a wooden tub filled with lukewarm water ready in front of her, for it to drop into. And that Danczura has an urgent question for me.

All right, I say, I'll be over in a minute. But first we'll have something to eat. You ask her what she wants and I'll start serving. She shouldn't be shy to tell you everything. Anyhow, you know she isn't my niece.

The food on Fabritius's plate has gone cold by the time he returns.

He reports that the baby plopped straight into the water in the wooden tub readied for it, and must have swallowed hard, but instead of bawling, it swam silently around the tub flapping its legs, as its long black hair floated on the surface of the water.

Let's eat, I tell him. I don't see anything remarkable in any of that.

And that Danczura! She gave birth without a single murmur, while her hair turned as glossy as a chestnut shell, the lines on her face smoothed out, all its lumps and pustules disappeared, her eyes shone like blue pearls. She sends her regards, by the way, and just wanted to say that today she heard us talking about some Nikita or other, that it's a nice name and she liked it. She thought that, boy or girl, the baby should be called Nikita.

12.

(STELIAN & FABRITIUS)

Anatol Korkodus is long dead but every year, with a slice of milk loaf and a goblet of blackberry wine in hand, I visit the meadow of the Paltin and spend the night before his name day at his place of rest, hot Spring No. 2. This day comes at the height of summer, and at this time, around midsummer night, the sky has a glassy sheen from sunset to daybreak, and the nights are gelatinous yet translucent. I can see my old man lying a fathom deep, a mirage afloating in the blue expanse of the nether world.

Years before, in the course of one of his surveys, he had caught sight beneath the silken surface of the water of a dead and completely blue wild piglet, which had not only been perfectly preserved in all its corporeality, but glittered in every imaginable hue of cornflower, as the mineral precipitates floating in the water settled on its bristles, providing it with an overlay of coloured crystals. It was then that it suddenly occurred to him that if death in this spot had such a glorious perpetuation, when his own time came, it should be in this place, the basin of hot Spring No. 2, that he should be laid to eternal rest.

His hair, straggly like seaweed underwater, has already turned blue, his beard, too, is blue, as are his bushy eyebrows, and in the water all around him silver-blue lacanthus beetles swim to and fro.

Three days before midsummer night, just a little after sunrise, since that's when the blade of a scythe can most effectively cut the grass and dew-degged reeds, I'm about to leave for the meadow of the Paltin to prepare for my watch the following night, when the unfrocked pastor Lorenz Fabritius makes an appearance.

I haven't seen him for the past several days, as for reasons best known to himself he hasn't shown his face; every evening I waited for him in vain to turn up at the gate with his draughts box under his arm. He's looking haggard and wan, his skin is moist, his beard cobwebby, only his eyes are ablaze, like those of Brother Wolf in Eronim Mox's book of stories. I should, says he, pick up my chainsaw at once and go out with him to the Czervensky water-mill to cut out of the ice the half-rabbit that he had had frozen last winter. The matter is urgent, since he promised Brigitta Konuvalov some rabbit meat in exchange for a duvet.

In the Czervensky water-mill, winter reigns eternal: it's enveloped in ice from the top of its turrets down to the bottom of its fieldstone walls. He's not the only one to keep provisions there; some lay aside a half-truckle of goat's cheese, or a whole chicken, or perhaps a little leftover game: from hooks hammered into the ice dangle curt signs on small birch panels indicating what's behind each and the name of its owner. You have to cut quite deep into the ice, carving out a wedge shape from two sides, and where the two cuts meet detach both the top and the bottom layer before the chunk can be lifted out. Once you've put your foodstuffs in it, the hole can be re-sealed with the top layer of the section that was removed. Since I own the only chainsaw in Yablonska Polyana, should anyone want to put away some small item of food for a rainy day, they have to call on me to cut them a suitable hole in the ice. And call me again when they want to take it out. I gladly do this for them and always go when summoned.

The various parts of the saw have spent the winter in the larder, with its chain soaking in the bottom of a bowl of machine oil and its fuel tank empty, so I tell Fabritius to be patient until I'm ready. He should take his time going home and be waiting for me in an hour or so in front of the hostelry, or out by the water-mill, beyond the Czervensky jetty.

Fabritius lives in the former hostelry, at the Sign of The Two Queans. After hostelry keeper Edmund Pochoriles set himself alight and rose to heaven commingled with the pungent fumes, Lorenz Fabritius moved into the place to join Danczura, my former niece. The three of them, Fabritius, Danczura and Nikita, have been living there since. Nikita, the little child prodigy, is the daughter of Danczura and the late hostelry keeper Edmund Pochoriles.

Fabritius seems not too happy about what I am saying and eyes me suspiciously, shifting from one leg to the other, giving in the end a dismissive wave of the hand and walking off muttering under his breath. It seems something is troubling him, something must have happened to him. In the past he took some care over his outward appearance, but now he is wearing the same wax-stained velveteen trousers and soiled blue cotton shirt that he wore several days ago, when I last saw him coming home from the woods. Everything he is wearing is creased, as if he slept in his clothes, too.

Though summers in Verhovina are short, there is now a brightness and a sussuration flowing down from the harsh crags and the early morning air above the housetops is already thrumming with life. Yet beneath the sussuration Yablonska Polyana is swathed in a mirage-like silence that fills its every nook and cranny, all that can be heard from somewhere in its depths are the shrieks of Jakab Gleznár's terrified guinea fowl. These days Damasskin Nikolsky's foxes, with their cocked, pointy ears, can be found lurking behind the fences even in broad daylight.

I pick up the parts of the saw, put them together, lift out out the chain from the basin, and hang it on a nail in one of the veranda's pillars. As it's drying, I fry up a few corn griddle-cakes in a little fat. While they're still hot I spread sour cream on two of them and chew them slowly, and put out another two, just as they are, on the veranda's balustrade, for the Stelian kid. But he didn't take even yesterday's portion and flies in a variety of strident colours are wheeling around above it. For some reason he didn't come this way even yesterday: he didn't want any breakfast. I look out towards the wash-house but see no sign of him coming this way.

These days people hereabouts don't get up that early, by the time they shuffle out and there are stirrings in the courtyards and the chimneys start belching smoke, it's generally getting on for the middle of the day. The Infantrymen's Street is deserted, likewise deserted are the hovels clinging to the hillsides; only from the door of the Augustins' abandoned place can a living ghost, my perfidious cat Tatyana, be seen skulking towards the gate that Fabritius had left open. She surfaced again a few days ago by the fences, grown old and emaciated, reeking of unfamiliar, choking smells, having spent years roaming lands unknown. Now she comes walking straight into the yard, and apart from a passing, sly glance she pays me no attention as she passes under the veranda. Reaching the garden, she stops in her tracks before the guinea pigs' cage in the shade of the plum trees, and slowly eases herself down onto her belly. Stock still, her whiskers agleam, she eyes the animals trembling in the corner of the cage.

Anatol Korkodus was still alive when Vandyeluk, the other reformatory kid, lured her away from the house. When she escaped his clutches, she turned up in Nikolina, spotted in vet Schwantz's courtyard, people said, but she must have spent most of her time gallivanting in the wild. Suspicious scars are etched deep in her ginger fur, her tail is now much bushier, and her ears have grown tufts like those of a lynx. A sour, choking, alien smell envelops her like some mysterious shroud. This is what the smell of death must be like. Tomorrow or the day after I'll dig her a little ditch under the plum trees.

In the old days I used to sharpen the blades before use, but since ice is softer than wood, this time I don't bother, and I stretch the chain over the sprockets. I leave the saw on the balustrade, by Stelian's two untouched plates. I look out above the fence, over the Infantrymen's Street, towards the public wash-house: if the kid should happen to come, I'll send him over to the Augustins' cellar to fetch a small can of petrol.

But even yesterday he didn't turn up.

Stelian sleeps in the public wash-house, coming over in the mornings and reporting to me. He asks whether there is anything for him to do that day and I tell him there isn't. That he can do what he wants to keep himself occupied, he should just make sure he doesn't hurt anyone. And if he should happen to feel like it, he can leave: he could start packing now, no one will stop him. He is here by accident; should he not feel at home, he's welcome to go and follow his nose.

But he doesn't leave.

Stelian was one of the last to be picked by my old man Brigadier Anatol Korkodus from the photographs in the reformatory catalogue, thinking he would take him on temporarily, and if he proved satisfactory after a few weeks' trial, he would keep him on the settlement for further training. Almost certainly his small, slim figure and his blond curls and round face reminded him a little of his favourite plaything, Roswitha. It was no use the instructors telling him in no uncertain terms that, angel face or no, Stelian was a "tub of lard", that is to say, smooth and round as a pebble, he offered no purchase, nothing and no one could have any influence over such a kid. Even so, he was the choice of Anatol Korkodus, who perhaps thought that the murmurings of the wild waters hereabouts and the cool, cleansing northerly winds would suffuse his soul, and then maybe the hectic in his blood would no longer rage. It was just that by the time the various papers had been passed to and fro, one stamp here, another there, and the official document allowing him to be released was ready and Stelian was finally allowed to leave, some people had done for my old man. One bitterly cold morning persons unknown had kidnapped him on a fiery sledge and the next time we saw him, on another morning, in front of the gate, he was lying at the bottom of an abandoned horse and cart covered in a blanket of hoarfrost, with only his frozen, bloodless white nose poking out of the straw.

And so Stelian just turned up one day. With his pink, dreamy look he has been hanging around us ever since. The moment he wakes up, he comes and takes his breakfast from the veranda. He gets a corn fritter or two fried in oil, which I prepare for him bright and early, putting it out for him on a tin plate on the veranda balustrade, so that I shouldn't have to let him into the kitchen. Nonetheless he knocks on the door and asks whether there'll be anything for him to do that day. Although I sometimes give him the odd job to do, like now sending him over to the Augustins' cellar for petrol, I'm reluctant to ask him to do anything. In the past it had happened that I sent him to fetch some diesel oil from the station, and once, when I didn't feel like seeing strangers, I sent him to the spring taps to deal with the water tank folk, but no one wanted to see him ever again. But even if I could make some use of him there wouldn't be anything for him to do here. Apart from selling the water of the Paltinsky meadow's hot springs, gathering toadstools, nuts, rose hips, mint, camomile and thyme from the slopes of the Medwaya, and dredging up the fine pebbles from the bed of the Yablonka by the cartload, there's nothing to do even for us.

We are waiting, in case anyone comes. Perhaps those who took Anatol Korkodus with them will come this way again. Horse-face, the big-footed vagabond who wanted to reopen the sunken mines, or the procurator Damasskin Nikolsky, who once came with a covered trailer and released six pairs of foxes on the Paltinsky meadow. Or someone else. Perhaps someone will come and tell us why we are here. Or perhaps no one will ever come here again.

If truth be told, we are just waiting for time to pass.

Stelian knows nothing about Horse-face, nor about Damasskin Nikolsky and his foxes, even if he sometimes hears talk of them, as such things are of no interest to him. Apart from the fact that he hangs around with us without uttering a word, we don't know anything about him either.

Unless it counts as knowledge that since the coming of spring, he spends all day with his hand stiffly sunk in his pockets propping up the fence of the former hostelry, at the Sign of The Two Queans. He fixes the kitchen door with his clear, stone-coloured eyes, as if wanting to see what's behind the opaque, blurry glass, or to make it crack by means of his stare alone. Then, when the door finally opens and Danczura in her yellow blouse, with the cloud of butterflies fluttering in her wake, walks barefoot through the yard, he follows her with tender looks, as the sun-dappled wall of the house can be made out between her thighs through her thin shift. Danczura enters Pochoriles's summerhouse, where she keeps her daughter Nikita hidden, closing the door behind herself when she gives her the breast or changes her nappy, often spending as much as half an hour indoors. When she comes out and adjusts her damp blouse above her bosom as she passes by the fence, she tries to look Stelian straight in the eye, but he continues to watch the play of the light under the girl's shift. And so it goes, day after day. Perhaps ten or fifteen times a day, without them exchanging a word.

Meanwhile the late hostelry keeper Edmund Pochoriles's mute husky continues to pant in front of its kennel and tearing at its chain.

Fabritius watches from behind the curtains in the house. Sometimes he opens the window and says to him in a low voice:

You have a sick mind, Stelian. You weren't made to live on this glorious earth. You ought to have died long ago.

But Stelian does not hear.

It's two days now since I last saw him. Flies circle above the tin plates left on the balustrade, the oil bubbles have burst on the fried fritters, having become just faded rocks on the tin plates. For some reason Stelian hasn't wanted breakfast for two days running.

And I won't be waiting for him any longer. In the Augustins' cellar there remains a little diesel fuel at the bottom of a barrel and I pour some into a container. As it isn't even half full, I pop over to the Man-Gold yard, to the Tatars. They trade in leather and rubber, so glue is something they always need: they always stock a wide range of solvents. While Akimofte takes the container to the larder, I sit down on a stuffed sack. I have a feel and look inside it: it's chock-full of brand-new brogues made of rubber tyres. I tell the Tatar that only a few of us are left here on the banks of the Yablonka, who does he imagine will wear them all. Akimofte grins: they could still come back into fashion. Not long ago, for example, Danczura was here and bought Stelian a pair.

Stelian?

Akimofte grins.

Through the open door of the shop one can see the spital-house's windows. On either side of the window, in wrought iron flower-holders, are two quite large sloe branches, bursting with ashen buds. They frame Nika Karanika, the blue-tit demon, standing there in her blue gown embroidered all over with little birds. As I stare and stare, a film glazes over my eyes and Nika Karanika begins to recede, her shape becoming fuzzy, while the blue tits and the warblers fly up from her gown and begin to circle above her head. The cloying scent of her jasmine oil percolates even through the closed windows.

Nika Karanika stands in her blue gown in the spital-house window, between the budding sloe branches, her right hand held high, her fingers aflutter, as if she were giving signals. As if she did indeed want something from me.

I walk over, whereupon she opens the window very slightly. Around her nose and beneath the enormous berry eyes are etched the purple lines of some secret sorrow, though it would seem that she is also smiling a little.

She says: Do come closer, Adam. May I say something?

Go ahead.

She continues: I think it was you who stuck these prickly, thorny branches in the window for me. Am I right? It was you, wasn't it?

Could be.

Then you can probably also tell me what you intended by doing so?

Only that they should frame you when you look out of the window. Because there is nothing more wonderful than the pungent scent of the blossoming sloe. And because thoughts of Miss Nika occur to me several times a day. This happened yesterday, too, when I picked these boughs. I thought you were sure to guess how they came to be there and then for a moment you would think of me.

A curious train of thought indeed. What occurs to me at the moment is that I won't forget you. For I can now tell you that I'm just about to leave this place. Some people, people of goodwill, came this way and promised that if I went with them they'd remove the knife blade that once broke off so unpleasantly and lodged in my vertebrae. Seeing as they are so kind, I'll go with them.

Do go, feel free. I shan't urge you to stay. In fact, it's for the best if I never see you again.

But who knows, Nika Karanika continues in a low voice, if you have the time and if you happen to find yourself walking this way in the evening, you could stop by under my window one last time. I mean, assuming night does indeed fall today. If I remember right it was you who told me that it says in Eronim Mox's book that the world will end when the sun doesn't set at all throughout the night and merely wanders along below the horizon. Now even I am inclined to say that it seems that time may not be so far off.

So, that was Nika Karanika. If she goes now, it will be as if she'd never been here, she will take with her the little birds, her cardamom scent, and in the intimate crannies of her body she will take with her all her glorious secrets.

The moment he saw her Anatol Korkodus declared: this is a demon, a veritable demon. Once my old man had explained to her the meaning of the word, she too was comfortable with the label. If anyone asked who or what kind of creature she was, she told them her tale: that she had been born far away in the south, on the limy soil of the barren lands inhabited by demons, where her father was a camp commandant, that's where she had to escape from, because once, in a time of drought, she had given the prisoners water to drink. When there had been no rain for the third year running and the prisoners tried to squeeze the dew of the morning mists from blankets they laid out in the open, she had taken pity on them and made water gush from a bare rock for them. Alas, the water was salty and hot, and stank, so they set off in pursuit, one managing to catch up with her bearing the knife of which the blade broke off in her spine and to this day shifts around between her vertebrae.

Seamstress Aliwanka's window is open wide, from the damp murk of the house the clacking of the sewing machine can be heard. Aliwanka is sitting at her sewing machine, beside her Brigitta Konuvalov is holding the end of a large bedsheet, so that it doesn't hang down and brush the floor as it's being hemmed. The moment they see me, the clacking stops and Brigitta Konuvalov lets go of the sheet. She comes over to the window, leans out, and grabs me by the sleeve of my jacket.

She minces no words in telling me that it's high time to do something about that Stelian. Things have come to such a pass that Fabritius no longer has anywhere to live and was obliged to seek shelter in the sacristy. They are just now trying to sew him a nice thick duvet cover so that the poor fellow doesn't have to spend the night shivering between the dank walls.

Because in case I hadn't yet heard, two days ago, late in the evening, while Fabritius was playing draughts under the statue of the Three-Legged Woman in the square with Begizdan, the owner of the bodega, Stelian had out of the blue moved into the hostelry to be with Danczura. Since then they have refused to let Fabritius into the house. They keep the gate and all the doors of the former hostelry firmly locked, and when Fabritius stops by the picket fence they stare at him uncomprehendingly from behind the closed windows, shrugging their shoulders: they don't know him, look at each other in surprise, asking what this person might want, have nothing to discuss, and in the end stick their tongues out at him. Meanwhile even through the closed windows it can be clearly seen that Stelian is already wearing Fabritius's favourite blue-and-green striped pyjamas.

And what is queerest of all, and at the same time the most frightening sign that something quite unusual is afoot, is that Nikita, the child prodigy hitherto thought to be mute, had found her voice. She bawls from morning till night and the only reason she cannot be heard from afar is that Stelian has stuffed her mouth with rags.

If only there were someone in the settlement, a real man, who could sort this useless kid out once and for all.

Stelian! That pink angel-face. So: that's how things stand.

I saunter out to the bank of the Yablonka, as far as the Czervensky jetty, the chainsaw slung over my shoulder. This is where Anatol Korkodus's water-level gauges once stood, but since no one has been coming to read the water levels, they have disappeared under the black elder, the wild sloe and the briars that have completely overrun the banks of the river.

Even now, at the height of summer's torrent of green, the watermill stands here, frozen in ice, shrouded in a foggy haze. It glitters diamond-like in the sunlight, all around it tongues of vapour rise and shimmer in all the colours of the rainbow, while its every purple cranny exhales the chill breath of winter.

Fabritius walks up and down before the entrance to the cellar, his collar turned up.

A good many years ago, back in the days of Anatol Korkodus, one September Balwinder failed to open the sluices in time, while in the far north the autumn fog began unexpectedly to unfurl and through its fissures came the bone-chilling cold of the polar nights, the floodgates suddenly froze up, and as the icy torrent began to build up behind them, the deluge gradually burst through the barriers and engulfed the mill, so that all of it – to the last brick – froze solid.

And there it stands to this day, enveloped in crystalline ice.

Though the mild breezes of the brief summer play upon it every year, so that sometimes it begins to iridesce with a velvety glow, just when it might actually begin to thaw, the brief season of light is over and the first frosts are already upon us. The summer merely illuminates it from within, only for the light to slowly dim and disappear from it: in the darkness of fogbound autumn nights, it looms on the edge of the settlement like Eronim Mox's giant magic lantern.

If you press your brow to the ice and shade your eyes to peer in, you can, if you are determined, see the furnishings of the time. Everything is in its place, as if cast in glass. The chests of corn, the millstones propped up against each other along the wall, the weighing machine, with the sacks of rye and corn beside it, the miller Filip Gleznár's table and, on top of the ice, as if swimming on it, his flour-caked hat.

And the mice. Apparently they tried to swim out of the icy swell through the closed windows and when they slammed into them, they froze solid on the spot. And there they are still, embedded in the ice like inquisitive little fish covered in grey fur, their mouths glued to the glass.

The half-rabbit that Fabritius had had frozen has been resting under the axle-tree of the millstone since the early winter. The exact location of the parcel, the name of its owner and its contents, are indicated by a brief inscription scratched on a small piece of birchwood dangling from the end of a nail: "Wild rabbit, half. L. Fabritius."

The ice surrounding it is full of blotches of grey and brown, virtually making it look like stone. At the onset of winter, having hidden the half-rabbit, Fabritius spent a whole day watering the crevice, until it froze over again completely. Now he has even brought two battery lamps with him, so that he can illuminate the ice from two sides at once, in case some trick of the light should make me stray over into some neighbour's patch by mistake.

I wait for him to say something but Fabritius remains sullenly silent. It seems he isn't yet ready to let me into his secret. He just indicates nervously how much space I should leave beside and above the frozen meat, a good two spans.

Two spans, he says. It's a little too much, but if that's how he wants it, for him I'll do it.

I start the motor and I'm well into the ice when Fabritius motions for me to stop.

I stop, pull the saw out gingerly, shake off the pieces of ice still clinging to it, and put it down beside me. Fabritius gives it a slight prod with the toe of his boot.

Let's see now. What does it run on?

Petrol, I tell him. But it does no harm if a quarter of the tank is filled with oil.

Let me have a look and see how you usually start it up.

Come now, you've seen it before. Oh, all right: you yank the string with your left hand a few times, and once it's firing, you let in some gas, like in a small ATV. Mind it doesn't catch your trouser-leg, because then it'll take your leg off as well.

With that, I start it again so that he can see how it's done. While I'm revving the motor, I lean over to say into his ear quite loudly that we'll soon need a crowbar so that once the block with the half-rabbit in it has been hacked all around, it can be pulled out: since there's no purchase on the smooth ice we can't do it with our bare hands. He'll find something suitable in Pochoriles's toolshed in the hostelry courtyard. Even the iron bar that Danczura uses to bolt Nikita's door at night would do.

Nikita is a wunderkind. Everyone says so, though in fact no one apart from her mother has ever seen her. She is now over five years old and Danczura still breastfeeds her. Until yesterday no one had heard her cry and she hasn't learnt to walk or talk. Not even to walk, though according to seamstress Aliwanka, who can see through walls, she has three legs. Danczura does nothing but wait to see what will become of the wunderkind: she keeps her incommunicado in the hostelry's summer kitchen, its door bolted with an iron bar. The iron bar is propped up against the doorpost during the day.

Fabritius shakes his head,

Not a good idea, he says. I'm not going to go there now.

But we're going to need a crowbar, we won't get anywhere without it.

Well then, go and ask Stelian for it, perhaps he'll lend you his. But there's no guarantee they'll let you into the yard.

And he tells me what had happened. That the kid, who until then had only been single-mindedly propping up the fence, suddenly jumped over it and made a dash for the house. God knows what got into him, to have taken Danczura into his clutches.

I let the motor cut out.

I did think something must have happened, I tell him. Even yesterday the kid didn't come for his breakfast, there are two days' portions shrivelling up on the veranda. So I think you've guessed what's to be done with someone like that.

Fabritius gives me a serious look and nods:

Nothing. Only one solution presents itself with regard to Stelian. I hope you appreciate that I don't want to say it out loud. The how and when I'll work out later today.

I nod in sympathy: it's a shitty business, that's for sure. For my part I can say that I too have had enough of this Stelian. But the crowbar I mentioned will certainly be needed now: he should go and fetch one from the Augustins' cellar.

The hollows and cracks in the ice exude a damp cold, a haze swirls in front of the steps. I enjoy the sun as I wait for Fabritius to return with the crowbar. The wind seems to have changed direction, for the shrouds of vapour from the hot springs, whose choking smell of sulphur invariably settles in the depressions of the valleys and on the courtyards, are now streaming towards the crags of Nikolina. The air is vibrant above the Paltin meadow, as the intoxicating smell of the wild roses is borne into the houses on the gentle breeze.

Midsummer night is approaching, the feast of the wild rose; at least that's what Anatol Korkodus used to call it. At around this time, or rather a day or two earlier, comes the shortest night of the year. And, as mentioned before, Eronim Mox writes in his book of stories that there will come a time when day will no longer be followed by night.

When even the Czervensky water-mill will melt. All of it.

In the old days, when I used to walk my cat Tatyana on a leash, I would sometimes bring her out here to the mill to show her the mice. I would sit her up on the ramp in front of the window, so she could see the miracle and admire them as was her wont. In their black, globe-like eyes, hugely magnified by the ice, there still shone the light of hope. She would pick out one of them for herself, and stare at it until the intensity of her glare melted the surrounding ice. Then, when the mouse, as if about to spring to life, tipped over slightly to one side in the melt, she would suddenly make a grab for it, her paw invariably sliding off the hard glass. She's a cat and cats never forget: she's been annoyed with me ever since.

Fabritius returns with a fair-sized iron bar, with a big letter "A" engraved on its flat end. Until that fatal disaster Augustin had been a locksmith and a worker in metal, he had spent his whole life pounding iron, there are still huge piles of iron bits and pieces in his cellar, rusting away.

I lever out the block of ice, hand Fabritius the crowbar so he can use it to hack the ice off. But he seems to be no longer interested in the rabbit: he's still shining his battery lamp into the purple of the gaping hole in the ice.

D'you think there might be some way of making the hole bigger?

There isn't. Out of the question. I'd be cutting into the Nyegrutzes' patch.

Not even a little?

I fix him with a glare:

You're not thinking of scuppering him here, surely? Get that idea right out of your head.

Fabritius continues to stare into the hole.

It did cross my mind. A lot of daft things come into one's mind at times like this.

I explain that it's summer, it's hot, there's no point keeping on pouring water on it, he won't be able to get the hole to freeze over again. While what he's intending to do is bound to smell. And you're supposed to write something on the birch-bark tag, too. Well, no: we're getting ahead of ourselves.

Fabritius keeps nodding in agreement, he knows he'll not have an easy time of it. He lacks experience in this field, which is why he keeps getting silly ideas. But today he woke in the sacristy having taken a decision which he would, if all goes well, soon be carrying out. Perhaps he won't be needing that duvet.

I let this pass and nod uncertainly:

There's no place for him among us. I too have been wasting my time, making fritters for him for two days on end. And if I hadn't found out what happened, I might well have made him some again tomorrow.

We are now standing out in the courtyard of the water-mill. The block of ice, with a dull brownish patch in it, is lying on the grass, glinting in the sunshine, with little multicoloured tongues of vapour licking the air above it. Fabritius is hacking away at it with the crowbar, to get it to fit the plastic bag he's brought with him to take to Brigitta Konuvalov. As he fills the bag and heaves it over his shoulder, he looks at me and then at the chainsaw in turn, with an air of expectancy. He gives it another little nudge with his foot while muttering, as if to himself:

This is the sort of thing: a nice bit of equipment. He might ask to borrow it. Would I lend it to him?

The Stihl chainsaw lies on the ground, the drops of ice on its sharp teeth shivering as they melt.

I mumble something by way of an answer. That I don't like lending it out; though to be honest on the spur of the moment I can't think of anything that could do a better job. I'm not surprised it occurred to him. At all events it's a delicate business, he should think twice, it wouldn't be sensible to just come up with something out of the blue. Should it really be needed, he would find it on the veranda under a piece of cardboard. But he should take care, he heard just now what an ear-splitting noise it can make. And he must promise that as soon as he's done, he'll hurry along with it to the public wash-house. After soaking it thoroughly in hot spring water, he should also hold it under the tap for a while.

In the courtyard of the ex-hostelry Danczura's head of red hair is ablaze in the sharp light of the middle of the day. She is hanging out some clothes, but sometimes doubles up, collapsing into a garden chair and basking in the sunshine. She is wearing her yellow blouse: she picks a butterfly off it every so often, puts it in her mouth, and sucks on it. Beside her there are familiar clothes in the basket, familiar items on the clothes line: Fabritius's clean underwear and checked shirts. If nothing is done, someone else will be wearing them from now on. I walk over to the fence. Danczura makes no move, as if she hadn't noticed me.

I tell her: have Stelian come outside.

Still she doesn't turn towards me, only muttering: he isn't home.

Get hold of him for me all the same. Now. This minute.

She says she's sorry but she can't. Perhaps in the evening, when he's back from the forest. Seeing as he went off to Ferny Hollow with Nikita. I do know, don't I, that it's nowhere near here. It will be evening at best before he's back.

And how come Stelian can just waltz off? And anyway, what's he thinking of, taking Nikita to Ferny Hollow?

Nothing. He'll just put her down and leave her there and come straight back. We've had enough of her howling into our ears all day and all night. And how much longer did she think she'd be on breastmilk, because I've now had it with the endless breastfeeding. It's time she stood on her own two feet. Nikita is a wunderkind, she has no business among ordinary people.

In the afternoon the water tankers arrived. The hooting with which they signal their approach can be heard from afar, ensuring one of us will be waiting for them out by the taps. They come every other day with three carts, taking the water from here in 75 hectolitre barrels, the water that bubbles up for us from the ground in the Paltinsky meadow. Whether they take it near or far, by the time they arrive, it's sure to have cooled down and turned cloudy. Who knows what they need the thermal spring water for, seeing as it's lukewarm and smelly. Since Begidzan, too, closed down his bodega, they are the ones who supply us with our bits and pieces, the various goods we need. We get ten thousand coupons per collection, on top of that we get paid in flour, sugar, fat, and seeds. We also get soap and washing powder, and they supply us with diesel fuel, too.

Someone provides for us by buying all these useless things. But one day, when they need us no longer, they'll stop. We'll never know who they were and what they wanted.

It takes a good hour-and-a-half to two hours for the cisterns to fill up. At the ford on the Yablonka the dredgers fill the carts full of gravel. I stay by the thermal spring taps throughout, because the end of the rubber hose has expanded from the warm, salty water, and although I tried to fix it tight with wire, it keeps slipping off the end of the pipe. When that happens it's best if I hold it with my hands until the filling is done. While this is going on we don't talk, the tankermen aren't really prepared to engage in conversation. Whenever we ask them something, they appear not to understand, hem and haw, mutter, stare at us and just shrug. They come from another world, it's as if we didn't speak the same language. But when they leave, they pay, and the ramp behind the two water tankers is covered with a pile of goods.

I put on a smock and start distributing the rations in accordance with the advance bookings. Everyone gets what they ordered in exchange for coupons.

Fabritius, too, is standing in line. He patiently waits his turn and gets what was down in his advance booking: cooking oil, curd cheese, apple compote, mixed jam, corn bran, and the like. He carefully puts everything in his basket, then leans closer, and says sombrely:

I need a bit of vinegar, too. As much as possible.

Vinegar? All right, I won't ask what for.

I don't yet know myself, he says grimly.

I promise to try and set some aside, if necessary by giving him someone else's ration. And it won't do him any harm to know: the person we were discussing earlier isn't home. He'll be back from the Mute Forest sometime towards evening. So if Fabritius sets off around dusk at a comfortable pace towards the heights, then more or less at the far end of the slagheaps, near the abandoned mine workings, their paths would cross.

As soon as the dust settles after the water tankers and the dredgers, the donkeys suddenly start to bray, and a torrid heat settles upon the walls. This is the time everyone hereabouts falls into a faint, this is the local horror, the hour of death beneath the slopes of the Paltin. I dig out Anatol Korkodus's hammock, tie it up between two plum trees in the garden, and stretch out.

For a while I gaze up into the cloudless sky as the wax from the plum tree's leaves drizzles down on me in a cool spray. Then I turn on my side. The breeze barely touches the boughs, their shadow shimmers on the ripped ginger fur of my cat Tatyana. The two guinea pigs, nervous wrecks, shiver in the corner of the cage.

The entire garden is filled with a verdant humming and buzzing. When I close my eyes, I am suffused by a joy that, for no reason at all, has taken over my soul. I sway atop the softness of the universe.

This lasts until the arrival of seamstress Aliwanka. Today the loaf in memory of Anatol Korkodus is being baked by Aliwanka. She now places it, covered with a cloth, on the balustrade of the veranda. The blackberry wine that sends one to the land of Nod still comes from Pochoriles's cellar. Tonight I eat milk loaf and drink blackberry wine.

At some point late in the afternoon, the gate once more gives a creak. It's Fabritius. The draughts box under his arm rattles now and again. He crosses the yard and climbs up the steps to the veranda. He knocks, looks in, turns around, and stops by the balustrade. His eyes alight on the chainsaw, he picks it up, weighs it in his hand, then puts it back. He eyes the plates of bread fried in oil. At length he turns towards the garden and notices I'm resting in the hammock stretched between the plum trees.

He says he has been in church. He talked it over with him.

I sit up: who the hell with? Isn't it enough that for the moment only the two of us are in the know?

Fabritius raises a finger towards the sky. Whenever he finds himself in difficulties, he always gets a hand from up there.

I nod in agreement: I've noticed that applying to me, too. Yet in the evenings, instead of praying, I've long been reading Eronim Mox's tales. By the way, I've put aside a bottle and a half of vinegar for him, I'm not sure it'll be enough.

He isn't sure either. He doesn't know whether it'll be needed and, if so, how much of it. He'll see. All he can say is that once, when some kind of meat of Nadja Kapustin's in the pit began to smell, she wrapped it in a piece of cloth soaked in vinegar. This business, too, would take some time. One must be ready for anything.

True enough. It's summer, and hot with it.

Fabritius opens up the box of draughts and empties the contents onto the rain-soaked, sun-seared table. He hides one black and one white piece in each fist.

He says: take your pick.

I ask: won't you have a bite to eat first? I could roast a guinea pig for you. At least I'd get rid of one of them. Because it's painful to see that all they do is pant, with their stupid noses quivering with terror from morning to night. If someone doesn't eat them, in the end I'll just have to dig them a little ditch.

Fabritius looks up: no, he's not hungry. But a spade, a light spade, that's something he'll be needing soon.

I tell him, fine, he can have his pick of the army spades in the toolshed. I look up at the sky. Still a good hour and a half or two hours to go, at least. If he sets off then, the two of them will meet face to face at the abandoned workings.

He nods. There's still time, that's how he figures, too. Again he holds out his closed fists with the pieces in front of me.

I tell him we should throw for it. Higher goes first.

To this he says: it wouldn't come out in my favour, because today he'd win whatever he threw. Heaven is on his side.

All right, I say, let's see, because you've made me really curious. Then let's have, say, the four and the six.

He takes the dice, shakes them in his hands, then rolls them. A four and a six.

He says again: a good sign. Heaven is with him today, whatever he may do.

We have been playing draughts for quite a long time, yet we were only having our third game. We keep looking away from the board, staring this way and that in silence, while taking sips of the drink I keep for special occasions, home-distilled sloe brandy. I suggest we switch to Trik-Trak, the high-speed version. But even playing that we barely get as far as the third game. Suddenly Fabritius reaches across the table:

Tell me, but honestly, mind: did you ever imagine I'd do such a thing?

Such a thing? What thing?

Fabritius bats it away dismissively. There's nothing to talk about.

We don't pursue the matter. Fabritius believes he's having a good day, he says so himself. In that case he'll reach a decision about his business all by himself. Even now, without paying any attention to the board, he's already in a winning position.

After a while Jakab Gleznár stops by the gate. Though he came without making a sound, Fabritius immediately turns around, eyes him suspiciously, and crosses himself.

What's got into you? You're Lutheran.

Not any more, he says.

Gleznár does not enter, he waits for me to give a sign that I've noticed him. I don't stir from my chair, so in the end he starts gesticulating.

His face has a Gleznárishly enigmatic look, a little mischievous but careworn. He says to go with him, because he has something to show me.

Now? This minute?

Yes, now if you can, later it won't be of interest.

Gleznár lives with his guinea fowl at the bottom of the slope, in the vicinity of the Czernovsky jetty, on the last but one plot. We pass in front of The Two Queans: the summer kitchen, where Nikita lived, is being aired, its windows and doors are wide open. The yard is already in shadow as dusk falls, and on the steps, amid the scent of the freshly washed clothes drying there, sits my niece Danczura. I call her my niece, though she isn't. I actually told her on one occasion, but she still doesn't believe it. Now she sees me passing by the fence, even looks up once, but without saying hello, without saying anything, she keeps her head down. Stelian is still far away and hasn't even set off on his return journey, but she's already out there waiting for him.

Gleznár's plot, full of wild pear, runs steeply up the mountainside, redcurrant bushes and gooseberry bushes alternating along his fence. But at the gate it's not the scent of the garden that welcomes you, but some choking, bitterish smell from the bushes at the forest's edge, where wild animals have been. Gleznár goes ahead, on tiptoe, as if afraid that what he wants to show us might slip away.

He gestures archly for me to follow him. He goes around the house, leading us to the back, the poultry yard, where he stops. Everything is covered in feathers, all stuck in the mud, as if one were walking on a grey duvet that had been slashed open. Not a guinea fowl in sight. Just feathers, feathers everywhere.

Gleznár says they were here in the afternoon, in broad daylight, in the hour of death. He watched it all happen with arms folded from the veranda: there were so many of them, he didn't dream of making a move. They scraped out the soil from under the shed, and at the same time, somewhere else, opposite, under the fence as well. In one hole, out the other, so they didn't collide amid all the jostling. They took no risks, really taking their time. Guinea fowl are no masters of the air, not one got beyond the fence. They took every single one.

I ask him: well, what did he think, what the hell would they do with all the guinea fowl at once?

Foxes are prudent and astute creatures, he says. They think ahead: they bury them.

Night is reluctant to fall, only the far corners of the garden sink slowly into some kind of translucent, bluish haze, while the languid light of the sun quivers still on the plum trees' waxen leaves.

Fabritius lies in the hammock, boots and all, his cap pulled down over his eyes. Leaning against the trunk of the plum tree, at a slight angle, lies the half-empty bottle of sloe brandy. No sign of Tatyana, at the moment she is not in her usual place in the grass, where she'd been on duty from early in the morning. Then I do catch sight of her after all, her ginger fur is visible behind the barbed wire, and the door of the cage is half open. In front of Tatyana lie two guinea pigs in a faint. While she prods them and smacks them from one side to the other with her paw, they keep panting and squealing, with their eyes closed, while ants gather on their pink, damp noses.

Fabritius says he made only a small gap in the cage door, being curious to see if Tatyana noticed. While he was taking a quick look at the hammock to see if he might return there for a rest, the cat had already entered the cage. But anyway, if he remembers right, I'd said I'd had enough of them. Or should he perhaps have waited for me before doing what he did?

I wave him aside, oh, no, you don't imagine that, do you. I close the cage door and push in the bolt. And from now on this is the way it will stay. I'm never opening it again.

But Fabritius should now beware. He will need to keep a clear head and he will also need a sure hand. Not a drop more; he can set off soon. He'll find the saw on the veranda. It's best if he walks over, taking a breath or two of fresh air. Then, if he climbs up by Klara Bursen's fence to the meadow of the Paltin, passing the hot springs and going all the way along the slagheap embankment, then in an appropriate place, near the abandoned mine, he will encounter the party concerned. Should he not yet be there, he should wait. Then – and don't make me say it twice – chainsaw in hand, the washhouse ahead.

He stares at me: Well, he doesn't know about that. By Klara Bursen's fence, say I? Because he would have gone via the Czervensky jetty. Whereupon I tell him off curtly:

You know very well which way to go. You're just putting it on. I can't stand that sort of thing.

I was just thinking how I should raise the matter? What would you, for instance, say to him?

What would I say? On occasions like that I think it's best not to say anything. Valuable minutes are wasted. You're an educated man, with some experience of the world, so why should I have to tell you what to do? And you can forget about the spade. Others will do that bit for you.

He stares at me blankly; he doesn't understand.

It's enough if you prepare small batches and leave them scattered over the meadow, under trees and bushes. Should you be inclined to take a walk there in the morning, you won't find any of them there.

So, I needn't take a spade? Fine, if that's what you think, I won't.

He clambers out of the hammock, smooths down his clothes, shaking off the plum-tree leaves. He looks about him, then stares into the distance uncertainly:

So, now, straight away? Is it really that late? I'm not so sure, we could talk about it a bit more if you like. Tomorrow is another day, I say. And so is the day after that.

I shake my head, look him up and down, then look up at the sky: tomorrow? Or the day after? Those days, too, are today.

His brow glistens, the tip of his nose gleams. His palm when I grasp it is sweaty. Off you go, you're a decent fellow, I tell him. I see him to the gate, my hand on his shoulder. He looks back once or twice on his way, and I give him a wave: may heaven be with him.

It's getting late, but the day doesn't seem to want to end. In the western sky there is the red wreath of dusk, while the eastern seems already to be a lightish yellow. Above me, up on high, a cloud is radiant with the light of mother-of-pearl, and there emanates from it, like a silken whisper from the next world, a quiet humming that descends on the valley of the Yablonka. A restless twittering, like pearl balls sussurating in a little velvet purse. Birds without a home circle the earth without ever landing anywhere. The silken starlings from Eronim Mox's starling story.

But this is no longer heard by anyone else, behind the open doors and windows of the houses only the sounds of sleep have been undulating for a very long time.

When I set off, with the milk loaf and the wine in my little basket, heading for Anatol Korkodus and the lacanthus beetles, into the night of the thermal Spring No. 2, I decide to drop by the Man-Gold courtyard for one last time.

In its depths, shaded by the sloe branches, stands Nika Karanika behind her closed window. She can see I'm there but doesn't open it. Her index finger is poised across her lips: there is nothing to talk about. Nonetheless, she approaches the window with an emollient stateliness, in the half-light the berries of her eyes swell up, her features dilate, until suddenly with her mouth half-open, she glues the tip of her glistening tongue to the windowpane.

Nina Karanika's tongue from Eronim Mox's book of recipes. The story about the taste of saliva.

About shivering Fabritius, the slinking foxes of Damasskin Nikolsky, about the milk loaf and the wine, about Brigadier Anatol Korkodus, who lies asoak in the blue waters of eternity, on the mist-laden Paltinsky meadow.

A story about the silken starlings, about the letters N glowing in the light of mother-of-pearl across the sky, about the eternal twilight at the end of days.

Yet the saliva of joy comes oozing tepidly through the glass, surging through my limbs, throbbing irresistibly at the base of my spine, until it suddenly sears my thighs and dribbles coolly down my legs, reaching beneath my heels, cold as ice.

13.

(GUSTY)

Anatol Korkodus once explained how at the weekly fair in Velky Lukanar they recognised Verhovina's inhabitants, particularly those from Yablonska Polyana, by their foul smell. That there is indeed something amiss with us in that department is evident if only from the fact that when a stranger arrives and settles among us, he covers his nose with a handkerchief for some while and may need several hours to recover and acclimatise to us and, above all, to the air surrounding him and which he too must hence perforce inhale.

Yablonska Polyana is surrounded by the thermal springs of the Paltinsky meadow, by waters that are not merely hot but also turbid, rather salty, tasting of fungi, and intensely sulphurous. Curtains of a steamy, nausea-inducing brownish haze ripple day and night above the meadow, unless some fierce wind from the north should happen to come and sweep it away, and shrouds the valley, settling on the courtyards and seeping into the houses, the larders, the wardrobes, into the very depths of the dresser drawers. This is the only air we have here, it's the air of the Paltinsky meadow that keeps us alive; we bathe in the waters of the thermal springs and wash our clothes in the reek of their steamy waters. At night the fumes percolate into our brains and invade our dreams so that we waken at dawn with memories of chimeras. But we have grown used to it, we would not exchange our fate for any other.

When years earlier one foggy morning I got off the local train leaving behind me the pleasant woodchip smell of the locomotive, I too was met by the choking smell of the hot springs. That was a long time ago. Trains no longer come this way, the sides of the embankment are covered with birches and hazels, and much of the track, too, has long since disappeared.

The person now panting lightly with his back against the woodpile in the courtyard of what was once the water conservancy brigade arrived in a two-wheeled, horse-drawn carriage. He is sitting in the shade on a tree trunk, his nose buried in his clothing, breathing through it while he gets used to the atmosphere hereabouts, so we can set off for the Paltinsky meadow.

He is wearing a cap with a checked peak and a carefully ironed shirt under his jacket – the pocket of which, as on an army tunic, is embroidered with his name, Gusty – and the scent of fine soaps lingers about him; his hands are smooth, his nails well-groomed, he is clean shaven and must recently have had a haircut. He carries a satchel and a small canvas rucksack bearing the legend "Nikon", as well as a leatherette case that closes with a band of velcro, with the ends of three aluminium rods poking out of it. A stand of some kind. He says he'll be taking photographs from the marshy plateau above the gardens, detailed ones, of the whole area, of every nook and cranny where the thermal waters bubble up. The two-wheeler has been left by the gate, the horse unbridled, grazing in the yard.

Still, I ask him whether he was sent by the suffragan bishop or perhaps Commissar Kodrin from the inspectorate, but the stranger labelled Gusty says nothing and just looks at me with a degree of curiosity: apparently, he has never heard of those I just mentioned, or even of the inspectorate. When I ask him once more who he is in fact working for, he again just stares at me uncomprehendingly. Then he asks me my name.

Adam, I say.

Listen, Adam. You don't know them.

He aks for some drinking water as he keeps mopping his brow with a damp handkerchief.

I'd be glad if you could come with me. I'm feeling a bit light-headed, I'd be grateful if you could take this pack. He points to the stand in the leatherette box. It would be good if we could finish by midday.

I glance up at the sky, then slowly and reluctantly survey the yard.

I'm in no great mood to go outdoors these days, I say. And I really don't know what all this is about. Did you happen to bring a small gift of some kind?

Should I have? No one mentioned it.

It's more something one senses.

He spreads his arms wide, looking in embarrassment towards the heights. From behind the tangle of the trees in bud it is possible to see out towards the marshy plateau, the Paltinsky meadow, with the sombre, mist-shrouded peaks of the Medwaya beyond. Meanwhile he keeps mopping his brow and massaging his neck, sipping water from his cupped palm. He keeps clearing his throat, trying to get rid of the bitter phlegm that has gathered there, spitting as unobtrusively as he can into a handkerchief. Eventually he manages to pull himself together, stands up, and says, fine, now we can go.

Out of the blue he says that as he set off early in morning without breakfast, and hadn't brought elevenses, he'd like some coffee and something to eat here, so it would be a good idea to drop by the hostelry on the way.

Not likely, say I. No such thing in these parts.

But he knows of a bodega, and for the moment he could manage with just a packet of Eugénia creams to have something to munch on while he was working. It would take quite a few hours to do what he had to.

I'm sorry, but he should be clear: he wouldn't be eating here. The shops had closed down and any food that people had they ate themselves. For those from the authorities or a lost traveller, I was, on request, sometimes willing to make lebbencs soup, with potatoes and smoked bacon, for forty or fifty coupons or a decent piece of clothing they'd be prepared to part with. But if I now went with him, there'd be no one to prepare even that.

As I can see he is still astonished, confused and doubtful, I urge him on:

Get a move on, time's passing. If I have to go with you, I would for my part like to get this over with as soon as possible. It would certainly take several hours to visit all nine thermal springs in the meadow.

Nine? He'd heard there were only eight.

Nine, I tell you. That we sell the water from only eight is another matter. At one time they took the hot water from here in tankers, but of course it had always gone cold by the time they got it anywhere. Anatol Korkodus could tell you what it might be needed for, but he's no longer alive.

They drank it, said Gusty at this.

Could be. No accounting for taste. But the water of Spring No. 2 is unsuitable for any purpose. If, for example, you dip a stick in it, after a while it gets covered in blue crystals, and once they've dried the solid deposit can be easily scraped off. And if you put it back in the water, the same thing happens again. Anatol Korkodus once said that if ever we were in dire straits, we would do nothing but dangle sticks into the water and sell the blue crystals until our dying day and put the money in the bank.

But this man by the name of Gusty is not interested in this stuff about the blue crystals. He just repeats: so, there are after all only eight springs. Then he asks about the person I have now twice mentioned by name.

My adoptive father. He was the brigadier here. But they killed him.
Impossible, he says to this.
You're surprised? The look doesn't suit you.
He gives me a long, pitying look: Adam, Adam.

On our way to the meadow of the Paltin we pass by the former hostelry. In the yard, leaning back against the old dog kennel, sits Danczura, the woman who for a long time thought she was my niece. Her legs are splayed out, her eyes closed as if she was asleep. But she is not, her eyelashes flutter from time to time; her blouse is covered in butterflies that she's watching. From time to time she picks one off her bosom.

Gusty stops and watches her.

I gesture to him, nothing to see here, just carry on, keep going. I even hurry ahead, let him struggle to keep up. He lopes along a few steps behind me but keeps looking back: did he really see what he thought he did. He gives me an expectant, inquiring glance now and again, but says nothing. He points out he may have to come again tomorrow, and then he would bring sandwiches and a soft drink, and coffee in a vacuum flask. He would bear me in mind, too; what would I like to have, for example?

Eating. Again.

But honestly, he means it. He was thinking maybe salami sandwiches, some apple juice and a packet of Eugénia biscuits as well.

I stop and look him in the eye: he can bring what he likes. But I still don't know who sent him here.

Those who sent him here are thinking of the place's future. That was another reason he'd be interested to know how many people still lived here, give or take.

I've never counted them. There are still a few of us left. A dozen or two, to be more precise.

And whereabouts would they be this time of day?

They're not in the habit of showing themselves. They're sleeping, and doing this and that.

Because he's thinking of the workforce angle. He's only asking because they'd surely be glad to make a bit of money.

Want to know the truth? What would make them glad is if no one came here.

Along the Boursin farm's fence we make our way out to the Paltinsky meadow. From the plateau rim all of the moorland comes into view, as far as the foot of the Paltin, with its steep ravines overgrown with dwarf birches and hazelnut bushes, and below them the steam from the thermal springs rises in long, extended swirls. At its far end the meadow merges into the slagheaps, and on the side of the embankment, amidst the fresh shoots of thistle, mint and burdock, here and there flicker glimmering lumps of metal.

There is no wind, the steam hovering above the hot springs extends along the moorland, shreds of it sink cobweb-like into the sprouting grass and sedge. Below us in the gardens the plum trees are just beginning to blossom, between the fretwork of bare branches twinkle the roofs of Yablonska Polyana. Behind them, in the distance, the fog-bound heights of Nikolina, while to their left the landscape merges serenely into an unending expanse of deep purple.

Gusty throws down his rucksack, takes a map out of his satchel, opens it out and spreads it on the ground, and though there is no breath of a breeze, he places a rock at each of its four corners. He also has a compass and turns the map under it until the edge of the paper is parallel with its needle. He takes a stalk of grass, turns it this way and that above the map, all the while glancing up at the peaks and heights around.

He asks me for the leatherette case, opens it, takes the Nikon out of its canvas bag, screws the top of the stand into the hole at the bottom of the machine, then spreads its legs out, sticking their ends into the soil until the bubble in the spirit level is centred. He opens up the camera and waits for the lens to pop out. The back of the camera is matt glass, a small window that shows the entire Paltinsky meadow and behind it much of the centre of the slopes. Gusty rotates the camera slowly, stopping every now and then at various points, taking his time. On the right-hand side of the machine he adjusts a small lever to the right or left, zooming in on a particular feature, now here, now there. He takes a few pictures, then develops them right away. He takes several pictures from every angle, writing things down in a notebook after each. He continues taking photos for a while, then suddenly turns around, and with a crooked index finger beckons me over.

He says that as he panned up and down the meadow he could see by the foot of the trees and shrubs a number of small wooden crosses, all with the same legend: STLN 2011. He guessed that they might indicate different plots of land, but all the numbers were the same, every little cross bore the same letters and the same numbers. So what's all that about?

You're not wrong, I say. What you see are small crosses marking graves. They mean no more than what they say. In these parts we don't use vowels. We write using consonants, the rest everyone adds in their head. STLN – does that mean anything to you? No? Then there's nothing to talk about.

He doesn't get it but stops grilling me. He sets off, taking a few steps along the moorland, then plants his feet on it and jumps up and down. He looks at me questioningly.

It's like rubber. What the hell makes it so springy?

It's full of gases. If you put a stick into it, it goes in of its own accord, the soil simply swallows it up.

Wow. Seriously? Then that'll be something useful to know before they start the building works.

What's that supposed to mean?

We're putting up a couple of buildings here. You know, because of the hot water.

Has that been discussed with anyone?

Once again, he just stares at me in amazement, unable to grasp my question. Apparently, the matter has been discussed. Or not, as the case may be.

He continues to take photographs for a while. In the end he looks up, satisfied, and looks around the meadow, arms akimbo, his glance coming to a rest at the end of the plateau. He notices the slagheaps.

Let's just go over there. It seems to me that spot was made just for me.

It takes a good hour for us to clamber over in complete silence to the far end of the plateau, at the edge of the sodden meadow, keeping clear of the awkward areas of the moorland. There Gusty clambers up onto the slagheap embankment, with me in his wake carrying the stand with the camera on it. This slight elevation offers a good view of the entire Paltinsky meadow. Gusty opens up the tripod, sets up the machine and takes pictures from this new angle.

For some reason this is everyone's favourite view. When he finished his survey in the evenings, Anatol Korkodus would always make a little detour to this spot: this is where he found the horse-faced vagabond more than once, where Damasskin Nikolsky, in his suit and city shoes, had rutted around, and once even Commissar Kondrin had shown his guests around here.

Having taken the photographs, Gusty walks to the end of the embankment, stops again, broodingly, hands on hips. Silently he gazes up at the sombre heights and even takes a few hesitant steps forward, as if expecting to have a better view of them from this vantage point.

Very well, Adam, he says out of the blue, from here on I can manage by myself. I thought I would put in an order for a lebbencs soup from you. And what about that bluestone spring you mentioned? I'd be happy to take a look at that, too.

Fine, I say, I'll take you that far and show you a thing or two. The lacanthus beetles.

Some local speciality?

Nowhere else on the globe do lacanthus beetles live, only in hot Spring No. 2. They subsist on the copper in the water, that's what makes them clink and jangle and sparkle like medallions when they collide; as they spark and arc above the springs they create a dome of bluish green that lights up the night. No living thing can survive in these springs except for the lacanthus beetles. They revel in this thick, deadly liquid. As for the price of the lebbencs soup, I am not interested in money, but I'd be pleased to have your cap.

We set off. The stand, with the camera on it, the satchel and the rucksack beside them, all remain on the embankment.

On the way he asks: they clink, you say? What they taught me at school was that water deadens every sound. I wouldn't like it if you took me for a fool.

We are all made different. If you're hard of hearing you may not hear it.

Hot Spring No. 2 is not the second but the third in the sequence, and isn't situated at the foot of the heights, but at some distance from the others, quite far in, on the part of the meadow's fringe nearest the settlement. It can be reached through varicoloured puddles, on an unused, overgrown path. This is the only pool that it proved unnecessary to fence off, no rushes grow around it, nor plants that like a modicum of moist warmth, and even wild animals take care to give it a wide berth. In days long past Anatol Korkodus had stakes driven into the ground around the other pools and covered them with wire mesh, as the badgers would go swimming there because of their fleas. They discovered that if they immersed themselves in water, that would get rid of them. But that was a long time ago and the fences had long since been chewed through, so around sunset once again they can be seen near the pools, shaking the water out of their fur.

Hot Spring No. 2 is more extensive than the rest, and it has the deepest pool: if you could bathe in it, you would need four or five strokes to swim across it. Since last autumn it has been covered by a layer of leaves from the birch trees, which have turned the entire surface of the water yellow.

I go back to fetch the wire broom from Spring No. 3. It was with such a long-handled wire broom that we generally swept the fallen leaves and the windborne twigs off the water's surface, to make sure the decayed, slimy debris of the leaves didn't block the drains and the sun's rays could penetrate the water to the very bottom of the spring. But we made no use of the water of Spring No. 2 and cleared its surface only in the spring, after the thaw.

Down beneath the yellow birch leaves there lies already the secret blue realm of the hereafter. As I sweep aside the layer of leaves, the silkily vaporous water glints dark blue and black. And as the opening widens the sky and the clouds pursued by the wind can be seen framed by the yellow leaves.

Gusty leans above the surface of the water, but it is not the scudding clouds that he is looking at.

Even the seaweed in it's blue, he whispers. Would you kindly pluck a few strands for me.

No chance, I say. That's not seaweed. That's Anatol Korkodus's beard. You see, there's something in the water that makes the hair and the beard keep growing.

Who is this Anatol Korkodus?

You've already asked me that. I shan't tell you again. It's somebody who wanted to be laid to eternal rest here. If you go on a little further, and stand on that rock, you can position yourself so that you don't block the light from the sky, you'll see in the depths a wild piglet coloured blue. Anatol Korkodus lies to its right. Once your eyes have got used to it, you can see his face as well. The crystal has no effect on human skin, so that's stayed white.

So just tell me again what I should do?

You heard the first time, I won't tell you again. Take your time looking at it and I'll go and make the lebbencs soup. When you've had enough, come on after me. You can make your way back on your own by following the line of the fence.

Through Gleznár's abandoned garden I descend to the settlement. On the way, from the foot of the fence, I pick some wild sorrel, a handful of wild garlic, and a bunch of nettle leaves.

The two-wheeler is standing in front of the gate, the horse is in the garden, amidst the plum trees.

I fry up the noodles on a bed of bacon strips, add the wild garlic, and as the mixture begins to brown, sprinkle it with a litttle flour, stir for a while, keeping it on the hob, and before topping it up, garnish it with a little paprika. The lebbencs soup is ready when the noodles in it are tender. Then I cover the pot and push it to the side of the hob.

As it's quite a bit past midday and there's still no sign of Gusty, I make my way up to the meadow again, through Gleznár's garden.

I can see from afar that the stand with the camera on it is no longer where we left it at the far end of the slagheap.

Gusty, in his chequered cap, is standing by the edge of the pool, the stand before him, the camera on it at a slight angle, so that it's pointed aslant at the water, directly at Anatol Korkodus. Beside it on the ground, next to the Nikon bag, lies a lock of blue hair, the thing Gusty had thought was seaweed. It's like a few strands of wet string dipped in blue-coloured granulated sugar.

Gusty can hear the sucking noises behind him produced by the moorland, but he's hard at work, noises are of no interest to him just now. He doesn't turn around even when he must surely feel my breath on the nape of his neck. He just keeps pressing the buttons on his camera.

Anatol Korkodus's hair and beard, like seaweed, undulate gently under the water. One lock of his hair lies on the bank, next to the Nikon box.

When I give the tripod a kick, for a moment Gusty freezes, perhaps unable to believe what he's seeing: with a soft splash the camera immediately sinks into the water.

If you still need it, you can go and fetch it, I say.

He says nothing and, breathing heavily, begins to strip: he flings his jacket to one side, kicks off his shoes, tears off his shirt, and stands there in his vest and boxers, then he strides into the water, sinking up to his neck into the spring's soft little tongues of vapour. From there he turns suddenly towards me, staring with his eyebrows jigging frantically up and down.

It's deep, he says so softly, as if the air was barely leaving his mouth.

I nod. Of course it's deep.

Then, as he sinks into the decayed dry leaves covering the bottom of the basin, he manages to whisper:

Your hand. Give me your hand, Adam.

I can't reach you. As you can see, I can't reach that far.

He doesn't plead, just stares at me in astonishment, eyes widening, no sound being prepared to leave his lips; nor could it, indeed, as it's precisely his mouth that has filled up with the water of Spring No. 2. He might even be willing to swallow it for a short time, but its corrosive bitterness so paralyses his tongue that he can't even spit it out.

Amidst a mute bubble or two he sinks without a sound. In the place where he had been the water creates gentle rings for a while, the waves slowly steering his chequered cap, which has remained afloat on the water, towards the shore.

I don't lift a finger.

Then the wrinkles in the water once again smooth out and the clouds reappear on its surface, scudding across the sky, edging from the northwest towards the southeast.

The layer of leaves that had been pushed aside also moves back and slowly prepares to close the gap across the water's surface. I take my time and wait for the dark blue of the sky to disappear beneath the yellow of the overlapping leaves.

For some reason, Eronim Mox, after providing instructions on how to prepare îles flottantes, in particular those little clouds of foam that float on its surface, touches in his story upon the times when humans will no longer inhabit the earth. That these clouds will continue to scud across the sky just as if there were someone admiring them down below. About why they should do so then, there's not one word.

I can see from afar that Brigitta Konuvalov is resting on her elbows in the window. The little diamonds in her two incisors sparkle and gleam. She can see me, too; she waves and shouts in my direction:

Hello, Adam! It's Saturday. You didn't open up the wash-house for me.

And in case I didn't hear her, she gestures vehemently towards the wash-house.

I shout back:

Saturday?

Brigitta Konuvalov takes a bath every Saturday. Saturday midday I open up the wash-house for her, let the coldish water out of the pipes, wait for the hot water to start flowing from the tap, then stay with her until she finishes her bath. On these occasions she generally asks me to wash her back.

Saturday, she shouts. Of course it's Saturday.

I don't know where she gets this from. I think she just makes it up when she feels like having a bath. But I don't argue.

Very well then, I'll expect you in half an hour. That's how long it takes for the cool water to clear the pipes and finally get hot water flowing from the tap.

I open up the public wash-house and turn on the tap above the tub where Brigitta will be having her bath. There is just one tub here used for bathing, the other stone troughs along the wall are only for washing clothes. The tub had been given a while ago to Anatol Korkodus by the Suffragan Bishop of Lemberg. It's slightly egg-shaped, almost circular, so that one person, even Brigitte Konuvalov for example, can comfortably fit in it. It was carved from pale blue marble with greyish-white veins, and a stippled black stripe runs around it below the rim. It was said to have served as a stoup in Ivano-Frankivsk's Basilica of St Chrysostom. Ivano-Frankivsk is a large city, 10 or 15 people could dip their fingers in it at the same time.

As I said, a good half hour. That's how long it needs for the sediment to clear from the conduits, the pipes to warm up, and the tub to fill with water. But when it is half full, I let the water out, so that the water Brigitta Konuvalov gets is really hot.

The tub is half full by the time she arrives. These days, since the coming of spring, she has been wearing a stained, moth-eaten, little waistcoat of Ukrainian green that she must have picked up after rummaging about in some musty chest. The waistcoat is tight, it squeezes her breasts upwards and outwards, the two mounds with their web of lilac veins swelling up beneath her chin as if they grew straight out of her shoulders. Since losing her beloved Zhedu Baba, she dressed in variety of fanciful apparel, as if anyone cared. But there's no longer anyone around who might desire her.

She says: I saw you this morning with a stranger carrying a rucksack, walking along the Infantrymen's Street. What the hell was he doing here?

I look her in the eye: Today?

All right, don't tell me if you don't want to.

She takes off her waistcoat, steps out of her skirt and blouse, rolls her stockings down, and is now stark naked. Released from the grip of the waistcoat, her breasts hang down limply. On her calves, too, the flesh sags, and beneath her flaccid belly the moss is considerably blighted. But she keeps glancing back over her shoulder and flashes the mirrors of her teeth at me before she steps into the tub.

Meanwhile the hot water continues to flow from the tap; I don't turn it off, even when it reaches her navel. She waits, facing me, sitting with her back to the wall. This, in her view, is the ideal position for having one's back washed. I think she is right. You lean above her, one hand resting gently on her shoulder, you bend down over her head, more or less embracing her with one arm, and with leisurely movements scrub to and fro, down from the neck all the way to the cheeks of her rear.

Meanwhile she positions herself just under my stomach, between my legs.

On two previous occasions she had reached up and begun to unbutton me, and I had to slap her on the wrist. Once she even tried to do it with her teeth. Because, really, just a little suck, she really counted on nothing more nowadays. This time, too, she can't control herself, she is breathing heavily, digging, sniffing.

Brigitta Konuvalov, lover of so many, was really never my cup of tea; in my mind I was always haunted only by the shining little moon of Nika Karanika's knee, ever since I caught sight of her as she leaned back in the wash-house.

But that, it seems, was a long time ago.

Now, as Brigitta Konuvalov is greedily snuffling about under my stomach, it does seem that some female warmth is wafting my way after all. Goodness knows what's happening, as my palms slide across her back, along both sides of her spine, up and down, from her neck to her padded recesses, I let her fumble around, find what she is looking for, do with it what she will.

The hot water gurgles gently, no other sound can be heard.

It's soon over. Quite an odd, giddy, slightly cold feeling. When it ends it's as if I'd lost something.

Now, now, Brigitta! Dammit, Brigitta Konuvalov!

I turn away while she towels herself down and gets dressed. I just hear the swishing of the glad rags, the leather flapping about lightly as she tries to cram her bosom back into the waistcoat.

So, we'll meet again, she says.

I let the water out of the tub and scrub it clean with the long-handled brush.

The water continues to flow and I suddenly notice that a little silver-blue lacanthus beetle drops out of the tap. It's a sort of trainee beetle, no bigger than a bean, perhaps a little flatter. It glitters, glowing silver-blue as it swirls round the plughole. Then another. Then a third and fourth.

Seeing the ninth, I turn off the tap.

It looks as if in one of the thermal springs the composition of the water had changed.

The lebbencs soup under its lid has meanwhile gone quite cold. The fat is swimming on its surface in solidified blobs. If I only eat half of it now, there will be some left over for tomorrow.

I don't heat it up but ladle it cold from the pot, making sure that at least half of it remains. It's turned out a little thicker than it should, and the pasta doesn't, in fact, sink to the bottom of the pan. I make sure that there is also plenty of pasta for tomorrow.

While I'm eating, Gusty's horse gives the odd whinny in the garden. From time to time there is something rooting about under the eaves, too. At first I pay it no attention: I don't let such small noises interfere with my meal. The rooting about continues, however, but I go out onto the veranda to take a look around only once I've washed the spoon, put away the tureen with the soup in it carefully covered with a lid, and changed into clean underwear and dry house trousers.

Ah, the red-tailed hawks!

They arrive with little sticks and twigs in their beaks, always at the exact same spot, a little hole between the eaves and the veranda's beams that's hard to see. Then they come again, with dry stalks of grass, and finally long strands of hair that they use to weave the little twigs and sticks into a nest. The little twigs and sticks and grass stalks they bring from the garden here; for the long strands of hair they fly long distances. Towards the former communal stables, where at the bottom of the wall there have lain in heaps for years the decaying manes of the shaven donkeys.

The way they fly, the rustling of their wings, radiates a sense of security, an innate feeling of peace; they can see well enough that I am there, staring straight at them, but they take no interest in me at all. A little stick, a little twig, then again one of each, then four or five stalks of grass. Again a little stick or two, a couple of twigs, four or five dry stalks of grass, then a long strand of hair from the mane of a donkey. Little stick, little twig, dry grass stalk, strand of hair. It is dusk by the time they stop.

The red-tailed hawks have arrived.

Also available from our online bookshop
www.JantarPublishing.com

CARBIDE *by* ANDRIY LYUBKA

Translated from the original Ukrainian by Reilly Costigan-Humes and Isaac Stackhouse Wheeler

CARBIDE explores the underbelly of the Ukrainian smuggling industry. The protagonist, Tys, a merciless yet loving parody of Ukrainian nationalism, concocts a hairbrained scheme to dig a tunnel from the imaginary western Ukrainian city of Vedmediv to Hungary and force the European Union to grant Ukraine admission by smuggling its entire population into a member-country. Hilarity inevitably ensues, along with danger, when Tys, the would-be 'Moses of Ukraine', recruits a gang of local smugglers, including a latter-day Icarus determined to fly over the border and a femme fatale who traffics human organs. This timely novel offers a funny, yet tragic take on increasingly urgent topics such as the meaning of borders, nationalism, and European identity.

BELLEVUE *by* IVANA DOBRAKOVOVÁ

Translated from the original Slovak by Julia and Peter Sherwood

Blanka takes a summer job at a centre for people with physical disabilities in the French city of Marseille, where her encounter with their severe conditions ends badly. A deeply unsettling, visceral tale of a young woman unravelling, evolving from carer to cared for. A novel about our own inability to escape 'our own private cages', imprisoned by fear, anxiety and mistrust, no less than indifference to others.

For further news on new books and events, please visit
www.JantarPublishing.com

Also available from our online bookshop
www.JantarPublishing.com

PRAGUE, I SEE A CITY... *by* Daniela Hodrová

Translated from the original Czech by David Short

Originally commissioned for a French series of alternative guidebooks, Hodrová's novel is a conscious addition to the tradition of Prague literary texts by, for example, Karel Hynek Mácha, Jakub Arbes, Gustav Meyrink and Franz Kafka, who present the city as a hostile living creature or labyrinthine place of magic and mystery in which the individual human being may easily get lost.

CITY OF TORMENT... *by* Daniela Hodrová

Translated from the original Czech by Véronique Firkusny and Elena Sokol

An intoxicating, personal journey through 1,000 years of European culture where history's losers bite back.

On one level, a family and generational novel, conveyed through the complex voice of a first-person female narrator whose subjectivity becomes elaborately intertwined with the main protagonist, Eliška Beránková (*Lamb*). Eliška/Daniela is searching above all for her dead father, but also for her dead mother and ultimately for herself. At the same time, on a more abstract level, Hodrová introduces a feminine structural dimension to a theme especially prevalent in 20th-century prose – the novel as a self-conscious genre, openly exploring the relationship of the author to her text. Hodrová's trilogy represents a distinct contemporary Czech voice in women's experimental writing, a genre first introduced to anglophone readers by Virginia Woolf.

For further news on new books and events, please visit
www.JantarPublishing.com